A MATCH
TO FOOL SOCIETY

Laura Martin

MILLS & BOON

First published in Great Britain 2022
by Mills & Boon, an imprint of HarperCollins*Publishers* Ltd,
1 London Bridge Street, London, SE1 9GF

www.harpercollins.co.uk

HarperCollins*Publishers*
1st Floor, Watermarque Building,
Ringsend Road, Dublin 4, Ireland

A Match to Fool Society © 2022 Laura Martin

ISBN: 978-0-263-30206-6

12/22

To the many inspirational female mentors
I've been lucky enough to have in life.

Your time and encouragement has always made a difference.

Chapter One

'I do declare, it has been a thoroughly successful year,' Lady Mountjoy said to the group of women gathered round her. 'And we have still got the main round of balls and events ahead of us.'

'How many matches have you secured?'

'Four. Four out of five of the debutantes I brought from Somerset are now married.'

Jane took a step back, wondering if there was any way she could fade into the background. Never was there a time she liked to be the centre of attention in a ballroom, but right at this moment she would have been happy to blend into the wallpaper. If any of the women in Lady Mountjoy's circle turned and saw her, there would be exclamations of pity and reassurances that she too would find her match. Even though that would be painful, it wouldn't be as bad as Lady Mountjoy's eyes turning to her in that affectionate but calculating way.

'What about number five?' one of the companions asked.

Number Five took a step to the left, wondering if she might make it to the door without attracting any attention.

'Miss Ashworth is a fine young lady and I have no doubt that we will see her happily married before the Season is out.'

Shuffling her feet, Jane inched towards the door and freedom from the inquisitive stares. None of this had seemed so bad when her friends had been there to experience everything with her, but now she was alone and exposed to the glare of curiosity without anyone to shield her.

Jane continued to shuffle, all the time wondering if she would be better to stride away, then all the group of matriarchs would see would be her squared shoulders and head held high.

Nearly at the door, she risked a look back, catching a snippet of the conversation.

'The quiet, mousy ones…'

For a moment she stiffened, allowing the frustration to course through her, revelling in the fire it stoked deep inside her, before she took a deep breath and banished the defiance that burned bright. Turning, she made the last two steps to the door quickly, already rejoicing in her smooth escape as she rushed through, looking over her shoulder to see if anyone had noted her exit from the ballroom.

Her body collided with something solid and, before Jane could even look round, she flew back through the ballroom doors, her arms spread wide, trying to grasp on to anything she could. There was a moment when she thought she might regain her equilibrium and keep her feet, but it was short lived, and instead she slipped anew on the shiny floor and landed with a hard bump on her bottom.

Every pair of eyes in the ballroom turned to her. Hands raised to mouths and smiles were suppressed. No doubt there were even a few genuine gasps of sympathy.

Quickly Jane leaned to tug down her dress. It had puffed up as she had tumbled backwards and the hem now sat just below her knees, giving everyone a glimpse of her practical white stockings.

Hating the way the blood rushed to her cheeks and the tears pooled in her eyes, threatening to spill out onto her lashes, Jane pressed her lips together in an attempt to maintain her composure.

'My apologies,' a deep voice said, stepping into her line of vision and offering her his hand.

Jane regarded the man for a moment, realising this was the solid form she'd so disastrously bounced off. He was smiling, although she didn't get the impression he was laughing *at* her, as many of the other guests were.

There wasn't anything to do but take his hand and allow him to pull her to her feet. She stood quickly, a little too quickly, and her body bumped against his before she could take a step back and put some distance between them.

'Are you hurt?' His concern seemed genuine, although the hint of a smile was still tugging at the corner of his lips.

'No,' Jane said abruptly. She turned to move away, surprised when the man caught her hand, stopping her from fleeing.

'You're in a hurry, Miss…?'

'Ashworth. Yes, I am.'

'Miss Ashworth,' he said, looking her over appraisingly. 'So, where is the guest of honour of tonight's ball running off to so fast?'

Closing her eyes for a moment, Jane tried to ignore the sideways looks they were getting from a group of young ladies Jane vaguely knew. Silently she dug her fingernails into her palms and summoned a tight smile. It was no use trying to flee now anyway. All eyes were on her. She had missed her opportunity to slip away unnoticed.

'Ah, Miss Ashworth, I wondered where you had got to. Did you injure yourself in your fall?' Lady Mountjoy hurried over and Jane turned to the older woman. Despite her penchant for match-making the countess was kind, warm and motherly and Jane knew her concern was real. 'Whatever happened?'

Jane's eyes flicked to her companion, wondering if he would let it slip that she had been fleeing the ballroom.

'Carelessness on my part, I am afraid, Lady Mountjoy,' he said, inclining his head in greeting. 'I wasn't looking where I was going and barrelled into Miss Ashworth.' He smiled at her and Jane felt the full force of his charm. 'A thousand apologies, Miss Ashworth, please forgive me.'

'Of course,' Jane murmured.

'Have you been introduced to Mr Stewart? No?' Lady Mountjoy beamed, and Jane felt as if a lead weight was sitting in her stomach. 'Miss Jane Ashworth, this is Mr Stewart.

Mr Stewart, this is Miss Ashworth, one of the young ladies who accompanied me to London this year.'

'Delighted to make your acquaintance.' Something sparkled in his green-blue eyes as he looked at her and Jane got the impression he found everything in life a little amusing. There was a certain warmth to his smile that sought to draw one in and an air of merriment she hadn't come across often.

'We are honoured to have you attend tonight, Mr Stewart, I have not seen you at one of these events for a long time.'

Jane's curiosity was momentarily piqued, and Lady Mountjoy must have sensed it, for she propelled Jane forward a few steps with a light touch on her lower back.

'Miss Ashworth is free for the next dance if you would care to take to the dance floor.'

'Miss Ashworth?' Mr Stewart murmured, showing no chagrin at having been so deftly manoeuvred into offering a dance.

'I have somewhere…' Jane began, choking back the response as Lady Mountjoy elbowed her gently in the ribs. 'I suppose a dance would be pleasant. Thank you.'

With an amused expression on his face, Mr Stewart held out his hand and led Jane to the dance floor where the other couples were beginning to assemble. As the music began for the dance, Jane sent up a silent prayer of thanks that it wasn't a waltz. She wasn't the most skilled at dancing, but the lively steps of a quadrille or cotillion were much more forgiving to disguise the odd misstep or stumble.

'You are frowning, Miss Ashworth, do you not like the dance?'

Jane looked up and missed a step, grimacing as she planted her foot on Mr Stewart's toes. He barely reacted, and his face remained impassive, but he couldn't suppress the flicker of surprise in his eyes.

'I like the dance,' she said, focussing on the numbers in her head as she counted her steps.

'Perhaps it is the company you find taxing?'

She stumbled again and Mr Stewart effortlessly caught her elbow and whisked her into the next turn. A chain of uncharitable thoughts started to run through Jane's head and she had to swiftly silence them. It wasn't Mr Stewart's fault he was attractive, charming and good at dancing. Some people were blessed in the endeavours that society found important, others were not. Usually it did not bother Jane that she found the idle chit-chat at balls difficult to engage in, and that her dancing wouldn't have anyone madly clamouring to partner her, but today she wished she had just a little more grace.

'I have to count my steps,' she said through clenched teeth. 'And I frown when I concentrate.'

'Ah. What happens if you don't count your steps?'

'I wouldn't be able to dance.'

'I don't believe you.'

'You think I'm here counting steps and treading on your toes for fun?'

Mr Stewart laughed, throwing his head back and letting the laugh rip through him. Jane looked around uncomfortably. People were beginning to look. Nothing about this evening was going to plan and Mr Stewart was not helping.

'Come,' he said, waiting for her to meet his eye once he had stopped laughing. 'Clear your head of all those numbers and all the nonsense your dance tutors taught you and feel the music. Feel how it flows through you and then put your trust in me.'

'I barely know you. Why would I trust you?'

'I am asking you to trust me with a dance, Miss Ashworth, not your life.'

She grumbled under her breath but realised

the quickest way to get rid of Mr Stewart and his enthusiasm was to play along. Soon the dance would be finished and, if at that point he realised what a truly terrible dancer she was, she was hopeful he would leave her alone. Then she would find a way to slip away and find some peace in the rest of the house.

'Fine. My head is clear.'

'You're lying.'

Her eyes shot up to meet his and she saw the determination there underneath the sparkle of humour.

Leaning in closer, he spoke quietly, his breath tickling her ear and sending shivers down her spine. 'I can see your lips moving.'

It took all of her self-control not to clamp her lips tightly together.

'Close your eyes, empty your head of all your thoughts and trust me.'

'Fine.'

They covered a few feet of ballroom floor before Jane panicked about the lack of control she had over her movement. In the same instant, her feet became tangled and she fell forward, this time thankful for Mr Stewart's solid form to stop her from tumbling from the floor.

'Whoa,' he said softly, allowing her to recover her own balance. Jane looked around, realising many of the people gathered around the dance floor were watching them, and that she had brushed far too close to a man she did not know.

Thankfully the musicians quietened, the couples stopped their lively movements and Jane was spared any further embarrassment.

'Thank you for the dance,' she said quickly, turning away before Mr Stewart had time to answer. She doubted he would ask her for another, not unless he secretly enjoyed getting his toes stomped on.

'Setting your cap a little high, aren't you, Miss Ashworth?' Mrs Farthington said as Jane hurried past. Mrs Farthington had started the year with Jane as one of Lady Mountjoy's debutantes, but had recently married the insipid Mr Farthington. Jane still thought of the woman as 'snide Miss Huntley', and found it difficult to believe she was now married. It was an odd match, with Mr Farthington rather in awe of his young bride. He boasted a fortune and a kind heart, but was rather a hapless soul, and nowhere near sharp enough to keep up with his fiancée. Even now he hovered close by as if not sure whether to stand with his new wife or not.

'I'm not setting my cap at anyone,' Jane snapped.

'*Everyone* saw that not-so-subtle stumble into his arms. I'm not sure you're his type, though.'

'I'm not trying to be his type.'

'Good. I hear he has a wicked reputation.'

Jane glanced back over her shoulder, catching a glimpse of Mr Stewart's dark hair as he bowed over a young lady's hand. He was attractive. Even she could not deny that. He had an air of confidence about him that seemed to pull people in, to make them want to be part of his circle. Then there were his eyes, that deep mix of blue and green that was adept at making you feel as if you were the only person in the room.

'Enjoy the ball, Mrs Farthington,' Jane said as she swept away, the effect rather ruined as she tripped on her hem and stumbled, but thankfully this time did not lose her footing entirely.

Chapter Two

Tom pulled the covers over his head and groaned, trying to remember where he had ended up the night before. The evening had started respectably enough at Lady Mountjoy's ball. There weren't many society events he attended throughout the Season, but Lady Mountjoy was a distant cousin of his mother and had always been kind, even indulgent with him, so he had dropped in on the way to his club.

After the ball had come far too many drinks with an old friend, and he had vague memories of ending the evening in his friend's tavern on the other side of the river, but had no recollection how he had got home.

The knocking on the door started again and Tom threw off the bed clothes in frustration. It was far too early for visitors—far too early for anyone honest to be out and about. Even his footmen were taking a while to get to the door, which meant either they were still in bed or at the very least downstairs taking an early breakfast.

He rose, moving to the window to see if he could catch a glimpse of who thought it was acceptable to wake a man with a hangover when the sun was not yet peeking over the horizon.

Whoever it was had positioned themselves too close to the door for him to see, and with his head pounding he decided to let his footmen sort it out and collapsed back into bed.

Two minutes later, there was a light tap on the door.

'Excuse me, sir.' Upton's voice came through the thick wood. 'You're needed downstairs.'

His servants normally required very little guidance. He paid well and ensured his staff were happy and motivated in their jobs. It meant he didn't need to worry about any of the day-to-day running of his household and made his life so much easier. It was unusual for one of them to seek him out to deal with something, and as such Tom knew it must be important. Even so, it was still a struggle to drag himself out of bed.

'Come in, Upton,' he called, pulling on a nightshirt and then lifting his dressing gown from where he had thrown it the night before.

'Very sorry to disturb you so early, sir, there is someone downstairs you need to see.'

It looked as though the footman had thrown on his livery, and as Tom peered at the clock on the mantelpiece he realised it was only a little after six.

'At this hour?'

'They insisted, sir.'

Tom raised an eyebrow but didn't argue further, deciding instead to hurry downstairs and sort out whatever misunderstanding had caused someone to knock at his door at such an unsociable hour. By the time he reached the bottom of the sweeping staircase, his mood had not improved, and he threw open the door to the dining room.

All the bluster was knocked from him by the sight that met his eyes. Sleepily curled in an arm chair was a young boy with a shock of dark hair. His eyes flickered open as Tom entered the room, but it was too much of an effort, and after a moment's assessment he closed them again.

Sitting next to the boy was a woman of middle age. She was wrapped up against the cold, the hood of her cloak still pulled up over her hair, and her cheeks rosy from the bite of the winter wind.

'Who are you?' If he was honest with himself, Tom knew without having to be told at least who the boy was, but his mind was struggling to wade through the shock of seeing the child here.

'My name is Alessia Endrizzi. You do not know me, but I promised a dear friend to undertake a journey for her, and she assured me we would be well received when we arrived.'

Tom felt his throat closing up and reached to loosen his collar, only remembering he was in his night clothes when his hand touched the soft cotton of his nightshirt.

'Your friend…?'

The woman smiled kindly and Tom saw the hint of sadness.

'I have a letter. Perhaps it would be best if you read that first.'

Tom nodded, taking the letter but unable to bring himself to open it for a minute. He stood by the fire one of the servants must have hastily lit when the guests had arrived and stared into the flames, trying to summon the courage to tear open the envelope.

My dearest brother,
How long it has been since I set eyes upon you. Often I think of home, of those childhood days we spent playing together. Always you could make me smile and laugh, even in the most dire of circumstances, and I will be thankful for ever for your love and companionship.

Next comes an apology. I am sorry I left it so long to contact you. I know you would have worried about me, and if I had been a better sister I would have returned sooner, but in truth I have been happy here hidden away in rural Italy. I know you would never have reproached me for my choice and I hope this will make what I ask easier for you.

My husband, my dear Giovanni, passed away three years ago. He has no surviving family and although I am surrounded by good friends I cannot ask of them such a momentous favour.

I am dying. The doctors cannot tell me exactly what is wrong, but I have a large growth in my belly. It is eating away at my life force and soon there will be nothing left of me. I do not have the strength to make the journey home even though I wish I could hug you one last time.

My kind friend, Alessia, offered to bring Edward to you. I am so sorry I did not send advance warning of their arrival, but things are happening so quickly. I know it will be a shock, but I beg of you to look after my darling boy for me. Love him, cherish him, tell him about his mama and how much he was loved by both his parents.

Edward is six. He is kind and loving and intelligent and funny. I know you will provide everything he needs, because I know the kind of man you have grown in to, but I beg you to love him as well. You know as well as I do what it is like to go through childhood without love, and at least we had each other.

I will bid you farewell now and hope one day we will meet again in heaven, and there you can tell me all about my wonderful son.

All my love
Rebecca

For a long moment Tom couldn't think of anything but his sister's sunny smile and he felt a searing pain shoot through him at the realisation he would never see her again. It had been twelve years since she'd left. For twelve long years he'd missed his childhood companion, but he'd always imagined one day they would be reunited. As always when he thought of Rebecca he felt a horrible mass of guilt and regret pushing down on him. He had not done the best by his sister, having abandoned her to save his own sanity, and he had never forgiven himself.

He glanced at the boy sleeping in the arm chair, noting the familiar curve to his lips and the shock of dark, curly hair, identical to Rebecca's when they had been children, impossible to tame.

'This is Edward?' It was a wholly unnecessary question, but Tom didn't know what to say. Never had he imagined he would start the day today with his nephew in the house. A nephew he hadn't even known existed.

'This is Edward,' Alessia said softly.

A kindness radiated from her and Tom could see why his sister had entrusted her son to this woman.

'The journey has been long, and he is very tired.'

'You must be tired too. Shall I ask one of the servants to show you upstairs to a bedroom to rest?'

'I cannot stay.'

'You've only just arrived.'

'Our journey was plagued by delays.' She smiled kindly at him. 'I have been away from my family for a long time already and I need to get back to them.'

'Do you have children?'

'Six. They are with their grandmother, but I must return as soon as possible.'

'Surely you have time to rest for one day?' Tom wanted to hear about his sister, about her life in Italy and the years during which she had disappeared.

'I have booked a passage on a ship that sails later this morning.' She paused and then reached out, took his hand and squeezed. 'You look just like her.'

'Was she happy?'

Alessia nodded. 'Very happy. She loved Giovanni very much and he worshipped her. Of course, when Giovanni died she was heartbroken, but her love for Edward helped her through.' Gesticulating to the hall, she continued. 'She wrote more letters, letters for Edward but also some for you. She had time to prepare. Her decline was gradual but steady and she wanted to leave something for Edward to remember her by. All the legal documents are in the bundle as well.'

'Thank you for bringing them.'

'I am sorry I cannot stay. I had planned to remain for a few days before returning, but as I say, it is impossible. I am happy to write, once you have read the letters, if you have any questions.'

Tom ran a hand through his short hair, enjoying the bristly feeling on his fingertips. Part of him wondered if he was in some terrible dream fuelled by too much alcohol the night before. Perhaps in a few minutes he would stir, woken by a sound in the real world.

No such relief came.

He could not force Alessia to stay, and understood the sacrifice she had made already in fulfilling her friend's last request. Even so, as the kindly Italian woman stood he felt a wrench of panic.

'He likes stories and make-believe, long hugs and to be sung to sleep at night,' she said, as if reading his mind.

'Thank you for everything you have done

for them both. Can I give you something to pay for your passage?'

'No. I couldn't do much for Rebecca, but I could do this.' She leaned over the sleeping boy and kissed him tenderly on the cheek. Edward stirred but did not wake and, with one final caress of the sleeping boy's cheek, Alessia left.

Staggering a little, Tom sat down, the reality of everything he had just been told starting to dawn on him. His sister was dead, and now he was guardian to her son, a vulnerable young boy who had lost so much already.

'I'm not the person you need,' he murmured as he looked across at his nephew. He knew nothing about children. Over the last decade he had steadfastly refused even to contemplate courting a woman with a view to settling down. He didn't want to continue the family line and had no intention of ever being anything but a happy bachelor.

A wave of panic washed over him, building gradually until he thought he might be crushed under the weight of responsibility. Tom pulled at his collar, feeling as though something was tightening around his neck, but there was only the loose fabric of his shirt.

He felt the sudden and overwhelming need to get out of the house. The walls were closing in around him and he needed to suck in the fresh air, to remind himself there was a whole world out there.

'Mrs Hills,' he called, certain his steadfast housekeeper would not still be abed, with all the commotion going on.

She appeared from the hallway instantly, her face drawn with worry but softening when she saw the sleeping boy.

'This is my nephew, Edward,' he said, the words feeling foreign on his tongue. 'He has had a long journey and I expect will sleep a while. Is there a bed for him?'

'The blue room is aired and ready.'

'Good. I will carry him upstairs. I want someone to sit with him in case he wakes. No doubt it will be disturbing for him to be in an unfamiliar house.' For one dreadful second he wondered if the boy spoke only Italian, then dismissed the idea. Surely Rebecca would have wanted to teach her son her language, to share that part of her with him? 'I will be back in an hour, maybe two. There are some things I need to arrange.'

'Of course, sir. I will ask Hetty to sit with him. She has half a dozen younger siblings and is wonderful with children.'

'Good.'

Tom hesitated before walking over to his nephew and threading his arms underneath the sturdy little body. The boy was warm and snuggled in to Tom's embrace as he lifted him, exhaling a soft breath and murmuring something inaudible. Something clenched in Tom's chest and he felt the flicker of recognition. It was as if he were holding his sister in his arms, picking her up when she had scraped her knee or fallen from a tree in one of their games.

Forcing his legs to move, he took one step and then another, moving slowly so not to jolt Edward awake.

As he placed his nephew into the soft double bed in the blue room, the young boy's eyes flickered open for a second, settling on Tom's face. He smiled, wriggled down under the sheets and promptly fell back asleep.

Chapter Three

Jane was glad of the darkness as she drew the hood of her cloak over her head and slipped out of the back door. It was a route she had taken many times now and she knew which floorboards to avoid and how to twist the key in the lock to prevent it from making a horrible screeching sound. She wondered if some of the servants were aware she sneaked out like this, choosing to keep quiet rather than inform their mistress, deciding it was none of their business what a country girl from Somerset was doing, creeping about London at all hours.

Outside the morning was misty and cold and a persistent drizzle fell from the sky, soaking her in minutes. It was mid March and sometimes in Somerset the spring flowers would be blooming, but this year the cold temperatures had delayed the first signs of spring. At this time, she knew she would have to walk a fair distance before there would be a hackney coach to hail. It was too early for most people wealthy enough to want a carriage for hire to be up and about.

She walked briskly, head bent against the weather, the package she carried held tightly to her body.

It was barely better in the hackney, once she found one. She was so wet from the walk that she shivered the entire way, feeling her damp skirts clinging to her legs.

Self-consciously she tried to smooth down her hair, telling herself it wasn't about appearance, but also aware that if she looked too bedraggled she would be thrown out before she had a chance to make her point to the man with whom she hoped to gain an appointment.

Jane watched the streets of London pass by, feeling a heaviness in her stomach as they crossed the river. Even country girls like her knew Southwark was not a place for gently bred young ladies. She might not be wealthy, but she had been raised in a certain way.

The carriage slowed and Jane peered out, suddenly unsure now she was so close to her destination.

'I can't take you no further, miss,' the driver said, jumping down. 'Streets are too narrow.'

A heaviness settled in her stomach and part of her wanted to stay in the relative warmth of the coach and tell the coachman to take her back home. With a glance down at the package she held close to her chest, she rallied. *This* was the whole reason she was here in London, the whole reason she had endured months of balls, dinner parties and trips to the modiste.

'Thank you,' she said as she stepped down, handing the fare to the driver. 'Can you direct me where to go on foot from here?'

'Down that street there, take the second left and you'll come into a courtyard. The address you want is somewhere there.'

'Thank you.'

Jane wished it was a little later in the morning. Although the sun had risen, the streets were still dark and a thin fog curled around her ankles. For a moment she didn't move, her eyes darting left and right, taking in the drunken man sprawled in a doorway and the two young children working up the courage to poke him with a stick. In the distance a group of women bustled through the streets, calling to each other, already well into their day, but here it was quiet.

The sound of the rolling of the carriage wheels beside her made Jane start and she had to move away quickly to avoid being splattered with mud and whatever other filth ran through the streets.

'Come on, Jane,' she muttered to herself, raising her chin and straightening her back. This had been her dream for so long. She wasn't about to give up now.

Blinking as he stepped into the bright sunlight from the gloomy interior of the tavern, Tom grimaced. Southwark wasn't his favourite place to visit at any time of day, but in the dim morning light one saw it for what it really was without the forgiving shield of darkness. The houses were built too close together, overflowing with families too large for the rooms they lived in. Worse still were the people who no longer had a roof over their heads, their eyes filled with despair when they managed to look up.

'Little slice of heaven my lord?' a woman called half-heartedly, as if she knew already her offer would be declined.

When he'd left his house a couple of hours earlier, he hadn't planned to traipse so far, but his feet had moved of their own accord and he'd found himself crossing the river into the less salubrious part of town.

'Remember that moment of pure dread just before the cavalry charge?' Western said as he followed Tom out of the tavern. The man was huge in stature, a giant of a man who took pride in having the deadliest punch in London.

'I remember,' Tom said quietly.

'If you could survive that, you can survive this.'

Without another word, Western gave him an almighty slap on the back, enough to have made Tom stumble if he hadn't braced himself, and then turned and went back inside the tavern.

Western might look as though he would be at home running a gang in the slums of St Giles, but his solid reliability and staunch friendship made Tom feel more grounded. He'd walked into the tavern a mess, his thoughts racing, jumping, not able to settle on what must be done about the surprise arrival of his nephew, the boy he was now charged with looking after. Western had succinctly told Tom to focus on the practical and everything else would fall into place in time.

'The practical,' Tom murmured to himself.

If only he knew something, anything, about children.

He looked around, taking in the bustle of the street, wondering if he would be able to find a carriage for hire to take him back home, where he could start making his plans.

At first his eyes skimmed over the well-dressed young woman walking hesitantly down the street, but after a moment he registered how out of place she looked, and his gaze darted back to her.

Her dress was covered with a dark cloak, the hood pulled up over her hair. There was nothing ostentatious about her clothes, but there was a quality about the fabric that one did not normally see in Southwark. For an instant the young woman turned her head and Tom caught a glimpse of her face. It looked familiar, although she had turned away so quickly he couldn't quite place her.

It was none of his business what this young woman was doing in this part of the city, but his protective instinct had been sparked, and he glanced around, seeing that he wasn't the only one who had taken note of the woman's fine clothing.

Making a decision, he started to cross the street, meaning to intercept the young woman and ensure she did not need any help, but before he could approach she moved way, walking briskly into a dark alley.

Cursing, Tom followed her, expecting to see her ambushed at any moment. She hurried along, looking up at the buildings as she went as if she was unfamiliar with this part of town. Not once did she look behind her and Tom marvelled at her lack of awareness of the danger she could be in. The alleys were narrow and dark, the buildings leaning inward and blocking out much of the light. Filth ran beneath his shoes and the stench was awful. He couldn't imagine what would induce a well-dressed lady to come to this part of town.

After a moment, she turned into a side alley, disappearing from view for a few seconds. Tom moved faster, darting round the corner. As he did, a fist came out of the shadows, connecting with his jaw and snapping his head to the side. It wasn't a particularly hard punch, but it had taken him by surprise and it took him a moment to recover. He did manage to dodge the second punch, the follow-through with the other fist, catching the hand in his before it made contact with his face.

The skin under his fingers was soft and the hand delicate so it was no surprise when it was a woman he drew out of the darkness. The hood of her cloak had fallen back and, as the light hit her face, he drew in a sharp breath of surprise.

'You?'

She frowned in recognition.

'Miss…' He fished around in his brain for the name from the ball the night before. 'Miss Ashworth.'

'Mr Stewart.'

'What are you doing lurking in dark alleys, punching people?'

Miss Ashworth spluttered. '*I* was doing nothing of the sort. I was going about my business, walking down the street, when you decided to follow me.'

'It's a dangerous part of London.'

'Hence why I darted into the alley and punched the man who was following me.'

Tom suppressed a smile at her defiant tone. 'I am sorry if I scared you. That was never my intention. I was concerned that you may not be aware of the dangers of walking alone in Southwark.'

Her fingers twitched in his and he realised he was still holding her hand. Quickly he released it and Miss Ashworth took a step back.

'What are you doing here?'

She hesitated. 'I have an appointment with someone.'

'In Southwark?'

'What are you doing here?' she fired back.

'I was visiting an old friend.'

He saw her raise an eyebrow, knowing the direction of her thoughts, but didn't disabuse her of the notion. People didn't understand the friendship between Western and himself at the best of times. It wasn't something he was about to try and explain in a dark alley to a woman he barely knew.

'You have a good punch,' he said, rubbing his jaw.

'Thank you.'

'I can't just leave you here, alone and un-chaperoned, Miss Ashworth,' he said slowly. There was a flare of defiance in her eyes.

'I have not asked for your protection Mr Stewart.'

'Yet I am honour-bound to give it.'

'Go home, or back to whatever warm bed you've hopped out of, and forget you ever saw me.'

'You know that is not possible. What if you were set upon by a band of thieves, or worse?'

'I can look after myself.'

Tom rubbed his forehead on either side with

his thumb and forefingers. He was developing a headache and Miss Ashworth's stubborn arguments weren't helping. He needed to go home to start organising whatever it was six-year-old boys required in life, not stand in an alley in the cold, arguing with a woman he had met only once before.

'How about I make you a deal?' he said, trying to keep the frustration from his voice. 'You allow me to escort you wherever it is you need to go, and ensure you get back home to Lady Mountjoy's house safely, and in return I will not tell anyone where you have been or what you are doing here.'

Miss Ashworth opened her mouth to argue but before she could speak Tom ploughed on.

'It is a good deal, Miss Ashworth, and I do not have the time or the inclination to negotiate. The alternative is I bundle you into a carriage, take you back to the Mountjoys and tell them where I found you.'

'Fine,' Miss Ashworth said after a couple of seconds. 'Keep up.'

Reaching down, she picked up a package Tom hadn't even realised she had dropped then spun on her heel and marched off down the alley, taking a couple of turns until they came out into a dreary courtyard. The buildings huddled around a cobbled square, ramshackle and grimy, the upper levels accessed by a set of rickety wooden stairs that looked as though they would barely hold a man's weight.

Miss Ashworth, who until this moment had managed to keep up at least a façade of confidence, faltered.

'Not what you were expecting?'

She ignored him, looking up at the doors on the upper level, turning in a circle as she did.

'Would you like me to go first?'

'I can manage from here.'

Despite her protests, Tom followed her up the stairs carefully, spreading his weight evenly so as not to crash through the rotting wooden planks.

Up close the upper level was even worse. The windows were covered in a thick layer of grime and some of the doors were rotting on their hinges.

'Are you sure you're in the right place?' Most of the buildings looked abandoned and beyond repair.

Miss Ashworth paused outside a door that looked as though it had been once painted dark green. She bent down, looked at a scuffed plaque on the door and then straightened with a grimace.

Tom stepped closer and peered at the sign, surprised by what he read: *William Highbury, Book Publisher.*

'A publisher?' Now he was even more confused than before.

She knocked.

'What do you want with a publisher?'

Ignoring him, Miss Ashworth stepped to the side and squinted through the window.

'What do you want with a publisher in Southwark?'

'That is absolutely none of your business.'

'There's no one here. These buildings are not fit for anyone to live in or run a business in.'

Miss Ashworth knocked again, this time louder and more insistent.

'There's no one there, love,' a voice from below called up.

They both moved to the edge of the upper walkway and looked down to the courtyard below.

'Do you know where Mr Highbury is now?'

'Dead. Buried two years ago.' The woman was already starting to walk away, a basket under her arm and a young child trailing in her footsteps.

'And his business—did anyone take it over?'

'He had no children. He had no one,' the woman shouted over her shoulder before disappearing into the alleyway.

Tom watched as Miss Ashworth closed her eyes and let her shoulders sag, unable to comprehend what could have been so important to cause her such disappointment now the chance was gone.

'What did you want with him?'

Miss Ashworth shook her head, glancing down to a bulge beneath her cloak. He remembered the package she had retrieved from the floor after dropping it to punch him.

'What is in that package?'

'It is none of your concern.' She gave an exasperated exhalation. 'In fact none of this is any of your concern. Good day, Mr Stewart.'

'We made a deal, Miss Ashworth,' he said, easily keeping up with her as she started to climb back down the rickety steps.

She turned to glare at him and in doing so her dress caught on a protruding nail on one of the wooden planks. As she turned back, the fabric snagged, pulling and causing her to stumble.

With a little cry she managed to regain her balance, just as Tom lunged forward to grab hold of her, but both their combined weight on one rotten wooden step was too much and there was an ominous crack.

They were only four steps from the ground and, preferring a twisted ankle to a flesh wound from the splintered wood, Tom jumped, grabbing on to Miss Ashworth's arm and pulling her with him. They landed heavily, their bodies crashing into one another. Tom could see he had sent Miss Ashworth reeling so, trying to correct his mistake, he reached out again, ensuring they fell together, and he cushioned the landing.

As he made contact with the cold, wet cobbles, he felt the jarring impact travel through his spine, made worse when Miss Ashworth's body landed squarely on top of his, pushing the air from his lungs.

For a moment neither of them moved, both too stunned to do anything but catch their breaths.

'What did you do that for?' Miss Ashworth asked after a few seconds. She was looking at him as though he were a maniac.

'The wood was splintering! Get cut by a piece of filthy wood, and at best you could lose your leg, perhaps even your life. I chose not to risk it, for either of us.'

Miss Ashworth looked over at the collapsed

bottom portion of the staircase, some of the indignation ebbing out of her expression.

'Filthy perverts, it's broad daylight,' a voice shouted from the end of the alleyway leading into the courtyard. 'Go somewhere private or at least wait until after dark.'

With horror Miss Ashworth looked down, only now realising the position they were in. Tom was lying on his back on the stone cobbles with Miss Ashworth straddling his hips. It wasn't comfortable, and no one in their right mind would choose this filthy location for getting intimate, but he could see from a distance, and in the right light it might look as though they had been overcome by lust for one another.

Quickly Miss Ashworth scrambled to her feet, backing away to put as much distance between them as possible. Tom took a little longer to get up, his back protesting after the jolt it had taken as they'd fallen.

'I'm going home,' Miss Ashworth declared.

'First sensible thing you've said all morning,' Tom muttered.

Either she didn't hear him or chose to ignore him as she stalked back through the alley to the wider streets. It didn't take too long to find a carriage for hire to take them back to Mayfair.

Miss Ashworth seemed to relax a little once the wheels were moving and they wound their way back towards the river and the more familiar parts of London.

They sat in silence for the journey. Normally Tom would have found a way to charm the serious young woman sitting across from him, but today he was too distracted. His mind was already back home, on the little boy with the dark hair and long eyelashes who was now completely reliant on Tom for everything with which a parent should be providing him.

'Can you tell the driver to stop at the end of the street?'

'Why?'

Miss Ashworth rolled her eyes and leaned out of the carriage window, shouting up to the driver. She looked satisfied as a carriage rolled to a stop and went to open the door.

'Thank you for a diverting morning,' Tom said dryly.

'Let us hope our paths do not ever need to cross again.'

She hopped down and without a backward glance began to stride along the street. Tom could probably have stayed in the carriage—it was well past nine o'clock and the streets were busy. It was only a couple of minutes' walk to Lady Mountjoy's house and Miss Ashworth had bowed her head in the drizzle and was making fast progress. Still, he knew he wouldn't feel easy if he didn't see she got safely indoors, so he followed her out of the carriage, quickly paid the driver and walked after her.

He wasn't all that surprised when Miss Ashworth eschewed the front door, instead slipping round the side of the house and into the garden, no doubt to enter the house via a back door, hopefully unnoticed.

'Strange morning,' he murmured, shaking his head. It had been one of the most bizarre mornings of his life.

He paused outside of the Mountjoy house, looking up at the windows, and then turned to leave.

'Mr Stewart! Mr Stewart!' a voice called.

With a sinking in his stomach, he slowly turned back. Lady Mountjoy was standing just outside her front door, waving over to him.

Chapter Four

It was far too early for visitors, but Lady Mountjoy was well known for her hospitality, and taking in those members of her circle who didn't have anyone else to turn to, so the servants didn't blink when she asked for tea and toast to be brought up to the drawing room.

'I just happened to glance out of the window and saw you standing opposite the house, and I thought you had the look of a man who does not know what to do,' Lady Mountjoy said as she poured the tea. 'It is early for visiting, but I am sure Miss Ashworth would be amenable to coming down, seeing as it is you.'

'Miss Ashworth?' Even as the words left his mouth, he knew his tone was a little too sharp, a little too defensive.

'She is the reason you are here, is she not?

You two did dance beautifully at the ball last night.'

Tom closed his eyes. Lady Mountjoy, consummate match-maker, thought he was a possible suitor for her last remaining debutante. His instinct was to rush in, to put her right immediately, but he was aware he needed to step carefully. As much as he didn't want to become embroiled in one of Lady Mountjoy's match-making schemes, equally he knew he couldn't betray why he had really been outside the house. Miss Ashworth might have been foolish to travel to Southwark for her mystery mission, but it wasn't his place to tell her temporary guardians.

'You have it wrong,' he said quickly. 'Pleasant as I am sure Miss Ashworth is, it wasn't her I came to see.'

'Oh.'

'I need your help. It is a delicate matter, but I thought you may be able to advise me.'

The older woman sat back in her chair, resting her tea cup in her saucer, and motioned for him to go on.

'I am sure you remember my sister, Rebecca.'

'Of course.'

'The official story my father liked to tell is that she married a foreign count.'

'Yes, I remember.'

'It was nonsense, of course. My sister fell in love with an Italian, but he wasn't a count, he was a musician.'

'She married him?'

'I don't know. She left with him quietly. My father was not a reasonable man, and if he'd had any notion of what was about to happen he would have locked her up and sent her away.'

Lady Mountjoy nodded thoughtfully. 'That cannot have been easy for you.'

'I loved my sister dearly, and missed her terribly, but I do not begrudge her seizing a chance of happiness. She would have been married off to one of my father's old friends and been under the control of another vindictive old man had she stayed.' He didn't speak of the guilt he felt every morning for the decision he had made at eighteen to leave her behind. It still plagued him, how quickly he had signed up to join the army, how quickly he had moved on with his life whilst she'd still been made to endure a thousand tiny psychological tortures every day from their father.

'You speak of her in the past tense.'

'I learned recently that she passed away a few months ago.'

'I am sorry, my dear.'

Tom nodded, feeling the prick of tears in his eyes. Throughout his childhood he had been schooled that gentlemen did not show their emotions and, although over the last few years he had been trying to do exactly the opposite of many of his father's lessons, showing true emotion was still difficult.

'I can trust your discretion, Lady Mountjoy?'

'Of course.'

'She and her husband left behind a son, my nephew. He has just been delivered into my care and, I have to be honest, I have not the slightest idea what to do with him.'

'Oh my. What a responsibility,' Lady Mountjoy said, reaching across the divide between them and touching him briefly on the hand.

'I know nothing about children. I have never had any desire to father a child of my own. My lifestyle is not conducive to raising a six-year-old.'

'Yet here you are, with a young boy waiting for you to step up.'

Tom closed his eyes. 'I do not have any close relatives.' He grimaced. 'And my friends are mainly men who live their lives in the same manner I do. I thought...' He trailed off, looking across at the older woman with anticipation. It might not have been the true reason he had come to the Mountjoy residence today, but he *did* need help, and Lady Mountjoy was not known as society's favourite matriarch for nothing.

'You thought I might be able to offer some advice?'

'Yes.'

Tom could see the countess was formulating an answer when the door flew open and Miss Ashworth burst into the room. She had changed. Her dress was clean and dry and her hair was pulled into a neat, low bun, although if he looked carefully he could still see some loose damp strands curling at the base of her neck.

'Mr Stewart,' Miss Ashworth said, her tone accusatory.

Tom stood. Even though he had spent less than an hour in total in her company, he knew she was going to make assumptions that were not true and likely expose both of them to unnecessary scandal.

'Good morning, Miss Ashworth, I trust you

enjoyed the ball last night?' he said, trying to convey a sense of calm.

'How could…?' She faltered as she registered his calm tone and serene smile. 'Yes… yes, I did. Thank you.' She glanced at Lady Mountjoy, who was looking at her curiously. 'It is rather early for a visit, is it not?'

'I apologise,' Tom said. 'I have had a lot on my mind and I thought it later than it is. Lady Mountjoy, generous hostess that she is, was too polite to turn me away.'

'Mr Stewart, if you would wait a moment whilst I find my address book, I have a few contacts that could help you.'

Before Tom could answer either way, Lady Mountjoy had risen and swept from the room, leaving him with Miss Ashworth.

'What are you doing here?' Miss Ashworth whispered as soon as she could be sure the older woman was out of earshot. 'You weren't meant to follow me in. Why are you interfering with everything?'

'Calm down.'

It was the wrong thing to say. The young woman pressed her lips together until they were almost white and colour flooded to her cheeks.

'So far today you have stalked me through

the streets of Southwark, injured my hand, drawn lewd comments from the local residents and now you're here to betray me.'

'You're being melodramatic. And wrong.'

'What are you doing here?'

'Firstly, I wasn't stalking you. I was concerned for your welfare. Secondly, you hurt your hand by *punching me*. Thirdly, you were the one who stomped down the rotten staircase and made us fall into the grime of the Southwark streets.' He paused, glad to see some of the defiance had left her. 'And fourthly, I wanted to check you got home safely, but Lady Mountjoy spotted me outside. I have told her I was here for another reason. I have not even mentioned you at all.'

'Oh.' She hesitated. 'Thank you.'

'Here we are,' Lady Mountjoy said as she breezed back into the room. 'I have written down a few essential contacts. There is an agency that provides nursemaids and nannies, the details of a couple of tutors and three tailors that are wonderful with children.'

'Thank you,' Tom said, taking the piece of paper and getting to his feet. He was ready to leave the events of this morning well behind him.

'You have younger siblings, don't you, Miss Ashworth?'

'Yes, five younger sisters.'

'Good. Tomorrow Miss Ashworth and I will call on you and if needed provide some practical and emotional support. You will get through this, Mr Stewart.'

He bowed, eager to get out of the house before he had to impart any more details of his personal life to either of the two women in front of him.

'Thank you for all your help, Lady Mountjoy. Have a pleasant day, Miss Ashworth.'

'Why don't you see Mr Stewart to the door, Miss Ashworth?' Lady Mountjoy said with a twinkle in her eye. 'My hip is paining me all of a sudden.'

Tom left the room, waiting for the footman to bring him his coat and hat before he stepped out through the front door. To his surprise, Miss Ashworth followed him, pulling the heavy wooden door closed behind her and accompanying him onto the steps in front of the house.

'Is something the matter?'

'I should thank you,' Miss Ashworth said quietly. 'For not giving me away. I know you didn't have to lie for me.' She didn't meet his eye as she spoke but her words were clear.

'It is not my place to inform Lady Mountjoy what you have been doing, but a word of advice—she is a sharp woman, *very* hard to deceive. I doubt she is completely in the dark as to what you are doing, even though I have not a clue.'

Miss Ashworth nodded slowly then turned to go back inside. 'I didn't know you had children, Mr Stewart,' she said over her shoulder.

'I don't.'

'But Lady Mountjoy said…'

'It is for my nephew. He has recently come to live with me. And now I must get back to him.'

Tom bowed, turned and took the steps two at a time, not stopping to look back over his shoulder. Enough distractions. Now he needed to get home and work out how he was going to cope with his life being turned completely upside down.

Chapter Five

'He is not going to want me bursting into his drawing room at a time like this,' Jane protested, even though she knew it was futile.

'Nonsense, the man has just become guardian to a young child he barely knows. He will be glad of any and all support offered.'

'Surely he would rather have privacy and solitude in this difficult time?'

'If that was what he wanted, would he have come to call yesterday?' Lady Mountjoy asked, and Jane quickly dropped her protestations. It was too late anyway, they were already drawing up to an impressive house on Grosvenor Square.

'Lady Mountjoy,' Jane said, knowing this might be her only chance to talk in private with her benefactor, 'Please promise me you are not going to try and match me with Mr Stewart.'

'Why do you ask, Jane? He is lovely, isn't he?'

'No.' She said it far too quickly and loudly, taking hold of her emotions and toning down her vehemence as she repeated the word. 'No. I mean, I am sure he is a perfectly pleasant gentleman, but on the couple of occasions we exchanged words there was nothing between us.'

'Really? I thought I saw a spark. That first flare of interest.'

'No.' Jane felt her heart sinking. Lady Mountjoy was thinking of pushing her and the irritating Mr Stewart closer together. 'I can promise there was nothing between us.'

'If it is meant to be, it is meant to be,' Lady Mountjoy said cryptically.

There was no time for any further argument as the carriage door was opened by the driver and Lady Mountjoy hopped out, spritely in step and not showing any hint of the hip pain she had complained of the day before.

Jane wondered about staying in the carriage, knowing it was pure fantasy to think she would escape this visit. With a groan she stepped down and followed the countess in through the front door.

A footman led them through the hall to a room at the back of the house, bypassing the grand drawing room. Instead they were shown into the library, where Mr Stewart and a young boy with the same shock of dark-brown hair and long eyelashes were poring over an atlas together.

For a moment the man and boy didn't realise they were being observed and they continued to talk in low voices. Then the child looked up, confusion on his face.

'Lady Mountjoy and Miss Ashworth to see you, sir,' the footman announced.

'Thank you. Would you see to it tea is served in the drawing room?'

He stood, motioning for his guests to go ahead whilst he turned and spoke to the boy next to him. The boy nodded, but looked crestfallen at having his uncle taken away.

'How is he settling in?' Lady Mountjoy enquired as they sat down in the drawing room.

Mr Stewart grimaced. 'He cried for his mother all last night, which is hardly surprising.'

'Poor child,' Jane murmured. She was lucky enough to have both her parents still alive, but she had lost her twin sister a few years earlier, and she still mourned Harriet every day. Losing someone you loved was terrible, but it was even worse for someone as young as Mr Stewart's nephew.

'This isn't the right place for him,' Mr Stewart said, running a hand through his hair, and for the first time since meeting him Jane saw his vulnerable side. Normally he was all glib comments and perfectly timed quips. Now he looked as if he was about to be bested by a six-year-old boy.

'Of course it is. You're his family,' Lady Mountjoy said.

'I know. And I know it is my responsibility to look after him but this house, this life in London, it isn't the right environment for him.' He motioned around the room. 'I have no toys, no books, nothing to interest a child. For the last hour we've been looking at atlases to see which route his ship took from Italy to here, but I cannot stretch out that activity any longer.'

'He's too young for school,' Jane said quickly, knowing it wasn't her place to tell Mr Stewart how to organise his affairs, but unable to stop herself.

'Why do you say that?'

Jane felt the force of his stare on her, as if he were probing her mind to see what secrets lay there. She thought of the day her parents had sent Harriet and her off to school, convinced they were doing the right thing by their daughters, furthering their education so one day they might become governesses or music teachers. In principle, it *had* been the right thing, but Jane would never forget the coldness of the teachers or the hostility from some of the other girls. She'd missed her family, missed her home, and she had been fourteen years old. She couldn't imagine being sent away at the tender age of six.

'He's young, and he's just lost everything and everyone he knows and cares about. Sending him to school before he can feel he has a home to come back to would be devastating for him.'

'It is early yet to make such decisions. Things will get easier,' Lady Mountjoy said. 'Did you have any luck with the agency that employs nannies?'

Mr Stewart grimaced. 'Three weeks is the soonest they can have someone available. Apparently it is a very busy time for them.'

'That is a long time,' Lady Mountjoy murmured. 'But perhaps we can help. Miss Ashworth is wonderful with children, and she is always complaining that I drag her to too many society events. Perhaps a couple of times a week she could come and spend some time with your nephew.'

Jane looked at Lady Mountjoy, completely stunned. She had anticipated some subtle manoeuvring, gentle suggestions that might place Mr Stewart and her together on a few occasions, but not to be volunteered for a job as part-time nanny to a boy she didn't know.

'I could not ask that,' Mr Stewart said quickly, and Jane would have been offended by the alarm in his eyes if hers had not reflected the same sentiment.

'Nonsense. Miss Ashworth loves children, and I am sure she would rather that than I line up a parade of suitors for her.'

Jane thought of her relative freedom in the Mountjoy household, the way she was able to take time to write in the afternoons, and her trips across London to visit various publishers in a bid for one of them to read her work. The last thing she wanted was to be under Lady Mountjoy's constant scrutiny, to be the one on whom the countess focussed her matchmaking eye.

'It is such a pleasant afternoon,' Jane said

quickly. 'Perhaps we could go for a walk, Mr Stewart, and discuss the idea. Your nephew could come too, of course.'

Mr Stewart looked surprised, and after ten seconds hadn't answered when Lady Mountjoy clapped her hands. 'What a wonderful idea. I would accompany you, but did I mention my hip is paining me?'

'It is raining,' Mr Stewart said.

'Mere drizzle.'

'And the wind is whipping up.'

'A little gust of wind never hurt anyone.'

'And there is talk of snow.'

'I am sure your nephew would be delighted to see snow.'

'Fine,' Mr Stewart said. 'As you are so enthused. Shall I see Miss Ashworth home after?'

'That is most kind of you, Mr Stewart,' Lady Mountjoy said. 'Perhaps you have a maid who could act as chaperon?'

Twenty minutes later they stepped through the gates of Hyde Park, their heads bowed against the wind.

'Is it always so cold here?' Edward asked, his voice quiet as it was whipped away by the wind.

'Not always, and certainly not normally in

March,' Jane said, trying to inject a note of cheerfulness into her voice. 'I expect you are used to much warmer weather in Italy.'

He nodded and shivered. Jane crouched down in front of him and adjusted the boy's coat. It was thin, not made for an English winter, and already looked to be getting too small for him. To combat this, he had two scarves wrapped around his neck and a pair of oversized gloves on his hands that kept slipping off. Pulled down over his ears was a warm woolly hat, also a few sizes too big.

'Mama said England was beautiful.' He screwed up his nose and looked at the bare trees and muddy grass. 'It doesn't look beautiful.'

'Not now,' Jane said, squeezing his hand. 'But just wait until it is covered in a thick layer of snow, everything white and fresh. Then it will look beautiful.'

'Will we have snow? Really?' His face lit up.

'Yes, without a doubt. If not this year then certainly next winter. And you will be able to throw snowballs and go ice-skating, and perhaps even go sledging.'

'I will be the best at throwing snowballs,' Edward said, becoming animated. 'I always play catch with Roberto and Michel.' Suddenly his face dropped.

'It is hard leaving people behind, isn't it?'

He nodded and Jane felt her heart squeeze for the little boy. Children were resilient. He would settle in his new home, and in a few years there would be no outward signs of missing what he'd once had, just an inner longing, a feeling of not being quite complete.

'Lady Mountjoy was right—you are good with children,' Edward said as Jane straightened up to continue their walk.

'It is not hard. You merely talk to them as another human. So many people think they do not understand enough to hold a conversation, but they are wrong. Children see everything and hear everything, even if they might sometimes need help interpreting what they have taken in.'

Mr Stewart was silent for a few minutes, his eyes locked on his nephew as they strolled through the park.

'I had an ulterior motive for agreeing with Lady Mountjoy that we should take a walk together,' Jane said as they rounded a corner and came out into a wide-open grassy area. There was no one else about so she could be sure they wouldn't be overheard.

'Go on.'

For a moment she hesitated, unsure as to how to continue now she had broached the subject.

'I am not looking for a husband,' she said, wanting to claw back the words when Mr Stewart's eyes widened in horror.

'And I am not looking for a wife,' he said quickly.

'Of course not,' Jane snapped. 'That is not what I meant. Be quiet and listen for a moment.' Her embarrassment made her speak sharply, but it had the desired effect; Mr Stewart remained silent and motioned for her to go on. 'I am not looking for a husband, but it is Lady Mountjoy's greatest wish to pair me off with some suitor. She feels everyone is happier when matched with someone else.'

'Yes, she does have a certain reputation for match-making.'

'I respect Lady Mountjoy greatly, but I do not have the time or energy to fend off her match-making efforts. She started with five debutantes, and everyone else is married. All she has left is me.'

'I can see why you would feel nervous,' Mr Stewart murmured.

'I have…things I need to be doing. Until

now, I have enjoyed a modicum of freedom, but I can feel that slipping through my fingers.'

'Things?'

'Yes, *things*,' she said, refusing to elaborate. He didn't need to know about her dreams, that this was her one chance to make everything she had hoped for and worked for a reality. 'I cannot spend every waking second of my day being paraded in front of an endless line of dull gentlemen who are never going to be interested in me anyway.'

'What is it you think we can do for each other?'

'If Lady Mountjoy believes there is a chance we are falling for each other, then she will leave me in peace when it comes to other suitors.' She risked a glance up at Mr Stewart and saw that so far he wasn't convinced by her plan. 'You need help with your nephew and, whilst I am no nursemaid, I enjoy the company of children. I would be happy to visit a few times a week, to take Edward on trips to the park or read with him quietly in the library.'

Slowly Mr Stewart nodded. 'You help me with Edward, and in doing so Lady Mountjoy assumes the reason you are so keen to spend time with me is because we are falling for one another.'

'I am sure we can be civil to one another in company and perhaps even attend a few of the same events to build the illusion.'

'What about at the end of the Season?'

'At the end of the Season I will return to Somerset and you will have your nanny and will have settled into a routine with Edward.' Jane risked another glance at the man beside her. He hadn't dismissed the idea outright so she was hopeful he might see the merit in it.

'I cannot see the harm in trying the idea, as long as we are both completely honest with one another. If an attachment begins to form...'

Jane laughed and then realised he was serious. 'Do women fall for you that easily, Mr Stewart?'

He shrugged.

'I promise I have no feelings for you except a mild gratitude that you might save me from the match-making machinations of Lady Mountjoy.' She held up her hand so he didn't interrupt. 'And I promise that if I find your... *charm*...so irresistible I will immediately let you know and we can sever our arrangement.'

'Then I cannot see a problem.'

'I will inform Lady Mountjoy that I wish to help you and Edward, as was her suggestion, and we will take it from there.'

Jane held out her hand and waited for Mr Stewart to shake it.

'I do have one condition, though,' he said, holding her eye.

'Name it.'

'You tell me what it is that is so important that you were sneaking around Southwark yesterday morning, and why you are eager for Lady Mountjoy not to scrutinise your every move these next few weeks.'

Jane held his eye, wondering if it would be the final straw if she shook her head and refused to answer him. For so long, her writing and her ambition had been private, something she had held close to her and hadn't let anyone see. She thought of Mr Stewart's steely determination when he had followed her the morning before and, even though she didn't know him well, she could tell he was a man used to getting what he wanted.

She paused, looking down and scuffing her shoe on the path.

'I write,' she said finally. 'And draw—illustrations for the stories I write.' Quickly she glanced up to see his reaction. It was unheard of for a woman of middling social status to have ambitions that stretched beyond marrying well and supporting her husband in his endeavours.

'What do you write?'

She frowned. She hadn't expected his interest to be beyond the superficial. She'd thought, one he found out her secret, he would immediately dismiss it as the dream of a naïve young woman.

'Stories for children.'

'And you draw?'

'Yes. And paint.'

He nodded slowly. 'You're looking for a publisher. That's what you were doing in Southwark.' He paused. 'Surely there are more reputable places to find a publisher than an alley in Southwark?'

Jane wondered what it must be like to be born into a life of privilege, a life where everything fell at your feet. Her family wasn't poor, but they did not have connections outside Somerset, and even if they had she wouldn't have had access to them as a woman.

Slowly he shook his head. 'I suppose you have tried them already?'

'They will not even meet with me when they find out I am a woman.'

'Ah.'

It was not an unexpected turn of events. She

had known it would be difficult, perhaps even impossible, to get her stories published, but she hadn't expected everyone to refuse even to look at her work.

'I am not afraid of rejection,' she said quietly. 'I know my stories and illustrations may never be published, but I wish they would be judged on merit, not on who has written them.'

'I could…'

She held up a hand to stop him. 'No. Whatever you are offering is kind, but I need to do this on my own. I do not want to succeed because I have passed my work off as someone else's.'

'I was merely going to suggest an introduction or two.'

'And have my stories published out of some favour someone owes you? No. Again, thank you for your kindness, but I if I do this it will be on my own.'

Mr Stewart looked as though he was going to say more but thought better of it.

'Can we go and see the ducks?' Edward asked, pulling on Jane's hand.

'Yes, let's see if we can spot any swans or geese too.'

Chapter Six

'**W**here is he?' Miss Ashworth asked as she burst into the house. She was trailed by a weary-looking maid who Tom didn't envy, it would be quite a job to keep up with the energetic Miss Ashworth, acting as chaperon as she raced around the city.

'He's upstairs in his bedroom,' Tom said, feeling a deep relief that someone else had arrived to share in his panic.

Miss Ashworth rushed towards the stairs and then caught herself, turning back to face him.

'Tell me exactly what happened.'

'I am told he woke in the night and started calling for his mother. The maid who has been sleeping in his room tried to comfort him, but he became more distressed and asked for me. I was…' He fell silent, the guilt of not being where he'd needed to be almost overwhelming him. 'I was not there and he has been inconsolable since.'

'Where were you?' Miss Ashworth asked, and then quickly shook her head. 'I do not wish to know the answer to that question.' She started back towards the stairs and Tom followed, feeling out of place in his own house.

The heart-wrenching sound of sobs led Jane along the upstairs hallway to a room at the end, and softly she knocked on the door. There was no answer, but she hadn't expected one, instead waiting for a moment before going in.

Edward was on the floor next to his bed, hugging his blanket as if it was all he had in the world. His face was tear-streaked and blotchy and his hair looked tousled.

Jane felt a rush of affection for the little boy and rushed to him, wondering if it was too familiar to scoop him up in her arms. She thought of her little sisters at six, at what comfort they'd got from a loving touch or cuddle, and she quietened her doubts and cradled the little boy in her arms. His sobs grew louder as he buried his head into her chest, as if he were overcome with emotion and finally allowing himself to let it out.

She sat there for a long time, holding him

tight, one hand gently rubbing his back, occasionally dropping a kiss onto the mop of dark hair. She let him cry, let him rid himself of all the overwhelming emotion, and only when his body had stilled and his sobs quietened did she try and speak to him.

'Did you have a bad dream?'

He nodded, a minute movement of his head against her chest.

'Did you want to tell me what it was about?'

'I can't remember.'

'Sometimes when I have bad dreams I just want to have a cuddle with someone.'

'I wanted my mama,' Edward said, his voice breaking and the tears starting again. 'I want my mama.'

'I know you do, little one,' Jane murmured, stroking his hair. She sang to him, a song she had sung hundreds of times before to her little sisters whenever they had scraped a knee or bumped a head.

'Lavender blue, dilly-dilly...'

Finally, after what felt like thousands of repeats of the gentle lullaby, the little boy's body grew heavy in her arms and his breathing deepened. Jane stayed in the same position for a while longer, ensuring he was deeply asleep before she set him down on the bed and tucked him in.

Mr Stewart shifted by the door and she realised he had been there the whole time.

'How did you do that?' He was looking at her in awe.

'He's a child. He needs comfort and security and someone to hold him tight and make him feel as though they will protect him from the world.'

'It's not me that he wants to do that.'

'Of course it's not. Edward wants his mother, but she isn't here, and you are.'

Mr Stewart closed his eyes and shook his head, as if trying to rid himself of the morning's events.

Jane knew she shouldn't push the man. He had suffered the bereavement of his sister and taken in his nephew, but even though she didn't know him well she thought he was capable of more for the child.

'Do you want children, Mr Stewart?'

'Good lord, no,' he said quickly as they walked side by side down the hallway.

'Any reason for the vehemence of your reply?'

He shrugged. 'It isn't in my plan for my life.'

'May I enquire what is in your plan?'

He paused and turned to her, and Jane felt the full force of his charm. He smiled at her and for a fraction of a second she saw what gave him the reputation of a rake. The women in ballrooms whispered about him whilst biting their lower lips and looking on longingly. It was ridiculous, but she could see the basis of their infatuation. Mr Stewart was an attractive man, with his dark hair and green eyes, but it wasn't just his appearance that made him so popular. There was something about his smile, the way he looked at you, something that made you want to be in on the joke he was telling or the tale he was spinning.

Quickly she caught herself. It was superficial, the gift of a charmer and no more.

'To stay blissfully free and single and unencumbered.'

'No wife, no children?'

'Are you volunteering yourself again, Miss Ashworth?'

'No. I'm just surprised. You are a wealthy and influential man. I thought the ambition of all wealthy and influential men was to marry a submissive young lady and then ensure their house is filled with enough heirs to carry on the family name.'

Leaning in a little closer, he smiled. 'You

may be right that is the wish of many gentlemen, but I have no title to pass on, no inflated
sense of my family name. I am quite content
with living *my* life to the full rather than ruin-
ing another generation.'

'You are dedicated to a life of pleasure,
then?'

'Is it so surprising?' They had reached the
stairs and he spun to face her. Jane felt a rush
of anticipation, as if she were being swept into
his confidence. 'What other purpose do we
as humans have? We are born, we work and
then we die. Surely the only way to make a life
worthwhile is to enjoy it to the full for the few
short years we are here?'

'Some people would argue that dedicating
your life to others, through charity or good
deeds, is a more worthwhile way to spend a
lifetime.'

He shrugged. 'It is exactly the same. People
do the things that make them feel good. Yes,
for some there is also an element of sacrifice,
that decision to put someone else's happiness
first, but in the end *that* makes them feel worthy.' He paused and searched her eyes with his
own. 'The only difference is I can admit my
life is about seeking pleasure.'

Jane regarded him for a long moment. It was

an interesting concept and, although she didn't entirely agree, she did see his idea had merit.

'Yet you have kept Edward here with you,' she said quietly.

'I'm not a monster. The boy has lost everyone he loves.'

'If you were truly dedicated to your own pleasure then you would have sent him away. I would wager you have a country residence tucked away somewhere, a comfortable house you could have sent him to with a couple of servants to keep him safe and looked after.'

'Is that what you think I should do with him?'

'No,' Jane said quickly. 'That would be devastating. You know that, and you are putting his needs ahead of yours.'

Mr Stewart gave her a quick smile. 'I said I seek pleasure, not that I am selfish.'

Together they walked downstairs, and Jane paused in the hallway. She knew she should leave. Her maid was peeking out from the door that led to the kitchens and it would be most appropriate if she returned home now Edward had settled.

'Stay,' Mr Stewart said. 'Stay until Edward wakes.'

'I could,' Jane said slowly. 'But I wonder if

it would be better if he woke and you were sitting beside his bed.'

Mr Stewart didn't argue, watching her silently as she ushered her maid into the hallway and to the door.

'I thought of taking Edward to Astley's later. Perhaps you would like to come?'

Jane hesitated. She had thought of trying to slip away that afternoon to visit some of the publishing houses she had been to when she had first arrived in London, hopeful and inexperienced. They had refused to even admit her then, but she was getting better at the patter that would gain her an audience with the right people.

'Astley's sounds lovely.'

'Bring whoever you would like as a chaperon.'

'Thank you.'

'Shall I pick you up at four o'clock?'

She felt a frisson of excitement. When she had agreed to come to London with Lady Mountjoy for the winter months leading up to the Season, her focus had been entirely on trying to find someone to publish her stories. But, as the weeks had passed and her friendship with the other debutantes had blossomed, she had begun to enjoy all the new experi-

ences. Not so much the balls and the dress fit-
tings, but the trips around London, the visits to
Vauxhall Pleasure Gardens, the strolls through
the park. Jane was well aware that after these
few months she would return to Somerset and
might never leave the county again. It was a
long way from Bath to London, and a journey
her family could ill afford.

Astley's was another place she had heard
much about, and she reasoned one afternoon
away from her mission wouldn't hurt.

'Thank you.'

She turned to go, a footman opening the
door for her, but before she could step outside
Mr Stewart caught her hand. Jane felt a jolt
of energy pass through her, making her skin
prickle and burn as if it were on fire.

'Thank you for coming this morning,' he
said quietly, sincerely.

Jane managed to nod, feeling her heart
pound in her chest, and forced herself to pull
her hand away and break contact. Out on the
pavement she risked a glance back, feeling the
breath being pulled from her body as he gave
her one last smile.

'Stop it,' she muttered to herself. Mr Stewart was a consummate charmer, a man she tol-
erated for the convenient agreement they had

made, and for the sake of his sweet nephew. She would not allow herself to succumb to the allure of his smile. She was stronger than that, shrewder than that.

'This is all very mysterious,' Lucy said, and Jane had to pull herself away from the window to reply.

'There is nothing mysterious at all about it.'

Lucy raised an eyebrow. 'A man with a reputation as a notorious rake has invited you to Astley's for the afternoon. I only moved out three weeks ago, and before that I am quite sure you had never once mentioned a Mr Stewart.'

'I didn't know him then.'

'How *do* you know him?'

'We were introduced—at Lady Mountjoy's ball. The one you were meant to come to, but were caught up in wedded bliss so missed it.'

'I have apologised a thousand times!' Lucy grinned. 'But when you marry…'

Jane snorted.

'*When* you marry I am sure you will understand how time slips away from you.'

'How is the delightful Captain Weyman?'

Lucy had married her childhood sweetheart three weeks earlier after an agonising wait whilst he'd been abroad with the army. Jane liked to tease her friend but was beyond ecstatic that Lucy had finally married the man she loved, overcoming all the hurdles that had been placed in their way.

'Very well. We are thinking of returning to Somerset soon to see if we can start to repair the relationship with his father. William will get his orders in the next couple of weeks, but we are hoping his next posting will be closer than his last.'

'Don't go yet,' Jane said quietly. 'I would miss you too much, and you don't want to start off your married life with the sourness of his family seeping into your happiness.'

'Perhaps we will wait until the summer. I do love Somerset in the summer months.' She smiled at her friend, looking pointedly at the window again, and Jane made an effort to pull herself away.

'Mr Stewart recently became guardian to his nephew, a lovely young boy who is six years old and called Edward. Being a man who has never spent any time around children, he claims he is out of his depth with Edward, although it would be unfair to say he is completely useless with him.'

'I hope you don't use such encouraging words with him.'

Jane smiled, pleased to have her friend back even if it was just for the afternoon.

'So how have you become involved in Mr Stewart's situation?'

'Lady Mountjoy suggested I might help him, as I have so many younger siblings and am used to the company of children.'

'Ah.'

'Ah indeed. She has this gleam in her eye.'

'She does have a nearly perfect record. Out of the five of us she brought to London, you are the only one unmarried.'

'Don't remind me. I don't wish to disappoint her. She has been more than generous with her time and money and affection, but she is not going to see me married.'

'Not even to the charming Mr Stewart?'

'Certainly not to him.' Jane felt the heat on her cheeks and hated that this line of questioning was making her blush.

'Let me see if I have this right. Lady Mountjoy wants to pair you with Mr Stewart, even though he has a reputation as a rake who has no intention of settling down. She has volunteered you to assist with his nephew and you are just going along with all of this?'

'If it isn't him it'll just be someone else. At least I can be sure he harbours no interest in me and I know I have no interest in him. His nephew is adorable, and if I manage to avoid an endless parade of suitors then I can tolerate a few hours a week spent in Mr Stewart's company.'

'You discussed it with him?'

'Openly. He agreed.'

'What is in it for him?'

'I spend some time with his nephew whilst he waits for the nanny the agency have promised him.'

Lucy pondered for a moment. 'Not a bad plan in theory,' she said after a minute. 'But what if one of you starts to develop feelings for the other? You will be in close proximity for a while.'

'That will never happen. Mr Stewart is a man who prefers his liaisons without emotional attachment, and I have absolutely no interest in any romantic relationship.'

Lucy looked as though she was going to protest further when Jane saw the carriage pull to a halt outside.

'Miss Jane!' Edward shouted with glee as she climbed up into the carriage, darting forward off the seat where he sat with his uncle and into her arms. 'We're going to see the horses and the acrobats. Zio Tom said there are trapeze artists and tightrope walkers.'

'How wonderful,' Jane said, laughing as she got caught up in the young boy's enthusiasm. 'I have never seen a tightrope walker before.'

'Good afternoon,' Mr Stewart said, lifting his hat as Lucy stepped up.

'This is my dear friend, Mrs Lucy Weyman,' Jane said quickly. 'This is Mr Stewart and his nephew Edward.'

'Lovely to meet you,' Lucy said as she took her seat, grabbing hold of Jane as she almost overbalanced as the carriage started to move away.

The streets were busy on the journey to Lambeth, even more so as they approached Astley's amphitheatre. Jane craned her head out of the window, hoping to catch a glimpse of the theatre, awed by the size of the building they were approaching. The crowd was all heading in the same direction and there was a buzz of excitement and anticipation for the afternoon's entertainment.

Once their carriage finally found a spot to pull over to allow them to disembark, Mr Stewart hopped down and offered his hand to Jane, Lucy and finally Edward.

'Keep your coin purse hidden and anything of value secure,' Mr Stewart said as a merry group of women jostled past them. 'It is not quite the same clientele as you get at the opera.'

Mr Stewart seemed unperturbed by the mixed group of people flooding along the pavement and joining the queue to get into the theatre. Jane remembered her encounter with him in Southwark and wondered if his life in pursuit of pleasure took him to other less salubrious areas of the city.

They joined the queue, Mr Stewart paying for the tickets and leading them up the stairs to a box that overlooked the circular level stage.

Already there was a man juggling brightly coloured balls as he walked around in a circle, every so often doing a high throw or spinning before he caught the balls and continued. Edward's eyes fixed onto the juggler immediately and he was smiling by the time he had taken his seat.

'Have you been here before, Mr Stewart?' Jane asked as he courteously helped her arrange her chair so she could see well.

'Yes, many times. I had a hankering to be a horseman when I was a boy. Whenever we were in town, my sister and I would always sneak off and come to watch the show.'

Jane caught the hint of sadness in his voice at the mention of his sister.

'Did you never decide to pursue it as a career?'

'Actually, I did, although in the only way that was open to me. I was in the cavalry division in the army.'

'Did you serve for a long time?'

'Six years. Then I was injured and it took me a long time to recover.'

Jane looked at him with interest. He had no outwardly visible evidence of a bad injury. He didn't limp or walk with a stick, like many of the men who returned from war. There was no scarring on his face or his hands, and he moved quickly, agilely. She desperately wanted to know what happened to him but knew it was rude to ask outright.

Fidgeting, she tried to focus on something else.

'You can ask me,' Mr Stewart said as he leaned in closer. Jane felt the heat of his body as his arm brushed against hers for a second. 'I can see you want to.'

She'd always thought she wasn't that easy to read, and the idea of this man being able to tell what she was thinking by a quick glance at her expression or posture was unsettling.

'How were you injured?'

'I was thrown from my horse and trampled by the rest of the regiment.'

'Surely you couldn't survive that?'

'I was very lucky.' He flashed her a smile, 'Or extremely unlucky, whatever way you look at it. I was bed-bound for nine months, and they tell me unconscious for the first few weeks of that.'

'Nine months!' she exclaimed, and the people in the next box turned to look at her.

'It's a long time, isn't it? At least, that's what I'm told. To me it seemed like only a few minutes had passed. The days blurred into one. I think there was an element of delirium.'

There were so many questions Jane wanted to ask. It was incredible to think he had survived such a grievous injury and she wondered if that had influenced his desire to live to indulge his pleasures.

Mr Stewart chuckled at her expression. 'This is why I don't tell anyone. Their reactions vary from disbelief to pity.'

'It is rather extraordinary. What happened to you whilst you were injured?'

'On the battlefield, a good friend scooped me up and took me to back to our camp. The doctor set the broken bone in my arm and told him that if I woke up in the next twenty-four hours I might have a chance at survival.'

'Do you remember nothing?'

'Nothing at all. I stayed in the medical tent in the camp for two weeks. I am told they managed to get some water into me, but my body was wasting away. When they thought I was hours from death I opened my eyes for the first time. From there it was a long road home, a long road to recovery. It took three months to transport me.'

'It must have been strange to wake up after so long unconscious.'

'It was. The first few days were a blur of confusion and pain, but I know I am lucky to be alive. Many of my regiment did not survive.'

'Did it take you long to recover, once you woke up?'

He grinned at this. 'Have you ever seen a baby deer, with gangly legs, all bone and no muscle?'

Jane nodded, thinking of the forest a few miles away from her home where they would go on picnics in the summer months.

'My muscles had wasted away to such a degree that I could not stand. I could barely raise a glass to my lips. I was much like a new-born fawn, stumbling around even after a few weeks. I did not start to recover until I was home, able to work on building my strength day by day, but even then it took a long time.'

It must have taken a lot of determination and work to have built himself up, and Jane felt a new respect for the man. He had no outward signs of his injuries, although she did wonder what hidden scars they had left.

'Didn't you want to return to the army after that?'

'I considered it, but I had been away for so long, and then it took months and months of work to get my fitness back to what would be required...' He shrugged. 'It was felt best I didn't return.' There was a glint of regret in his eye and Jane got the impression someone else had made the decision for him. She was about to try and probe further when there was a long blast on a trumpet and an excited gasp ran through the crowd.

Edward turned to her and grabbed her hand, his eyes shining with excitement.

'Do you think the acrobats will come first, Miss Jane?'

'Perhaps. Or maybe the trapeze artists.'

Jane felt the energy in the audience as a well-built man stepped out into the ring, raising a top hat and welcoming them to the show.

He promised wonders such as they had never seen before, and as he spoke a group of performers tumbled out from back stage and began the first routine.

For an hour and a half Jane sat on the edge of her seat, enthralled by the performance, but also by the look of wonder on Edward's face. She often liked to watch her younger sisters when they tried something new for the first time, enjoying that expression of sheer magic on their faces.

In time the show neared its climax and four horses broke into the ring, galloping in a circle, hooves thundering in time, and Edward let out a squeal of delight. Jane found herself leaning forward in her chair, and next to her she felt Mr Stewart shift as well. Glancing up at his face, she saw an expression that mirrored his nephew's as he watched the acrobats standing astride the horses, swinging themselves down to the ground and back up in a show of excellent muscle control and perfect timing.

Gently she touched Mr Stewart on the arm, not wanting to spoil his enjoyment, but keen he should share it with his nephew. She motioned for them to swap chairs so he was sitting next to the young boy, and after a moment she saw Mr Stewart bend his head towards his nephew's and begin to point out something that was happening below them. For half a minute, Jane watched them together, uncle and nephew brought together by their love of horses.

Chapter Seven

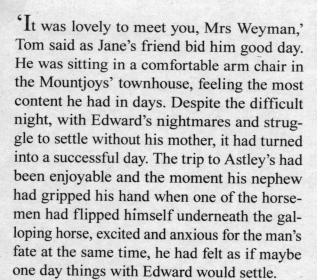

'It was lovely to meet you, Mrs Weyman,'
Tom said as Jane's friend bid him good day.
He was sitting in a comfortable arm chair in
the Mountjoys' townhouse, feeling the most
content he had in days. Despite the difficult
night, with Edward's nightmares and struggle to settle without his mother, it had turned
into a successful day. The trip to Astley's had
been enjoyable and the moment his nephew
had gripped his hand when one of the horse-
men had flipped himself underneath the galloping horse, excited and anxious for the man's
fate at the same time, he had felt as if maybe
one day things with Edward would settle.

He knew much of the success today had
come from the woman sitting opposite him.

'What are you looking at me like that for?'
Miss Ashworth looked relaxed, as if she

wanted to kick off her shoes and curl up in the comfortable arm chair. It was strangely comforting to see her like this, prim and upright as she normally was.

They were alone together in the drawing room now Mrs Weyman had left, although Lady Mountjoy was next door in the library with Edward, and Lord Mountjoy a little way down the hall in the study. The door was open, so there could be no suggestion of impropriety, but Tom had the sense of intimacy. It was as though he had been permitted to enter the private family cocoon and, although it wasn't something he was used to, right at this moment it felt quite comforting.

'Thank you,' he said softly.

'What for?'

'For today. For earlier this morning and for the trip to Astley's.'

'I didn't do anything this afternoon. I should be thanking you for inviting me.'

'You have a way with Edward. It makes everything easier.'

Jane smiled and he could see she was pleased with the compliment.

'I am grateful. I know you refused the other day, but my offer to help you find a publisher still stands. You are doing so much for me.'

Jane looked sharply at the open door and he realised quite how in the dark Lady Mountjoy was about Jane's ambition to get her work published.

'No,' she said quickly. 'That won't be necessary. All I need from you is what we originally agreed.'

He inclined his head. He wasn't sure why she was quite so reluctant to accept help, especially when it seemed her search for someone to publish her work wasn't going very well. They hadn't discussed details, but it was already mid March. She could only have a few more months in London until she returned home, losing her opportunity to wander the London streets with the package she was hopeful someone would take a chance on one day. Still, it wasn't his place to push the idea. He had put forward his offer to help twice now. She would ask him if she did want any assistance.

With a surreptitious glance at the door, Jane stood and moved closer to him, crouching down next to his chair and leaning in.

'We should ensure our deception is believable, though. Visiting Astley's was a good start, but perhaps we can endure a ball or two to make Lady Mountjoy really think she does not need to start parading me in front of other suitors.'

'Do you find balls something to be endured?'

'Don't you?' She looked up at him, her eyes wide under the dark eyelashes, and he felt something stir inside him. He realised he'd never properly looked at her before, never noticed the clarity of the green of her eyes or the fullness of her lips. Her skin was smooth, marked only by the few freckles dotted over her nose.

Tom frowned, wondering why he hadn't noticed her this way before. It was true he tried to steer well clear of gently bred young women. There was no point even considering a dalliance when he was not interested in marriage, but still, he normally noticed an attractive young woman.

His eyes drifted from the top down, noting the severe way she parted her hair in the middle and pulled it back from her face and the dress that was too big and shapeless on her form. Miss Ashworth was hiding and doing it quite successfully. Thrown into a world where all the other debutantes wanted to shine, wanted to be noticed, Miss Ashworth was doing her best to fade into the background.

He had the urge to reach out, to run a finger over her smooth cheek, to draw her closer and get her to spill all the secrets she was holding deep inside. She intrigued him, with her obvious dislike of social events and single-minded focus on her aims.

'I don't go to many,' he murmured. 'The privilege of answering to no one but yourself. I can choose what I attend and what I do not. It means the few I do attend I quite enjoy, but only because they are a rarity.'

Miss Ashworth let out a little sigh and then bit her lower lip. It was mesmerising to watch this close up, and Tom was well aware he was staring. Luckily, Miss Ashworth seemed preoccupied with the idea of doing exactly what one wanted and had a dreamy, faraway look in her eye.

'What do you say, then?' she said, snapping back to reality. 'Will you attend a few balls with me, dance a couple of dances?'

'Of course, it is the least I can do. I shall send you details of what events I am free to attend. Perhaps you might like to accompany me to Lord and Lady Parson's dinner party tomorrow night?'

'That sounds like a good idea. I shall check with Lady Mountjoy if we have been invited.'

She looked up at him, seeming to realise for the first time that she was leaning in so close. He expected her to jolt away but he saw her hesitate for just a moment, tucking a stray strand of hair behind her ear.

'Your nephew has quite outfoxed me playing draughts,' Lady Mountjoy said as she breezed into the room, stopping abruptly as she saw Miss Ashworth crouching by his chair, her face angled up towards him.

It looked intimate, there was no denying it, even though they had only been talking about society events.

Lady Mountjoy coughed to hide her surprise and then he saw her work very hard to suppress the smile of satisfaction that was trying to work its way across her face.

Miss Ashworth rose to her feet, colour flooding to her cheeks.

'We were discussing balls,' Miss Ashworth said as she rushed back to the seat she had been sitting in originally.

'Of course, of course,' Lady Mountjoy said quickly. 'Will you be attending Lord Framlingham's ball on Friday?'

There was no reason he couldn't. He hadn't made any plans with friends on Friday, and he wasn't quick enough with a deception to lie convincingly.

'Yes,' he said, telling himself it was only fair. *This* was how Miss Ashworth was asking him to support her—he needed to step up and do as she asked. Even if it meant society thinking they were romantically inclined.

He shuddered at the realisation of the impact of this agreement. Even when it became apparent he and Miss Ashworth were not heading for marriage, his reputation as a man with no interest in settling down would be rocked. No longer would the debutantes and their mothers avoid him completely.

'We can share a carriage, if you would like,' Lady Mountjoy offered.

It was an ingenious ploy on the part of the older woman. There was no good reason for him to refuse. His residence was not far from hers and they were going to the same destination, but it did mean he and Miss Ashworth would be seen arriving together, which would set tongues wagging. Added to that, it would be harder for him to leave after an hour or two. Politeness would oblige him to stay until the ladies were ready to depart.

He smiled, impressed with her skill. If he and Miss Ashworth had not been playing a part, if there'd been a flicker of true attraction between them, he could see how Lady Mountjoy and her little tricks would go about fanning those flames.

'That is most generous,' he said. 'What time will you be leaving?'

'Why don't we call for you en route?'

'Thank you.' He hesitated, wondering if organising two events in one conversation would look too keen, but he caught a glimpse of Miss Ashworth's encouraging look and forced himself to speak. 'I have been invited to Lord and Lady Parson's dinner party tomorrow night. I wonder if you and Miss Ashworth will be in attendance?'

Lady Mountjoy looked as though it was Christmas morning and she had just received the most fabulous gift. 'Yes, we will be. I shall have a word with Lady Parson, speak to her about the seating arrangement.' She clapped her hands in excitement. 'How fabulous.'

Tom gave an unconvincing smile and nodded, glad when Lady Mountjoy turned her attention away from him.

'Now I must see what book Edward has chosen to take home with him. We have such a collection of children's books sitting unread in the library. I said he must choose one.'

The countess glided out of the room and for a long moment both he and Miss Ashworth sat in silence.

'I'm sorry,' she whispered after a moment, 'I never meant to push you. A dinner and a ball all in one week. I'm sure you have other more exciting plans.'

'I am looking forward to it.'

Miss Ashworth scoffed. 'Do not go too far, Mr Stewart. We all know it will be a bore, but I am grateful all the same.'

'I will make you a promise,' he said, leaning forward in his chair. 'If you give me your word you will be open to enjoying yourself at the ball later this week, I promise you I will make it fun for you.'

'At a ball? With everyone watching our every move?'

'Do you not believe my reputation?'

She shifted in her seat, glancing at him and then quickly looking away.

'Go on, what do people say of me?'

She shook her head.

'I will not be offended, Miss Ashworth. I know very well people's opinions on me.'

'They say you are a rake. A man devoted to the pursuit of pleasure. They say you will often shun polite company in preference for less desirable companions.'

'There must be more.'

'I can't repeat it.'

'Of course you can.'

'They say you leave a trail of broken hearts behind you...that you must hypnotise the women you conduct your affairs with because no one you are close to has a bad word to say about you, even though you are obviously a sinner.'

'What do you think?'

She looked over at him and shifted in her seat. For a long while she was silent and he thought she might not answer at all.

'I think so many people believe that living a life of pleasure and indulgence means you cannot be a decent person. They think only those who are outwardly pious or charitable can be good. Of course, that is not true—we've all heard of the charitable patron swindling the poor or the vicar dipping his fingers into the collection pot.'

Tom liked how much thought Miss Ashworth put into her answers. He never knew what she was going to say, but he knew she would never stick to the merely superficial.

'In the same way, they think a man who has

lots of affairs, lots of mistresses, a man who refuses to play by the rules of polite society, must be inherently *bad* in some way. They're wrong, of course. You can make questionable choices but still be a good person.'

Raising an imaginary glass, he grinned. 'To questionable choices.'

'I am quite interested in seeing if you are viewed as a reformed character when you do start to socialise more.'

'The gossips love nothing more than a story of salvation.'

'You will be in demand, no doubt.'

'But I only have eyes for you.'

She laughed at this, and Tom saw her finally relaxing in his company. Miss Ashworth worked hard to keep up her wall of defence. She scared people off with her severe expressions and frumpy way of dressing and styling her hair. She worked hard to exude an air of bookishness, to ensure people thought she would not be fun company, but when you dug down beneath all of that there was so much more underneath.

Miss Ashworth was quick-witted and sharp. She had views on things other than the latest fashions or society gossip and was a keen observer of human nature. It had never featured

in his plans to pretend to be courting a debutante this Season, but if it had to be with anyone he was glad it was Miss Ashworth.

'I will show you a ball can be enjoyable, if
only you keep the right company.'

'I will look forward to it.'

Chapter Eight

It was at moments like this that Jane missed the protective shield the other debutantes had provided before they had all married, when they'd gone out in a gaggle to dinners and balls. She stood out, alone with Lord and Lady Mountjoy, and it felt as if all eyes were on her.

'Good evening,' their hostess said as she welcomed them into the drawing room where there was already a crowd of people.

'What a lovely group you have here,' Lady Mountjoy said. 'Thank you for the invitation. Your dinner parties are always a highlight of the Season.'

'You are too kind, Lady Mountjoy.' Lady Parson lowered her voice a little and leaned in, as if imparting a secret. 'Mr Stewart has not arrived yet, but I have arranged the seating so he and the young lady will be next to one another.'

'Thank you. I shall not forget this, Lady Parson.'

Jane almost rolled her eyes at the hushed voices of the two older women and quietly excused herself, stepping in to the room and seeing if there was anyone she recognised.

With a groan, she saw too late the closest person was Mrs Farthington with her hapless husband. Jane wondered whether it was too late to quietly back away, but as she took her first step Mrs Farthington turned and caught sight of Jane. Knowing she could not show any weakness, Jane summoned a smile.

'Miss Ashworth, you look…' Mrs Farthington trailed off as her eyes flicked up and down, taking in Jane's pale-green dress and simple hairstyle. 'Well. You look well.'

'As do you, Mrs Farthington. Lovely to see you, Mr Farthington.'

Her gaze darted around the room as she spoke, wondering if there was someone else she knew, someone to latch on to so she didn't have to spend her time talking to the woman in front of her.

Mrs Farthington was having none of it. She linked her arm through Jane's and started to stroll leisurely around the room as if they were old friends. Her husband trailed behind, carrying his wife's glass of wine.

'You are a secretive little mouse, aren't you?' Mrs Farthington said. 'When I teased you the other day about pursuing Mr Stewart as a possible suitor, I really was joking, but I hear he has agreed to come to this dinner party because of you and insisted you sit together.'

Jane closed her eyes for a moment, wondering how gossip and rumour spread so easily throughout the *ton*.

'Is it true, then?' Mrs Farthington probed. 'How interesting. I wonder what he wants from you.'

Jane knew it was an insult, as were most things coming from this woman's mouth, but she needed to keep her composure and not let anything slip.

She shrugged. 'I'm sure I do not know.'

'You do know his reputation?'

'Yes. I know what people say about him.'

'He doesn't really attend society events, not beyond one or two balls a year. He's handsome, of course… You can see why all the ladies sigh as he walks by, and I hear rumours he is a magnificent lover.'

'Mrs Farthington, I must protest,' Mr Farthington said, trying to insert himself next to his wife, but she flicked him away with a dismissive hand.

'I hear he has the choice of partner and I can only wonder what he wants with you.'

'Perhaps he enjoys my scintillating conversation or my impressive wit.'

Mrs Farthington laughed.

'I understand why you are suddenly so eager to capture yourself a husband, Miss Ashworth, with Miss Greenacre and Miss Stanley married to lords and Miss Freeman now a captain's wife.' She paused and by the glint in her eye Jane knew the next barb was going to be particularly sharp. 'But a little friendly advice—perhaps you should lower your expectations a little.'

'Or perhaps not,' Jane murmured as Mr Stewart walked into the room. All eyes were drawn to him as he greeted their host and hostess and then made his way directly to her. He was attractive, Jane couldn't deny it, and he had a presence that commanded attention.

'Miss Ashworth, it is a pleasure to see you again.' His eyes flicked over Mr and Mrs Farthington, and he nodded in greeting, but Jane was glad to see he did not seem inclined to stay and talk.

'Please excuse us,' he said with a blinding smile. 'I have the urge to speak to Miss Ashworth alone for a moment.'

Without waiting for their answer, he whisked Jane away.

'Thank you,' she murmured as they paused on the other side of the room.

'You looked uncomfortable.'

'Mrs Farthington is not a pleasant person. She was one of the debutantes Lady Mountjoy brought from Somerset. The other three were absolutely lovely, but she has always been cruel.'

'What did she say to you?'

'She was curious as to why you would suddenly be interested in me.'

Mr Stewart frowned, glancing over at the young woman and her husband on the other side of the room.

'Apparently you could have your pick of women, debutante, married or widowed. She does not see what would ever induce you to pick me.'

'I am sorry, Miss Ashworth,' he said, shaking his head. 'Some people baffle me in how they come out with such rude things. I particularly dislike bullies, and Mrs Farthington is a bully.'

'I suppose she is right, in a way, but there is no need to say it.'

'She's not right,' he said quietly, waiting for Jane to look up at him. 'Believe that. You are not worth less than I am—if anything I think you are probably worth more. It is just some people judge by the wrong standards.'

'I know.' Jane thought back a few years, to the time when her twin sister had been alive. Harriet had been beautiful, with dark-brown eyes and blonde hair. Her lips had been full and rosy and her skin soft and clear. They'd not been identical twins, and when they'd been young Jane had often wondered how two sisters born minutes apart could be so dissimilar.

They had done everything together, but even from a young age Jane had seen how they had been treated so differently. Things had been easier for Harriet—people had wanted to help her more, wanted to give her more. Not once had Jane begrudge her sister the benefits of being attractive, but Jane had learned as a child she was going to have to work twice as hard to achieve the same, being *the plain sister*.

She often wondered if it was this that had encouraged her to pursue her writing and illustrating, this need to stand out in some way against Harriet's superior looks and grace.

Then her desire to write and paint had only intensified after Harriet's death as Jane had looked to find something to focus on outside her own deep grief.

As always when she thought about Harriet, she felt the sadness threatening to pull her down and she quickly supressed it, grasping instead for one of the happy memories of her sister.

'Everyone is going through to dinner. Shall we?' He offered her his arm and together they walked through the double doors to the resplendently decorated dining room.

Tom was actually enjoying himself. Dinner was delicious, and he reminded himself to accept more invitations when he was in want of a fancy meal. Now the sweet course was being served, and the steamed pears with cinnamon smelled divine.

He had been seated in between Lady Mountjoy and Miss Ashworth, but at the beginning of the meal Lady Mountjoy had leaned in to him and whispered that she was going to break all the rules of dinner party etiquette and focus on talking to the man on her left so Tom need not worry about conversing with her. Instead, he could focus on Miss Ashworth. He had to applaud Lady Mountjoy's commitment to her cause as she was sitting next to Lord Willoughby, a notoriously dull man who only liked to talk about his time in the army forty years earlier.

Miss Ashworth was a delightful dinner companion, especially after a little coaxing and few glasses of wine. They had spent much of the meal with their heads bent together, discussing the other guests. Her observations were sharp and witty, and he was surprised that underneath her meek and mild exterior there was a woman who would be able to run rings around most of the other distinguished guests here tonight.

'That is incredible,' Miss Ashworth said, tasting a mouthful of the steamed pears.

Tom had been around far too many women who were so preoccupied with their figure that they would have refused pudding along with half the meal. Miss Ashworth had committed to enjoying every bite. She was slender but not skinny, although it was hard to tell under the loose dresses she wore. He got the impression she was trying to hide her figure, trying to stay as invisible as possible, and he wondered why. Now was not the right time to ask. They did not know each other well enough for a question like that, but perhaps one day he would work it out.

'Thank you for joining us, Mr Stewart,' Lady Parson said from the head of the table, catching his attention with a wave of her hand. 'It is wonderful to see you at an event such as this. I wonder, with you attending more society events, are we to assume you are looking to find a wife and settle down?'

Tom cleared his throat, having to resist the urge to glance at Miss Ashworth. He needed to tread carefully. He couldn't laugh at the notion and destroy the carefully curated picture he and Miss Ashworth were trying to build, but equally he didn't want to confirm the rumours and be besieged by debutantes thinking they might be the right match for him.

He gave his most charming smile. 'Who amongst us knows what the future holds, Lady Parson?'

'Indeed.' Sensing she wasn't going to get the answer she wanted, Lady Parson moved on, dropping the subject.

'Very diplomatic,' Miss Ashworth murmured as he turned back to her.

'I didn't think the truth would help our deception,' he whispered.

'The truth?'

'That I will never marry.'

'"Never" is a long time.'

'It is, Miss Ashworth.'

She looked at him curiously, but thankfully didn't push him to explain why he was so adamant. Some things were too private. Tom had decided long ago he would never marry, even before his accident. He couldn't trust himself with another person's happiness, another person's wellbeing.

For a moment he closed his eyes and pictured his sister. She looked young in his mind, just seventeen years old. That was the last time he had seen her, the last memory he had of her. After years of aggression and cruelty from their father, Tom had joined the army as soon as he'd turned eighteen. He had done it to escape, to rid himself of the feeling he was always doing wrong in his father's eyes. He'd always been afraid of angering him. He had joined the army and breathed a sigh of relief when he'd been sent away to fight. Of course he had thought about Rebecca, but the urge to escape had been too strong, and he had bought a commission even though he knew it meant leaving Rebecca behind with their father.

When she'd disappeared, the guilt he'd felt had been overwhelming. The situation must have been so bad to make her leave with nothing more than the clothes on her back. For years he had carried the guilt and self-recriminations. He knew he couldn't be trusted to put someone else's needs before his own, so he had vowed to never marry, never be in the situation where someone was reliant on him.

After his injury, he had become more determined, deciding to live every day as if it were his last, but to keep to his pledge of not developing any lasting connections.

It had all been going so well until Edward had turned up on his doorstep.

Thankfully, the conversation around them had moved on, and as everyone finished their pudding the gentlemen all settled down for drinks whilst the ladies withdrew to the drawing room. As Miss Ashworth stood, eyeing the other female guests warily, he caught her eye and winked, feeling inordinately happy at the momentary smile this elicited. Then the doors to the drawing room closed and he was swept into a world of business deals, estate management and parliamentary matters.

Chapter Nine

Jane touched her hair self-consciously as the carriage rolled to a stop outside Lord and Lady Framlingham's house. She had asked her maid to try a different style, something a little less severe than the centre parting she normally opted for. The curls that bounced around her face felt foreign and distracting, but when she had looked in the mirror before leaving she had felt a flush of pleasure in the change in her appearance.

'Shall we?'

Mr Stewart was sitting opposite her and jumped agilely down from the carriage as it rolled to a stop. As usual he looked devastatingly handsome with his dark hair swept across his forehead and his clothes cut to display his enviable physique.

The house was grand, even by London standards, situated out of the centre with more land around it. It meant it was larger than many of the townhouses Jane had visited in her time in London, many of which had to make do with throwing open the doors of the drawing rooms and dining rooms to make space for a ball.

As they walked inside Framlingham House, it was apparent no expense had been spared for the evening. Candles flickered inside glass lanterns to line the route up to the house and inside the decorations continued. Fresh flowers had been placed in every possible location, giving off a beautiful aroma and making the guests feel as if they had stepped into a painting of spring time. Despite it being mid March the weather this year was far too cold for these flowers to be blooming naturally and Jane wondered how they had achieved such an effect.

They were greeted by their hosts and guided to a magnificent ballroom with walls painted in light-blue and gold. A magnificent chandelier sparkled above their heads and already the musicians were playing gentle music to welcome the guests.

'All very civilised,' Mr Stewart murmured in her ear, and Jane had to press her lips together to stop a laugh bursting out.

She felt giddy and a little reckless tonight, very unlike her usual self. She knew part of it was because of the man holding her elbow, the man she realised was slowly becoming her friend.

Throughout all the balls, dinner parties and the operas she had disappeared into the background, overshadowed by the three other beautiful debutantes Lady Mountjoy had brought to London. Jane knew it was mainly her own doing—she hadn't wanted to be centre of attention and had done everything to ensure she wasn't the first to be asked to dance or the one the gentlemen clamoured to sit next to at dinner. Until recently she had still managed to enjoy a few of the events, swept along by her friends but, with Lucy and Eliza happily settled with their husbands, it had been looking like a grim few months as the Season started properly, observing solely from the edge of the room.

With Mr Stewart by her side it felt as though someone was seeing her, truly seeing her, for the first time. It felt thrilling to know that later on he would ask her to dance and she would actually enjoy the experience.

'Go, go,' Lady Mountjoy urged as she waved to an acquaintance across the room. 'You two young things take a walk around the room and enjoy yourselves.'

'She's planning the wedding already,' Mr Stewart murmured in Jane's ear as they obeyed, slipping into the crowds of the ballroom.

'I think she had it all planned out the moment you visited her drawing room after the last ball where we danced together.'

'A big celebration or a small family affair?'

'A big celebration, certainly. I am the fifth and final debutante she sponsored for the Season. She would want a party to match the scale of her achievement.'

'St George's?'

'Without a doubt, with a gathering after in the gardens of the Mountjoys' townhouse.'

'A fair engagement, then, for a summer wedding?'

'These things can't be rushed. Not when it should be the wedding of the year. Mr Stewart, the infamous rake, and the woman who finally enticed him to settle down.'

They both laughed and Jane saw a few people looking in their direction.

'Good evening, Mr Stewart,' a pretty young woman said as she glided up to them, resplendent in a dark-blue dress that draped beautifully about her shoulders, making her look like a Grecian goddess.

'Mrs Harper, lovely to see you. Are you well?'

'Quite well, Mr Stewart. Although surprised to see you here tonight.'

'May I introduce Miss Jane Ashworth, a friend of mine?'

'Delighted to meet you, Miss Ashworth.'

'And you, Mrs Harper.'

Mrs Harper's eyes raked over Jane and Jane had to resist the urge to pat her hair and smooth her dress. Instead she adopted a serene half-smile that she hoped gave her an air of confidence she didn't quite feel.

'How is Mr Harper?' Mr Stewart asked, and Jane thought she saw a darkening of the other woman's eyes.

'His gout ails him this evening. He has stayed at home.'

'Please send him my best wishes.'

Mrs Harper reached out and touched Mr Stewart's hand. 'You've always been so considerate. Do let me know when we can welcome you at our home again.'

'Was that a little strange?' Jane said as the slightly older woman smiled and walked away.

'It felt a little strange, although I don't think she said anything outrageous.'

'It was a little strange.'

Jane followed the pretty young woman with her eyes and then gasped. 'She's one of your mistresses!' It sounded so dramatic, but she couldn't believe the realisation had only just occurred.

Mr Stewart grabbed her hand and pulled it down from where she was covering her mouth.

'That is how rumours start,' he muttered.

'Is she not one of your mistresses?'

He coughed uncomfortably.

Jane felt a surge of envy and quickly tried to suppress it. It was absolutely none of her business if Mr Stewart had a dozen mistresses dotted about London. Still, she looked after the beautiful and confident young woman who had melted into the crowd and felt a stab of sadness that she would never have that confidence.

'But she's married.' Quickly Jane held up her hands. 'No, no, no. It is not my place to judge. You have always been very open about how you conduct your life and your philosophy for how you live it.'

'Stop. Please,' Mr Stewart said, again taking her wrists and lowering them to down, his fingers lingering on her skin for just a second

more than they should have. With a glance over
his shoulder he guided Jane to a quieter area of
the ballroom where they were shielded from
the view of most people by some well-placed
arrangements of flowers.

'You don't need to explain yourself to me.'

'I know,' Mr Stewart said, but continued on
anyway. 'I knew Mrs Harper before she married her second husband. She was widowed
young and spent a year or two enjoying the
new-found freedom of being wealthy and independent and allowed to make her own decisions for the first time ever.'

'And she chose you?'

'We spent a little time in one another's company.'

'She seemed very keen to renew your acquaintance.'

Mr Stewart sighed and swept a hand through
his hair. 'I don't have many rules in life, but I
do refuse to dally with innocent young women
and married women. There is no need. There
are plenty of people unattached and eager for
a liaison outside of those groups.'

'The beautiful Mrs Harper doesn't have the
same rules, I assume?'

'She married a much older man and I can
only assume he can't keep up.'

Jane glanced up, seeing Mr Stewart's wicked smile, and thumped him on the arm.

'You're trying to embarrass me.'

'You look so pretty when you blush.'

'Hasn't anyone told you it is wrong to corrupt the minds of innocent debutantes?'

'But it is so much fun.'

'If you don't behave, I will find Mrs Harper and tell her you will climb through her bedroom window in the small hours tonight.'

'A threat indeed. Come, Miss Ashworth, we should return to the main area of the ballroom or someone will think I'm ravishing you behind here.'

This did make the blood flood to Jane's cheeks, as she couldn't help herself from imagining Mr Stewart's lips on hers, kissing her until she didn't know who she was any more. Quickly she tried to push the thought aside, but the image had become lodged in her mind, and she found it impossible to look at her companion without being drawn to his perfectly shaped lips.

'Would you give me the honour of the first dance?' Mr Stewart asked as the pace and volume of the music the musicians were playing changed, indicating the couples should take to the dance floor.

'Of course,' she said, and then hesitated as she realised it was a waltz. 'Or maybe we can sit this set out and try in the next one.'

'Don't you like to waltz?'

'Do you remember our last disastrous dance?'

'It wasn't disastrous.'

'I can just about make it through a quadrille or cotillion,' Jane said, wondering why they were still heading to where all the couples were assembling. 'But a waltz is so much harder.'

'You've just never had the right partner.'

'It's nothing to do with my partners. *I* can't dance it. My feet get all in a muddle, then I overthink it and end up stumbling. You *do* remember the last dance we had together?'

'Do you trust me?'

Slowly she nodded, realising that even though their acquaintance was short she was starting to trust him.

'Then give me one more chance.'

For a long moment she didn't answer. It was foolish. She was going to end up in a tangled mess with the whole room staring at her, laughing that, not only did she think she could have a chance with a charming and handsome man like Mr Stewart, but she couldn't dance a simple waltz either.

'Fine. But if I fall you will have my eternal embarrassment on your conscience.'

She allowed him to lead her to a space in between the other couples and tried not to look at all the people gathered around the edge of the dance floor.

'Relax,' he said, slipping a hand around her waist. Jane shifted, aware of the heat of his skin through the thin material of her dress.

'I'm trying to.'

'People trying to relax do not clench their jaws.'

With a gargantuan effort Jane relaxed her jaw and let out a deep breath.

'Better... Now make your grip a little looser. It'll be nice to leave the ball this evening with a few of my fingers still attached.'

He was smiling at her, and Jane felt some of the tension ebb away.

Leaning in, he dropped his voice so only she could hear. 'Do you know the best way to forget you're nervous?'

She shook her head.

'Imagine everyone around you has come to the ball in their underclothes.'

A laugh burst from Jane's lips at the absurdity of it.

'Go on, try it. I promise it'll work. How about Mr Leggety?'

'Stop it,' Jane said as they started to move.

'Or Mrs Waterbeach.'

'Don't, this is cruel.'

'To them or to you, having to imagine it?'

'Both.'

'What about Lord Penrose?'

Jane laughed again and then looked down, realising that they were waltzing and had been for some time.

'It's working, isn't it?'

She panicked, not knowing what beat she was on, and tried to start counting.

'Stop,' he said firmly. 'You do not need to count. You are dancing beautifully.'

She stumbled again as she glanced down at her feet.

'Look at me, Miss Ashworth.'

She did, feeling the pull of his dark eyes and feeling a shiver run down her spine as he leaned in closer to her.

'If it helps, imagine me in my underclothes.'

Jane spluttered, even though she hadn't been about to say anything.

'Oversized bloomers, double layer of vest, perhaps even a thick nightshirt.'

'You don't wear any of that, do you?' she

managed to say, aware her eyes were raking down his body, trying to imagine exactly what was underneath the well-tailored jacket and trousers.

For a long moment Jane thought he wasn't going to answer and then he leaned in even closer so his lips were almost up against her ear.

'Nothing at all.'

He spun her, whisking her round and round, his eyes locked on hers as if she were the only person in the world.

Jane had no idea how long the dance lasted. It felt as though everything else had faded away into nothing. Even the music was a faint melody in the background. When Mr Stewart stopped moving, she stood for a moment, completely still in his arms, her chest heaving from the exertion and the heightened awareness.

'Thank you for the dance, Miss Ashworth,' he said, and Jane managed to mumble something as they stepped away from the dance floor.

'You look a little flushed. Would you like a glass of lemonade?'

She nodded, glad of the suggestion. She needed a few minutes alone, a few minutes to reason with herself, to try and claw back some of her sanity.

As Mr Stewart left her, Jane stayed still for a few seconds, and then as he disappeared out of view she let out a deep exhalation and turned to leave. She planned to find a quiet corner, perhaps on the chairs set out for chaperons and spinsters, to get her breath back and reset her equilibrium.

Instead she barrelled right into a tall man. Apologising quickly, she rushed away, not even looking the man in the eye.

Feeling as though the crowd of people was closing in, she decided she needed some air and hurried towards the ornate glass doors that led onto the terrace.

Outside the air was cold and the sky was a deep inky black. There was no moon and no sign of any stars to illuminate the gardens below. The candlelight from the ballroom spilled out onto the terrace, but a few feet from the doors everything was plunged into shadow.

It was quiet on the terrace, with two couples strolling arm in arm along its length, but no one else venturing out of the heat of the ballroom so early in the night.

Closing her eyes, Jane leaned on the stone balustrade, glad of the darkness so no one could see her expression. She was still shaking, still hadn't recovered from the dance with Mr Stewart. It had started so well, with him distracting her, making her laugh even, and then twirling her until she'd felt as though she were dancing on thin air, floating above the floor of the ballroom. Then he had looked at her with those dark, enticing eyes and invited her to picture him without his clothes on.

Even now Jane got a flush of heat flood through her body as she thought of it.

Do not do this, she ordered herself. It was not a helpful reaction to have to the man who was assisting her. She needed Lady Mountjoy to believe in their fake attachment for one another, not to build it up herself into something that it wasn't. *He is doing you a favour.*

Mr Stewart was kind and generous, more so than he liked people to know, but she knew there was no way he would ever be attracted to her.

Even as she shook her head to try and rid herself of the images, another flooded her brain—the picture of Mr Stewart wearing very little, leaning in as if he were about to kiss her.

She spun abruptly, startling a couple that was walking arm in arm along the terrace behind her. Managing a smile she hoped didn't look too deranged, Jane hurried further away into the darkness at the end of the terrace, breathing a sigh of relief when the cold night air became too much for the other people who had ventured outside. Finally alone, she closed her eyes and took a few deep breaths.

Soon she would have to return to the ball, to Mr Stewart and his charming smile. She would have to pretend nothing had changed, to laugh, talk and dance as if her whole world hadn't just shifted under her feet.

Don't be so dramatic, she told herself. It was a flicker of desire no more. Objectively, anyone would have to admit Mr Stewart was an attractive man. It was not remarkable to feel a pull, a desire, to be close to him. Perhaps it would be stranger if she didn't feel anything at all.

Knowing she had to return to the ballroom, Jane was about to step out of the shadows at the end of the terrace when the door opened once again, momentarily making the volume of the music flare for a few seconds. It was a young couple with their heads bent together and their voices lowered to breathy whispers.

Not wanting to intrude on an intimate moment, Jane went to step into the light, but before she could move she saw the woman reach up and pull the man into a deep kiss. Jane froze, not knowing what to do for the best. The couple must have thought they'd snatched a rare moment of privacy and surely would be mortified to be caught like this.

For a moment she wondered if they were married, but the furtive way the young woman kept glancing at the door to the ballroom made it obvious they were not. Jane felt paralysed, knowing that every second she remained hidden, the more she would see, the more the couple were compromising themselves, but already feeling it was too late to stroll out of the darkness and announce her presence.

As the couple continued to kiss, Jane spun, wondering if there might be another way. The glasshouse sat at the end of the terrace and there was a door right behind her. Perhaps if it was open there might be another route into the main house and no one need ever know what she had witnessed.

Almost crying with relief as the door shifted, Jane slipped inside, closing it silently behind her. The air was warmer in there and a little humid despite the cool, crisp conditions outside. At first it was hard to see anything, and the darkness seemed all-consuming, but after a few seconds her eyes began to adjust and she could begin to make out the outlines of things.

Much of it still looked unfamiliar, but Jane reasoned that was probably because the glasshouse was filled with exotic plants and flowers. Carefully she felt her way through the foliage, trying to be as quiet as she could.

The glass house was massive, three long interconnecting buildings attached to the edge of the main house. There was a sickly sweet smell pervading the air and Jane realised this must have been where all of the flowers for tonight's ball had been grown.

She had just stumbled her way through the first glasshouse when she heard the unmistakable click of the door opening and closing and then the giggle of the young couple who had been outside.

Jane stiffened, unable to move, surrounded as she was by the leaves of a palm tree. Even the tiniest movement made the fronds rustle and would give away her presence immediately.

Cursing her poor judgement for not stepping out of the shadows as soon as the young couple had ventured outside, she closed her eyes and waited, listening as the couple giggled and crept through the glasshouse. At one point they passed right by her, the young woman in touching distance.

For a moment she thought they might carry on all the way through the glasshouse, perhaps seeking the door Jane had thought to use at the other end, but nothing was going in her favour tonight and they paused a few feet away from her and began to kiss again.

Ever so slowly, Jane started retreating, feeling out each step as she did and barely breathing until she felt the cool glass under her fingers.

Before she could open the door and slip out to freedom, she looked up, surprised to see a figure approaching the glasshouse, relieved beyond words when the familiar features of Mr Stewart came into focus.

'What…?' he began, his voice booming through the quiet night air.

Jane grabbed the handle to the door, pulled it open and pressed a hand to his lips.

His lips were soft beneath her fingers and for a moment she was distracted, unable to think of anything but how they would feel trailing across her skin.

'There's someone in there,' she whispered, 'Well, two people.'

Mr Stewart glanced over her shoulder, his frown deepening. 'What are you doing in there?'

'Trying to avoid them.'

'By joining them?'

'No,' Jane said, a little louder. 'Don't be ridiculous. We need to get back to the ballroom. I'll explain once we're in there.'

Mr Stewart looked as if he was going to protest, but with one last glance over Jane's shoulder he nodded.

Jane stepped forward, glad to be out of the heat of the glasshouse, and dreading what a state she must look after panicking for ten minutes in the humid air. She had only taken one step when the door to the ballroom opened again and a group of women flooded out onto the terrace.

'What do we do?' Jane felt the evening couldn't get any worse. Here she was standing in the shadows with a notorious rake, probably looking dishevelled and as if she had been up to no good for the last half an hour. Mr Stewart hesitated, looking her up and down. He must have come to the same conclusion, for he groaned quietly and pulled her back into the glasshouse.

He shut the door gently behind them and then gripped her hand, leading them away from the windows so they would be less likely to be observed.

'Stay quiet,' he murmured in her ear, leaning close so his voice was just audible. Jane felt the heat of his body and had to resist the urge to reach out and touch him.

They were standing behind a raised bed, planted with exotic flowers, the petals bigger than anything Jane had ever seen before. It would be a fascinating place to see in the daylight, but right now she wished more than anything to be back in the safety of the ballroom.

'We'll be out of here soon,' Mr Stewart whispered, misjudging the distance between them and brushing his lips against her ear. A shiver of anticipation ran down Jane's spine and she found herself recklessly reaching out into the darkness. Her hand found his shirt and she felt his muscles tense as he became aware of the contact. She was surprised when he didn't move away. Instead, he shifted his stance just a little so he could rest his hand on the small of her back.

Jane felt all the breath leaving her body. It felt exquisitely intimate, standing here in the darkness with Mr Stewart, his fingers tracing gentle circles on her back, separated only by the thin fabric of her dress. She wanted more than anything in that moment to tilt her chin up and seek out his lips with her own.

Trying to banish all thoughts of kissing Mr Stewart, she shifted again, a small gasp escaping her lips as her hip bounced off the raised flower bed and the ricochet pushed her further into the arms of the man behind her. Glancing up, she could only see his silhouette in the darkness, but she had the impression he was feeling the same pull, the same attraction she was.

'Jane,' he murmured, one hand pressing into her waist and pulling her tighter to him. She wasn't sure if it was the darkness, the heat or the heady scent coming from the flowers but she felt as though reality was being swept away and she was floating into a place where anything could happen.

Jane raised herself up on her tiptoes and at the same moment Mr Stewart lowered his head, seeking out her lips in the darkness. The kiss was gentle, so full of promise that Jane yearned for more. His lips were like velvet on hers and as he kissed her she felt her body surrender and melt into his.

They both stiffened as the door to the glasshouse opened and light flooded inside. Quickly, they moved apart as much as they were able, but Jane's body was still pressed against Mr Stewart's in the confined space.

For a long moment Jane could think of nothing but how right it had seemed, being in his arms, and then the reality of their situation came crashing down upon her.

'This is my pride and joy,' the voice of their hostess, Lady Framlingham, rang out clearly. 'Of course, it is better viewed in the daylight, but I do often walk through here at night, marvelling at the flowers and the exotic plants.'

'It has the feel of a jungle,' another woman said as the group entered, closing the door behind them.

'Over the years we have collected more than four hundred different exotic plants. I would wager we have the most comprehensive collection in England.'

Jane wondered if they might pass by into the second of the interconnecting buildings, allowing Mr Stewart and her to slip out. As much as she secretly yearned to be kissed again, the sensible part of her knew it would be disastrous to be caught by the group of matrons traipsing through the glasshouses. It would mean certain ruin for her and, even though she did not plan to marry, she did not want to be sent home from London in disgrace and shunned evermore by polite society.

The group of women took their time admiring the flowers by lantern light. At one point one of the ladies moved closer to where Jane and Mr Stewart were standing, hidden by the drooping leaves of some exotic plant. Jane felt Mr Stewart's arm tighten around her and pull her closer, as if instinctively trying to protect her, but thankfully the woman moved away before they could be discovered.

'We need to get out of here,' Mr Stewart whispered into her ear as the ladies moved further into the glasshouse.

Jane nodded, looking over at the door. It was no distance away, really. Perhaps twenty long strides and they would be out in the air.

Carefully they picked their way back through the plants, stopping every few seconds to ensure Lady Framlingham and her friends were still occupied elsewhere.

They were almost at the door, almost to freedom, when Jane felt her nose begin to itch. There was a lot of pollen in the glass house, and she must have brushed up against one of the flowers. The urge to sneeze was overwhelming, and despite her best efforts Jane could not hold it in.

She sneezed. The sound was so loud it was as though someone had let off a gunshot in the enclosed space.

Mr Stewart didn't lose a second. He grabbed her by the hand and pulled, running out of the glass house and along the terrace. Whipping open the door to the ballroom, he stopped only to release her hand and place it lightly on his arm, and then, as if they had been doing nothing more than strolling on the terrace, he escorted her inside.

Jane felt a mess. Her hair was flattened to her head, damp with the moisture from the glasshouse, and she knew her skin would be flushed. If anyone took a closer look at them, it would quickly become apparent something untoward had happened.

'Ah, it's our second dance, Miss Ashworth,' Mr Stewart said, calmly leading her to the dance floor.

'We're dancing? Now?'

'It's a quadrille,' Mr Stewart said, the pleasant smile not dropping from his lips. 'By the end, every dancer will be gently perspiring and we will not look so out of place.'

The had taken their first steps when there was a commotion at the door leading to the terrace from the ballroom. Jane tried her hardest not to look, not wanting to catch anyone's eye. A murmur of excitement was slowly spreading through the ballroom as Lady Framlingham imparted her news.

'Don't look,' Mr Stewart instructed, 'But Lady Mountjoy is waiting for us to finish dancing.'

'Oh no, what have I done?'

'No one could have seen us. Perhaps Lady Framlingham caught the other couple you heard in the glasshouse.'

'Why would Lady Mountjoy want to talk to me so urgently if that was the case?'

'You must hold your composure.'

'So must you,' Jane shot back, irritated he thought she would be the one to let something slip she shouldn't.

'You do not need to worry about me.'

'Nor you me.'

He gave her a long, hard stare.

'Don't look at me like that. I will have you know I can lie very well.'

'Hmm.'

'I would wager I am a much more believable liar than you.'

'I doubt it,' he said, the easy smile returning to his lips. 'I've had a lot of practice.'

'We should talk about…' Jane trailed off, knowing she should not even mention the kiss they had shared in the glasshouse.

'Yes,' Mr Stewart said, his eyes searching her face. 'A moment of madness?' He phrased it as a question and Jane felt a mild pang of disappointment in amongst the relief.

'A moment of madness,' she agreed.

There was no time to discuss it further as the dance ended and the couples thanked each other, but she promised herself she would revisit the subject later, once Lady Mountjoy had been dealt with.

'Have you heard?' Lady Mountjoy said with no preamble as Mr Stewart escorted Jane from the dance floor.

'Heard what?' Jane tried to make her voice nonchalant, her whole demeanour relaxed.

'Lady Framlingham was giving a tour of her famous glasshouse to some of her friends and they disturbed a couple in there.'

'No!' Jane gasped and felt Mr Stewart exert a little pressure on her arm. Perhaps she was overdoing the enthusiasm. Normally she would say she didn't have any interest in gossip or something similar. 'Who was it?'

There was a long pause whilst Lady Mountjoy scrutinised Jane and Mr Stewart. 'No one knows,' she said eventually. 'Yet.'

'What a thrilling mystery,' Mr Stewart said quietly.

'Indeed. You were out on the terrace, were you not?'

'A while ago,' Mr Stewart said, 'But we were back before the quadrille was called and didn't see anyone heading into the glasshouse.'

Lady Mountjoy was silent again, searching them both with her eyes for some weakness.

'What's this?' she asked, leaning forward and looking at a tiny mark on Jane's dress. It was from where some pollen had rubbed against the fabric, a miniscule brown mark on the bodice, something anyone less observant would have easily missed.

'I don't know,' Jane said, trying to feign lack of interest. 'I am sure Mary will be able to get it out. She managed to make my dress look as good as new when I threw lemonade all over it at the Osbornes' dinner a few weeks ago.'

'Did you hear?' A woman bustled up to them, grasping Lady Mountjoy by the arm. 'They found a woman's glove in the glasshouse. It is only a matter of time before it is matched to the owner.'

In unison Lady Mountjoy and Mr Stewart looked down at Jane's hands where they rested by her side. Feeling some of the panic leave her, Jane smiled serenely as she lifted her arm to tuck a stray strand of hair behind her ear.

Both her hands were encased in delicate satin gloves, the fabric covering her forearms and buttoned at the elbow.

Lady Mountjoy gave a suspicious tut.

She leaned in towards Jane and Mr Stewart. 'Best behaviour,' she said firmly. 'Everyone will be watching everyone else. It will be like a chapter in one of those awful crime stories Lord Mountjoy likes to read.'

'Best behaviour,' Jane promised.

'I wouldn't dream of anything else,' Mr Stewart said.

Lady Mountjoy tapped him on the chest with the end of her fan. 'You may be charming, Mr Stewart, but remember you are an honourable man as well.'

The countess spun and walked away.

'What did she mean by that?'

Mr Stewart shook his head. He had lost his smile and looked a little worried.

'What did she mean?'

'I do have honour,' he said quietly, 'And that means if we had been caught…' He trailed off.

'You would have done the honourable thing,' she finished for him.

He shook himself, as if trying to rid his mind of that terrible thought.

Chapter Ten

'I'm not cut out for this,' Tom murmured as his nephew burst into tears at the sight of him. He had been playing a game with one of the maids, some complicated version of hide and seek, where Edward seemed to be at once both the person who hid and the person who searched. There had been squeals of joy and laughter, but as soon as Tom had entered the room and suggested they get some fresh air, mostly out of concern for the exhausted looking maid, his nephew had started crying.

He would have to remember to pay his staff extra this week. They had all quite happily taken on extra duties to help him with Edward, not once complaining about the work involved, and he knew he had to show his appreciation. He was a fair and generous employer, but he didn't want any of his servants leaving because they felt their extra efforts were going unappreciated.

Pressing one hand against his eye where the first pulses of a headache was brewing, he took a moment before he crouched down, bringing himself to Edward's level.

'It's such a lovely afternoon, I thought we might go to the park. We could take your sailing boat and try it on the Serpentine.'

There was no response from Edward, only a continuation of the tears.

'I don't mean to interfere, sir,' Hetty, the young maid who had been playing with Edward, said. 'But I don't mind playing with the young master.'

'You're good to say that, Hetty.' He hesitated. The boy was his responsibility, but his head was starting to throb, and he had an overwhelming sense of being trapped. He needed to get outside, to gasp in lungfuls of cool air, and arguing with Edward until he was ready to come wasn't going to speed things up. 'I'll be back in an hour or two. Be good for Hetty.'

With a mounting feeling of guilt, as if he were abandoning the boy for good, he grabbed his coat and hat and quickly left the house. He walked briskly, as if he were being chased, only slowing when he had put a good distance between himself and home.

Forcing himself to try and forget all the troubles that were plaguing him, he tried to focus on the things he could see and hear. It was a trick taught to him by an old army friend during his recovery from the head injury. Then the frustrations of the slowness of his recuperation, the mountain of effort it had taken even to take a few short steps outside the front door, had been overwhelming. He had been on the verge of giving in to the melancholy and despair that had threatened to consume him when this old friend had suggested he try looking outside of himself, even just for a moment.

Now he made himself slow down and empty his mind of everything except what he could see, hear and smell right at that moment. He let the noises of the street wash over him, the clatter of carriage wheels and the clopping of hooves, the chatter of groups of women as they passed him and the excited whoops of joy from children out with their nannies. Slowly he felt his heart rate slow and some of the stress seep from his body.

'Mr Stewart!' a familiar voice called.

He wondered whether he could get away with ignoring it, pretending he hadn't heard.

All he wanted was to be alone now, to have a few minutes of peace before he allowed himself to start thinking of the future, to decide what he needed to do with his nephew.

It was Lady Mountjoy, and he knew she wouldn't let him slip away, pretending he hadn't heard. He glanced up and had to suppress a groan. Walking beside her was Miss Ashworth, looking poised and serene, and actually smiling at him as if pleased to see him. It had been a week since he had last seen her, sending a note and telling her it might be best for him to keep his distance after their near miss at the Framlingham ball.

Now a week had passed, there would be no harm in being seen strolling together out in public, chaperoned by Lady Mountjoy. Suspicion had never really fallen on them anyway, but he had needed a few days' space to try and work out what exactly had happened in the glasshouse. There had been one moment, no more than a few seconds, when Miss Ashworth's body had been pressed against his. He had been able to feel her heart hammering in her chest and the heat of her skin through the fabric of her dress. She'd looked up at him and in that moment he had wanted nothing more than to kiss her, to claim her as his own.

It was not the first time he'd felt attraction for an unsuitable young woman, but it was the first time he'd acted on it. Normally he had complete control of himself, complete restraint, but there in the glasshouse he had been unable to do anything but brush his lips against Jane's. He should be thankful that the group of ladies had entered when they had or who knew what could have happened?

These past few days he had kept his distance, fearful of what he might feel when he saw her, even though he knew he was being ridiculous. It had been circumstance, nothing more. A combination of the dark, exotic atmosphere in the glasshouse and the thrill of almost being caught.

'Good afternoon,' he said, turning to face the two women, trying to summon a smile.

'Good afternoon. Is something amiss, Mr Stewart?' Miss Ashworth asked, her forehead crinkling with concern. 'You look pale.'

He cursed himself for being so easy to read and gave a nonchalant little shake of his head.

'I came out for an afternoon walk. It seemed a shame not to get out in the sunshine.'

Miss Ashworth and Lady Mountjoy both glanced up at the sky dubiously. It was grey and overcast with only one or two small breaks in the clouds where weak rays of sunshine were managing to filter through. Hardly a day that would inspire a spontaneous need to get into nature.

'How fortuitous! Miss Ashworth has been eager to get out for some fresh air all day. I said I would accompany her, but my hip is starting to pain me again.'

Miss Ashworth gave the older woman an incredulous look and then flashed an apologetic smile at Tom.

'Perhaps you could escort her for a short stroll whilst I rest a while on one of the benches in the park?'

'Of course. It would be my pleasure.'

They walked together into the park and found a suitable bench for Lady Mountjoy to sit and observe them from as they then carried on along the path.

'She only ever seems to complain of her hip when you are around,' Miss Ashworth said when they were far enough away from Lady Mountjoy so the countess would not hear the comment. The younger woman studied him for a moment. 'Something is wrong. You look like you haven't slept for a month. Is it what happened in the glasshouse?'

'No,' he said a little too quickly, forcing

himself to slow down and summon a more serene expression. 'Although I am tired. It is Edward.' He grimaced. Sleep had been hard to come by these last few days.

He was finding the scent of lavender coming off Miss Ashworth's hair every time she turned in his direction distracting. It made him think of the night in the glasshouse and stirred something deep inside him.

'Is he unwell?'

'No, but he is not happy. I fear I am not doing the right thing by him.'

'Why do you say he is not happy?'

'Take today—I suggested we go for a walk and he burst into tears. There are a hundred instances like that throughout the day from when he wakes up until when he goes to bed.'

'What was he doing before you suggested you go for a walk?'

'Playing hide and seek with one of the maids.'

Miss Ashworth shrugged. 'There it is, then. It has nothing to do with you.'

'What do you mean?'

'What do you enjoy doing most in the world?'

He hesitated for a moment and Miss Ashworth looked at him, eyes wide.

'No, perhaps don't tell me,' she said quickly.

'I was trying to choose between riding and driving my curricle,' he said with a smile, his spirits already lifting a little in Miss Ashworth's company. 'My mind clearly isn't as corrupted as yours.'

'I am an innocent debutante.'

'Clearly not in mind,' he murmured.

'Imagine you are riding your horse,' she ploughed on, resolutely looking ahead. 'Enjoying yourself in the great outdoors, and then suddenly without warning someone comes and tells you instead you need to dismount and you are going to the opera.' She paused to see if he was following her, glancing up at him with her lips pursed. 'It isn't that you dislike the opera, or that you don't want to go with the person who is suggesting it, but in your mind you are focussed on the thing you are enjoying in that moment. For someone to come along and tell you to stop immediately, even for an adult, is a bit frustrating. For a child, it makes them feel as though they have no control over their lives.'

Tom considered Miss Ashworth's words for a long moment.

'Is there a better way of doing it?'

She shrugged. 'Watch the nannies and nursemaids in the park. The ones with happy, contented-looking children lay out their expectations. They tell them even before they get to the park that they can stay and play for half an hour, walk around the Serpentine and feed the ducks. After that, they will return home.'

He nodded slowly. It made sense, and he couldn't really understand why he hadn't realised it himself. It was obvious when he thought about it, but in the moment when Edward had started crying, and Tom had felt as though nothing he could do was right, it had been so hard to be logical.

'It may be worth trying to give him time to get used to an idea before saying you are leaving immediately.'

'I'm no good at this.'

'You are.'

He shook his head. 'I'm not. *You* are good at this. You will make an excellent mother, but I am not a fit guardian for Edward.'

'You're talking nonsense,' Miss Ashworth said, and Tom couldn't help but smile even though he still felt morose. Miss Ashworth, the woman dismissed by most of society as a quiet little mouse, didn't tiptoe around but instead said exactly what she was thought. Everyone else's opinion of her was so wrong, it was laughable.

'If you did these things—upset him and then didn't worry about it—then you would be entitled to question if you were a fit guardian. The very fact that you are out here, feeling awful and wanting to do better, shows you are exactly the right person to be looking after him.'

'Hmm.'

'When is the nanny due to arrive?'

'Ten more days.'

'That is no time at all.'

'He's so distant much of the time. I feel awkward around him.'

'Most people do around children other than their own,' she said with a shrug.

'Do they?'

'Think about it. Your own child, you know from a little baby. You learn what they like and what they don't like, how they respond to you, how to handle them, through every stage of childhood. Edward has just appeared in your life. You need to give it time.' She smiled at him, and Tom felt some of the self-doubt ebbing away.

'I would love to see him again,' she said. 'I know we were keeping our distance so society doesn't suspect we were in that glasshouse, but I haven't heard our names attached to any of the rumours circulating. I think we are safe.'

For an instant she glanced up at him and he saw a flicker of remembrance in her eyes. As she bit her lower lip, he knew in a flash that she had felt that same pull he had, that same flare of attraction. The same thing he was trying to deny every time he looked at her.

Clearing his throat, he nodded. 'Of course. I was going to take him riding, or at least introduce him to some horses. Perhaps you would like to accompany us tomorrow?'

'That would be lovely.' She smiled at him again and her eye held his just a fraction too long before she looked away quickly. He knew he had flustered her but he was too preoccupied with his own interest in this serious young woman to try and put her at ease.

'I will take you back to Lady Mountjoy. No doubt she is getting cold sitting for so long in this weather.'

They walked in silence back to the countess, Tom quickly taking his leave and heading out of the park.

It was late and Tom knew he had consumed far too much alcohol for one night. He gambled like most men in his social circle, but had a hard rule that he never did so after more than five drinks. He had seen too many men ruined from their lack of self-control at the gaming tables, forced to sell their homes or go begging to wealthier relatives to cover their debt.

Tonight, though, he had been close to breaking his rule. He'd thrown back whisky after whisky and had then been tempted to linger at the tables.

'Leaving so soon, Stewart?' Lord Rowlinson called as he pushed back his chair and bid the people at the table good night.

'My skill is no match for yours but I do at least have the good sense to know when I am beaten,' Tom said, reaching for his coat.

He was drinking to forget, gambling to forget, and that could be dangerous. Stepping out into the cold night air, he hesitated, first turning left and then shaking his head and reversing his decision. A month ago he had made the acquaintance of a beautiful young actress who had given him a key and an open invitation to join her in her rooms any night he desired company. It would be another way to forget the thoughts that plagued him, to lose himself in carnal pleasure, but he knew it was the wrong decision tonight, so instead he slowly made his way over the river to Southwark.

Even the streets here made him think of Miss Ashworth, of following her into the dark alleyway and being punched in the jaw, and then her desperate attempts to find the long-dead publisher. He quickened his pace, as if trying to outrun his own thoughts, and almost burst through the door of The Hangman's Noose.

'You being chased or just eager to see me?' a tall, slim woman called out to him from behind the bar.

'You know I can't keep away, Mrs Western.'

'Come on over and pull up a chair. He's changing the barrel but he'll be up in a minute.'

She poured him a beer, the liquid a deep amber and the top frothing, setting it down carefully on the bar in front of him.

'You look awful, Tom.'

'We can't all be radiant all the time, Mrs Western.'

'Stop flirting with my wife, you scoundrel, I can hear you from down here.' Western's voice came from somewhere behind the bar, making Tom smile.

'Is it the headaches?'

He shook his head. 'They haven't been too bad. Only had one in the last few weeks.'

'Your fancy doctors still haven't got to the bottom of it?'

'No. I stopped going to see them when they

suggested leeches again.' They both shuddered at the thought.

'You've visited us twice in a fortnight. We are blessed,' Western said as he emerged from the cellar, wiping his hands on a cloth. 'You're right, he does look awful,' he said, turning to his wife.

'It'll be a woman,' Mrs Western said as she started to wipe down the bar.

'No doubt some poor girl has fallen in love with him and he's feeling the pressure of letting her down.'

'I can hear you,' Tom murmured, although he didn't mind their gentle teasing. It felt familiar and comforting and some of his troubles lifted from his shoulders as he watched his friends smile at each other.

'Is it a woman?'

'No,' he said a little too quickly, trying unsuccessfully to push the image of Miss Ashworth from his mind.

'Your nephew, then?' Western asked.

'He deserves better.'

'Nonsense,' Mrs Western said, motioning out to the street. 'Those children out there, the ones forced to work from the age of five climbing chimneys or worse—they deserve better.

The ones so hungry their bellies hurt and their teeth fall out—they deserve better.'

'I can't argue with that,' Tom said quietly.

'What did you have as a child?' Western said, coming round the bar and sitting next to him.

'A mother who died when I was a baby and a father who was cruel and controlling.'

'Look at you—a bit rough around the edges with some questionable decisions behind you, but all in all you've turned out all right.'

'Don't feed my conceit too much, Western, I might get too confident.'

'You're already too confident by half.'

'He's got a good home, a warm bed, plenty of food, people to take care of him and the chance of an education,' Mrs Western said, her voice a little softer, 'And an uncle who loves him.'

'Not like a parent would.'

Western clapped him on the back. 'Drink up and I'll pour us a whisky.'

'I don't even think it is your nephew you are feeling morose about,' Mrs Western said, eyeing him with a probing look on her face. 'It *is* a woman, isn't it?'

'Who is it this time? An actress? An opera

singer? One of those widows that seem to be so eager to get to know you intimately?'

'There is no one.'

'I don't believe you,' Western said as he reached for the bottle of whisky and poured them both a glass.

'Perhaps it is something a little more than that,' Mrs Western said, motioning to a new customer that she would be along in a moment. 'Are you thinking of finally settling down, Tom?'

'Good Lord, no,' he said, throwing back the whisky and then wishing he hadn't. 'Let's talk about something else. The horse racing, business—even the damn weather. I don't care as long as it isn't about the women in my life.'

'I think you touched a nerve, my dear,' Western said to his wife while clapping Tom on the back. 'I'll wager there will be wedding bells within the year.'

'I thought a tavern was somewhere a man could come to get peace.' Tom growled, standing and grabbing his coat.

'Come back and see us soon,' Mrs Western called from the other end of the bar. 'And bring your lady friend, whoever she may be.'

Chapter Eleven

The morning was cool and crisp as Jane hurried into the park, but there was a hint of warmth when the sun shone making Jane wonder if spring might be just around the corner. Her maid was shivering beside her despite the thick coat she wore and had already asked three times how long they would be out.

Not for the first time, Jane silently cursed the rules of society that meant she couldn't walk alone through a park or go for a ride with a gentleman without having another woman with her. It seemed ridiculous, especially in a public space. Luckily, her maid was open to a bribe if the price was right, and on more than one occasion Jane had paid the young woman to allow her to slip away when she was meant to be accompanying her.

Today, though, there was no need for a bribe

as she was going for an innocent ride with Mr Stewart and his nephew. Refusing to acknowledge the thrill of anticipation that flooded her body as she thought of Mr Stewart, she started to walk even faster, revelling in the burn in her lungs and her calves. Today she would not be overcome by foolish desire and she would remember the sensible young woman she really was. She didn't swoon at the first provocation, she didn't partake in the gossip of the ballroom, and she most certainly didn't lose her head over a man, even if he was ridiculously attractive and too charming for his own good.

The last thing she was going to think about was the kiss they had shared in the glasshouse at the ball. If Mr Stewart could act as if it had never happened, she would too.

'Miss Jane,' Edward shouted as he spotted her, running towards her at full speed and flinging his arms around her in a show of affection.

'How are you, Edward? Excited to see the horses?'

'Zio Tom said he has an extra-special surprise for me.' He lowered his voice. 'I think maybe he will let me do acrobatics, like we saw at Astley's!'

'Have you ridden before?'

'Our neighbour had a donkey called Ranun-colo who she would sometimes let me ride.'

'Never a horse?'

He shook his head.

'Then this is an exciting day.'

Hand in hand, they crossed the grassy area to where Mr Stewart was waiting, discussing something with a groom.

'Miss Ashworth, thank you for coming.'

'I would not have missed this for the world.'

Mr Stewart looked a little dishevelled this morning, as if he had not slept well, but still there was a sparkle in his eyes, something Jane found drawing her in.

'Ah, here they come,' he said, turning away.

Jane turned to see three horses being led across the grass by a groom. One was large and sleek, its coat a shiny mahogany colour. The second was lighter in colour and a little smaller, whilst the third was a little pony, trotting along happily to keep up with the two bigger horses.

'This is Sapphire,' Mr Stewart said, and Jane watched as the young boy's eyes lit up.

'Hello, Sapphire,' Edward said solemnly, waiting for the little pony to stop moving before reaching a tentative hand up to stroke her.

He was gentle and Jane could see from that very first moment he was in love.

'I am told Sapphire is very good for first-time riders. Do you think you would like to ride her?'

'Yes, please.'

'Let me help you.'

Jane moved so she was standing to the front of the pony, stroking the animal's soft nose whilst Mr Stewart crouched down and adjusted his nephew's coat to make him more comfortable.

'It will feel strange the first time you sit in the saddle. Remember to sit straight, but relax as much as possible, and do not hold the reins too tight.'

Edward nodded seriously as he absorbed the instructions.

'Someone will be holding Sapphire all the time, so there is no reason to worry about her bolting, but if you are afraid at all, you tell me.'

Lifting his nephew off the ground, Mr Stewart settled the young boy into the saddle, helping him adjust his position until he was comfortable. A wide grin spread across Edward's face and Jane felt her heart squeeze with affection. She might only have known

him for a short time but the little boy had made
an impression on her.

'Shall we go for a walk?'

'Yes, Zio Tom.'

Jane stayed where she was, watching uncle
and nephew walk in a large circle, the little
boy relaxing more with each step.

'You're a natural, Edward,' Jane said as they
looped back round.

'This is wonderful.'

After another loop, Edward looked much
more confident as Mr Stewart brought him
to a stop.

'What do you think about going for a ride
with Miss Ashworth and me?'

'Will someone be leading Sapphire?'

'Of course.'

The groom stepped forward and took hold
of the leather strap Mr Stewart had been using
to lead the little pony.

'Can I help you mount?'

Jane eyed the side-saddle and swallowed
hard. She had ridden before, dozens of times,
but only once in a side-saddle. Her parents
hadn't had enough funds to own and house
their own horse as Jane and her sisters had
grown older, so the opportunities to ride were
few and far between. The last time she had rid-

den side-saddle, she had fallen from the horse, but that didn't mean it would happen this time.

Mr Stewart stepped close behind her and for a moment all thoughts of being thrown from a galloping horse and breaking her neck disappeared. He boosted her up as if she weighed nothing at all, standing close until he was sure she was settled in the saddle.

He looked at ease as he mounted.

'Your injury didn't put you off riding?'

'No, I got back to riding even before I could walk properly,' he said with a grin. 'Nothing could keep me away from Rupert here.'

'Rupert?'

'I named him after a friend. Everyone ready?'

They set off at a very sedate pace and soon some of the anxiety Jane had felt when she'd first mounted subsided. The side-saddle was not the most comfortable way of riding, but she didn't feel as precarious as she had feared she would.

'We'll head down to the Serpentine and back. That will probably be enough.'

For a while they rode in silence, both Jane and Edward focusing on their horses, and Mr Stewart seemingly happy in their company.

'You can relax your grip a little. Your horse

is very well behaved,' he said quietly, leaning over towards her after a few minutes.'

Jane looked down and saw her knuckles were white on the reins where she was clutching them so hard. Making a conscious effort to relax, she loosened her grip and lowered her hands a fraction.

'Do you get to ride much in Somerset?'

It was the first time Mr Stewart had asked about her life back home and she felt a sudden pang of homesickness. When Lady Mountjoy had given her the opportunity to come to London, she had quickly accepted, but with mixed feelings. She'd wanted the chance to come and find a publisher, to see if this dream of hers was ever going to be achieved, but equally she had dreaded the social events she would be forced to attend.

'Not much. We don't own a horse,' she said, wondering if he would find that strange. Mr Stewart might not be an earl or a viscount, but he was from a very wealthy and influential family who would likely have had a stable full of horses.

'Shame. I bet there are some beautiful places to ride.'

She nodded, thinking of the rolling hills behind their house, the gentle countryside always so lush and green. A lump formed in her throat and she was surprised to feel the sting of tears in her eyes.

'Is something wrong?'

Shaking her head, she sniffed and wiped away the tears.

'I never thought I'd miss home as much as I do,' she said quietly. 'Before I left, I didn't even think about it, I didn't even consider I might feel a pang of sadness when I thought of snow on the hills or the way the sun lights up the countryside as it is setting.'

'Is it your family you miss too?'

'Yes. Our house is chaos with my five younger sisters. It feels like there is never a moment of peace, never a place to think or be quiet.' She shook her head, 'I even pine for the noise and the disorder.'

'Do you have someone close to you age in amongst your sisters?'

'No. I had a brother, born two years after me, but he died of a fever when he was very young. My parents didn't think they would have any more children after that.' She closed her eyes and thought of Harriet, her twin, the person she had been closest to in the world. She wasn't quite ready to tell anyone about her yet.

'I am sorry.'

'Meredith, the next oldest, is ten, Abigail is nine, the twins Caroline and Elizabeth are seven and Sybil is three.'

Mr Stewart raised his eyebrows. 'No wonder you are so good with Edward.'

She glanced over to the young boy who was sitting happily in his saddle, every so often getting up the courage to lean forward and give the pony a hug around her neck.

'You seem more relaxed with him,' Jane said.

'I went to see a friend last night, the friend I told you about in Southwark. His wife has never been afraid of speaking her mind and I think this time some of her words actually got through.'

'What did she say?'

'She told me Edward may miss out on certain things in life but so many children have it harder. He has a warm bed to sleep in at night, food on the table and will get an education to allow him to make the most of his future.'

'You're forgetting something,' she said quietly.

'What?'

'Someone who loves him.'

With a glance at the young boy next to him,

Mr Stewart nodded, and Jane saw true affection in his eyes. She had known it was there, right from the start, but it was wonderful to see this man allowing himself just to be with his nephew, to slowly build that relationship.

'He's lucky to have you.' She waited for Mr Stewart to look at her so he could see the sincerity in her expression. 'You may not have much experience with children but you have a good heart, Mr Stewart, and that is more important than anything else.'

'I have been complimented on one or two things before,' he said, looking across at her with a spark of mischief. 'But never has anyone taken any notice of my heart.'

'More fool them,' Jane murmured.

Her eyes flicked up to meet his and for a long moment she couldn't look away. There was an intensity there like never before and she felt as though her body might catch alight. His eyes were always bright, but today they seemed even brighter, and Jane felt their hypnotic pull.

They were almost at the Serpentine and thankfully Mr Stewart had to look away so he could instruct the groom where to lead Edward's horse on the trip back. Jane took advantage of the lull in Mr Stewart's attention to spur her horse forward a few steps so she could have a minute to herself. As she did, there was a shout from a hundred feet away, and then a few seconds later a brown furry animal came dashing towards them.

It was a large dog, running at such speed it looked like a blur until it got closer. It was barking and showing no signs of slowing down.

'Hold Sapphire,' Mr Stewart said, his voice calm but with a commanding edge to it. Jane glanced back and saw the groom take hold of Sapphire's bridle and start to stroke the horse whilst murmuring soothing words. The little pony didn't seem overly fazed by the approaching animal.

Jane turned back round just in time to see the dog hadn't stopped and was now running fast towards her horse. She froze, not knowing whether to lean forward to try and comfort the animal and risk losing her precarious balance in the side-saddle or stay still and hope the dog came under control.

Out of the corner of her eye she saw Mr Stewart dismount quickly and run towards her, but it was too late. The horse panicked, taking a few quick steps backwards, and then reared up, kicking out its front legs. The dog barked even louder and then the horse bolted.

Jane tensed every muscle possible, clinging on tightly and wondering why she hadn't hit the ground yet. The cold air whipped against her face and pulled her hair loose so it was flying out behind her, streaming across her shoulders.

At first she squeezed her eyes shut, not wanting to see the world spin as she tumbled to the ground, but after a few seconds, when she realised she was somehow still in the saddle, she quickly opened them again. The world was travelling by in a blur and she wasn't even sure what direction she was going in. Every time the horse's hooves hit the grass, Jane felt a jolt travel through her body and push her a little further out of an ideal riding position. A hundred more feet and she would be holding on with her hands alone.

The horse showed no sign of slowing and she was not experienced enough to know what to do for the best. Her heart was thumping in her chest and she could even feel the pulsation in her temples.

A flash of dark brown caught her eye and she risked turning her head a fraction, regretting the move as she slipped a little more in the saddle. Tom was galloping up beside her, although she didn't know what he planned to do other than pick up her broken body once she fell from the horse. He was gaining ground and then suddenly he was beside her, picking up the reins from where she had dropped them and pressing them into her hands.

'Gentle pressure,' he shouted across at her. 'You need to show the horse you are calm and in control.'

It was hard to resist the urge to pull on the reins with all her strength, but she managed to follow the instruction, exerting a firm but steady pressure on the reins. The result was almost instant. The horse did not stop, but Jane could feel some of the panic ebbing away, and gradually the gallop became a canter and then the canter became a trot.

When the horse had slowed enough, Mr Stewart leaped from his saddle and took hold of the bridle, holding the animal steady and placing a calming hand on his neck.

'I've got him…you can come down.'

'I can't,' Jane said.

'Are you stuck?'

She nodded and Mr Stewart took a moment to look her over to try and assess what was preventing her from getting down.

'You're not tangled. You should be able to slip down.'

'I can't,' she repeated.

He started to speak again and then went still, his eyes meeting hers and understanding blossoming in them.

Jane took in a ragged breath as he stepped towards her and placed his hands on her hips.

'You're safe,' he murmured, smiling at her softly in reassurance. 'I've got you.'

Gently he lifted her down, holding her as he placed her feet on the floor, as if knowing her knees would buckle underneath her.

'You're safe,' he said again, and this time Jane felt it.

For a long moment they stood body to body with his hands on her hips and then he reached out, placed a finger on her chin and tilted her face up towards him.

Jane felt an overwhelming surge of desire and as she looked up into Mr Stewart's eyes she knew he was feeling the same. In that moment she didn't have the ability to question it. All she knew was she wanted to be kissed more than she had ever wanted anything else before.

Slowly, as if savouring the moment, Mr Stewart moved towards her and then his lips were on hers. At first he was gentle but, as Jane moaned and swayed into the kiss, he gripped her tighter and kissed her harder.

Jane felt as though her knees might give way again, but Mr Stewart's strong arm around her waist held her up, pulling her even closer. She felt the irresistible draw of his body and without thinking pressed herself against him. He groaned and tangled his free hand in her hair.

Jane never wanted this moment to end. She pushed away all rational thought, refusing to allow any thought of consequence or scandal cross her mind. Instead, for perhaps the first time in her life, she allowed herself to be ruled by her desires.

Suddenly Mr Stewart pulled away and Jane felt herself almost topple. She felt naked, empty, as if half of her had been ripped away.

For a long moment they stood face to face, just looking at one another. Jane saw the panic in his eyes, the uncertainty, the regret and all the warmth from a moment before left her. He looked horrified to have kissed her.

'I'm sorry,' he said, taking another couple of steps away, only realising he was tethered in place by the reins he was holding on to when they went taut. 'I'm sorry,' he repeated. 'I shouldn't have done that.'

She wanted to scream at him, to tell him she had been as much to blame as him, to do anything to wipe the look of horror from his face. Surely kissing her hadn't been all that bad?

He looked around, as if only just remembering they were standing in a public place, that anyone could have seen them. Jane did the same, noting thankfully that the relatively early hour meant this part of the park was deserted and no one could have witnessed their indiscretion.

'I'm sorry.'

'Stop saying you're sorry,' Jane snapped.

For a long moment he gave her an assessing look and then turned away, ostensibly to see to the horses.

Panicking now, Jane tried to stop the thoughts racing at speed through her mind and allow a little space for something rational to materialise. She knew she was so unsettled because she *wasn't* sorry. For the past couple of weeks, an undeniable attraction had been building, and after their kiss in the glass house she had craved another, wanting it more than anything else.

'We were flustered,' Jane said slowly. 'Shaken by the shock of the horse bolting. I have heard people do irrational things when emotions are heightened.'

'Always so practical,' Mr Stewart murmured. For a moment something flared in his eyes and Jane wondered if he was thinking about kissing her again.

'We should return to Edward and the servants and pretend this never happened.' It hurt her to suggest it, but she knew it was the only thing to do. Especially given Mr Stewart's reaction to kissing her. She wouldn't let him see how much his immediate regret had upset her.

'Yes, good plan.'

He took hold of both sets of reins and began leading the horses, turning back when he saw she wasn't following him.

'Are you hurt?'

'No,' Jane said, forcing herself to move.

At home, in the privacy of her room, she would take the time to understand the roiling emotions inside her, but right at this moment she needed to act as though nothing was phasing her.

Chapter Twelve

'Jane, come sit with me. I am so excited about the show tonight. I can't believe after all these months in London we are finally going to the theatre.'

Jane squeezed through the crowd and took the vacant seat next to Lucy, taking a moment to look around her. It had taken weeks of persuasion to convince Lady Mountjoy that a trip to the theatre in Islington would not tarnish their reputations. They had attended the opera many times, but at first Lady Mountjoy had been resistant to a night at the theatre, saying it just wasn't a thing well-bred young ladies did.

'Where is Mr Weyman?' Jane strained her neck to see if she could catch a glimpse of Lucy's husband, but if he was close he was hidden by the bodies of all the people present.

'He suggested we might like a drink whilst

we watch the performance. I'm sure he will be back soon.'

After weeks of making plans, Lady Mountjoy had finally given in and allowed Jane to go and see a play tonight in the company of Lucy and her new husband.

'I love that as a married woman you are enough of a chaperon for me,' Jane said as she shuffled closer to her friend. 'It is so freeing to be able to be out with you and you alone.'

'It's strange, isn't it?' Lucy said, smiling broadly. 'So much has changed now that I am married. I do like the freedom of it.'

'I am pleased you find marriage freeing. You chose well, Lucy. Captain Weyman is a wonderful man and he seems to be happy to give you more trust and freedom than many men do their wives.'

'I wonder if it is because we have known each other for such a long time? I couldn't imagine him telling me what to do, even though he is quite used to ordering the men in his regiment around.'

Captain Weyman appeared through the crowd, smartly dressed for the evening, his lips set into a broad smile. It was impossible not to like him. He was affable and relaxed and never had a bad word to say about anyone. He and Lucy were so well-matched, Jane thought theirs must be the happiest marriage of the decade.

'Miss Ashworth, you are looking radiant this evening. I am delighted you could join us.'

'Thank you for inviting me. I know you are not in London for much longer and time with Lucy is precious.'

'Three more weeks,' Lucy said, suddenly looking sad. 'But I suppose this is the reality of being the wife of an army officer.'

'It will feel like no time at all, and I will be back again,' Captain Weyman said, but Jane could see there was sadness in his eyes too. 'Ah, I see Potters and Gillespie. I won't be a moment, my dear, but I had better go and say hello.'

Excusing himself, Captain Weyman sidled along past the other people sitting nearby to the two friends he had spotted, leaving Jane alone with Lucy.

'So, tell me, how are things going with the delectable Mr Stewart?'

'Stop,' Jane said, feeling a blush start to bloom on her cheeks despite her best efforts to maintain a nonchalant façade. 'There is absolutely nothing to tell because there is nothing going on with him.'

'I don't believe you. Look at how much you are blushing.'

'I'm not blushing.'

'It is no use denying it.'

Jane shook her head. 'Perhaps I should just tell you the truth,' she said slowly.

'This sounds intriguing.'

'Mr Stewart is helping me, and I him. We have made a mutually agreeable deal. I assist him with his nephew, accompany them on a few days out, provide a little advice until his nanny from the agency arrives...'

'And what do you get in return?'

Jane hesitated. Lucy knew that she drew and painted—they had shared a home for months and Jane would often cloister herself away in her room with her paintbrushes. What she had never confided to any of her friends was her ambition, her desire to see her work published, to try and make a living out of the stories she wrote and the pictures she painted to accompany them.

'Have you ever wondered why I decided to come to London?'

'Once or twice,' Lucy admitted. 'You never seemed that interested in the balls and the dinner parties and have expressed your reluctance to find a husband more than once.'

'It is not an environment I feel comfortable in. I don't have Eliza's easy charm, or your amiable nature, or Charlotte's good looks. I am not made to be a debutante.'

'Did your parents push you into it?'

Jane shook her head. 'No. Although they were delighted when I suggested I might approach Lady Mountjoy and see if she might consider me as one of her debutantes. With five younger sisters at home, I think they despair as to what might happen to us.'

'So, why then?'

'I wanted to come to London…' She looked around and then lowered her voice. 'I have a dream. Over the last few months I have been visiting publishers and printers to see if any might consider my work.'

'Your painting?' Lucy looked a little confused.

'I write stories to go with them. Children's stories.'

'Jane, that is wonderful, but how have you kept it secret all this time?'

'I didn't know if there was something worth pursuing with it but, now I have nearly exhausted all of the publishers in London and none will even give me an audience, I am close to giving up.'

'You can't give up, not if this is something you're passionate about.' Lucy shook her head vehemently. 'What I don't understand is what this has to do with Mr Stewart and your deal with him.'

'He caught me visiting one of the less desirable areas of London whilst I was searching for a publisher's shop. He escorted me home and Lady Mountjoy now thinks there is something between us. We agreed to use that, to allow me some freedom from her match-making efforts, to give me more time to work on finding a publisher.'

'That is quite a scheme, Jane,' Lucy said, puffing out her cheeks as she sat back in her chair and considered all she had been told.

'So you see, there really is not anything between me and Mr Stewart.'

'I understand how this began,' Lucy said slowly, dropping her voice as someone came and took one of the seats directly behind them. 'But that does not mean feelings cannot develop.'

'You're as bad as Lady Mountjoy.'

'Would it truly be that terrible if you were to fall in love?'

Jane closed her eyes for a moment, remembering the way his lips had felt on hers, the soaring of her heart as their bodies had come together. In those moment she had allowed herself to wonder, but it had been a short-lived fantasy both times.

'Perhaps one day it might happen,' Jane said, wishing the play would hurry up and start. 'But Mr Stewart has a certain reputation. I am not one to believe every titbit of gossip that comes my way, but he is a very charming man, and I have no doubt he could have his choice of women.'

'You're putting yourself down again, Jane. *You* are marvellous. You are interesting and quick witted, you're funny and a joy to be around. You're talented and beautiful…' Lucy stopped as Jane scoffed.

'I am well aware of my talents and my shortcomings,' Jane said quietly. 'And I have made my peace with them.'

'You are beautiful.'

She thought of the flare of attraction in Mr Stewart's eyes, the way she had felt when she had seen desire in his expression. It was the first time in her life she had wondered if she was more than a plain young woman, the least desirable of the debutantes, the one always left to one side at the ball. She knew much of it was her perpetuating the cycle. She felt plain, so she dressed in a way not to draw attention to herself—that way she could pretend it was because she didn't want anyone to notice her. It was a way of protecting herself.

Jane shook her head. She desperately wanted to confide in Lucy about the kisses, but she hadn't been able to get the sequence of events straight in her own mind, let alone work out what any of it meant. Every time she thought of it, she felt something stir deep within her, a desire to be back in that moment, to enjoy again and again the kisses they had shared. Her only kisses. Then she thought of Mr Stewart's reaction after the kiss in the park and she felt a deep embarrassment, as though she had somehow got everything so wrong. How could she crave another kiss when he seemed so aghast about the last?

Thankfully the hum of chatter in the theatre started to settle, the last few members of the audience took their seats and the curtain at the front of the stage began to move.

'We will continue this conversation later,' Lucy whispered as she settled back into her chair, smiling over at her husband as he reappeared.

The play was entertaining and had Jane laughing out loud through much of it. This was one thing she loved about her stay in London—getting to experience things she otherwise wouldn't have in her sleepy Somerset village.

'That was *exactly* what I needed,' Jane said as the actors and actresses came out onto the stage to take a bow to a rousing round of applause. For two blissful hours she hadn't thought about anything but what she was watching. It had been wonderful not to obsess about the kiss, not to worry about the next time she saw Mr Stewart, not even to feel down about her dwindling chances of getting her children's stories published.

'It was entertaining, wasn't it?' Lucy said, smiling back.

'Shall we let a few people leave so we're not in the press of the crowd?' Captain Weyman suggested. They remained in their seats for a few minutes as some of the audience slowly drifted away, standing once the auditorium was half-empty.

As they made their way out of the theatre, Jane looped her arm through Lucy's.

'Thank you,' she said, leaning her head in to speak to her friend.

'You're welcome. It has been a lovely evening.'

Jane was about to say more when she glanced up and felt her whole body stiffen. Ahead of them, walking directly towards them, was Mr Stewart. He noticed her a second or two later and Jane could see the surprise on his face. No doubt he thought himself safe from bumping into her here, in his world. The theatre wasn't a hotbed of scandal, but the audience was mainly made up of smartly dressed middle class people, not the small group of the wealthy and titled that made up the *ton*.

Jane's eyes flicked to his and she saw a flare of panic before he quickly recovered his composure. On his arm was a beautiful young woman with striking red hair and deep-blue eyes. She was dressed in a flowing emerald-green dress that fitted her body perfectly, showing off every curve without offending the more conservative of theatregoers.

She hated the flare of jealousy she felt as she saw how this woman turned to Mr Stewart with a question in her eyes, placing a hand on his arm as if to claim him. At the same time, Jane caught a glimpse of the shapeless lilac dress she had chosen for the occasion, choosing comfort over style when she had dressed a few hours earlier.

'Mr Stewart,' Lucy said, filling the silence

that stretched out. 'How wonderful to see you again.'

'And you, Mrs Weyman, you look well.'

'May I introduce my husband, Captain Weyman?' Lucy waited as the two men stepped forward. 'William, this is Mr Stewart, a friend of Jane's.'

'A pleasure.'

There was a pause as they all looked expectantly at Mr Stewart, waiting for him to introduce his companion.

'This is Mrs Catherine Burghley,' he said eventually. The young woman glanced at Mr Stewart, as if surprised at his reluctance to introduce her, and then cast a brilliant smile over the group.

'How lovely to meet some friends of Mr Stewart's. Did you enjoy the play?'

'It was fantastic,' Lucy said after a moment when it became apparent Jane wasn't going to answer.

Jane felt as though her tongue had become stuck to the roof of her mouth. She couldn't tear her eyes away from the intimate way Mrs Burghley stood with her hand resting on Mr Stewart's arm. Inside was a bubbling mix of jealousy she had no right to feel and shame at allowing herself to succumb to such an ugly emotion. Mr Stewart had never promised her anything. On the contrary, he had been very open about the sort company he preferred. Never had he denied his reputation as a rake. Never had he pretended his life was about much more than seeking out pleasure.

For a moment Jane closed her eyes. This shouldn't even be an issue. She and Mr Stewart were at most friends—friends who had shared two incredible kisses, but friends all the same.

She tried to give a friendly smile, but as Mrs Burghley recoiled she realised it had been more like a grimace.

'I'm a little warm,' she managed to mutter. 'Lovely to meet you, Mrs Burghley. I think I'll meet you outside, Lucy.'

Without waiting for a response, she turned and fled, darting through the groups of people still lingering in the foyer of the theatre.

As soon as she had taken her first few steps, she knew she was heading in the wrong direction. The main entrance was back the way she had come, back past Lucy and her husband, back past Mr Stewart and the stunning Mrs Burghley. In her haste to get away from everyone, she had chosen the wrong way, and now she was striding through the narrowing corridor towards areas where the public wasn't allowed.

'Miss Ashworth.' Mr Stewart's familiar voice came from behind her, close enough for her to know he had followed her. 'Miss Ashworth, stop.'

Determined not to obey, she pushed through the doors to the backstage area, surprised by the darkness. There were a few steps leading down to a narrow corridor which looked as though it ran the depth of the stage before turning abruptly at the end. There were voices in the distance, but no one visible. Jane hesitated, and at that moment Mr Stewart pushed through the doors behind her and caught hold of her wrist.

'Jane,' he said, his voice dropping now he had her to himself. It was the first time he had called her anything other than 'Miss Ashworth', and Jane felt a shiver of longing course through her body. She frowned to hide it, wishing her subconscious would behave itself.

'You followed me.'

'You looked upset.'

She shook her head, wondering exactly what she was going to say to make him believe she hadn't been fleeing from the sight of a beautiful young woman and him arm-in-arm.

'I'm not upset.' She found it best to be brief, abrupt even, in this sort of circumstance. Silently she grimaced, realising how ridiculous her thoughts were; she had never been in a situation even vaguely similar before in her life.

For a long moment neither of them spoke. She felt his eyes on her, searching her face, but she refused to look up. She was afraid if she did he might see something in her eyes, something to confirm what he was thinking.

'We never discussed our kiss,' he said after a minute. His voice seemed loud in the darkened corridor, echoing off the empty walls.

'Which one?'

'Either. Both. We need to talk about them.'

'Don't shout about it.'

'There's no one here, Jane.' There it was again, his use of her first name and the illusion of closeness it summoned.

'Someone could burst through those doors at any moment.'

'Fine,' he said, lowering his voice to a theatrical whisper. 'We never discussed our kisses.'

'What is there to discuss?'

He cleared his throat, looking uncomfortable.

'I didn't know if you were upset tonight because you saw me with another woman…' He trailed off.

Doing her best to channel the new Mrs Farthington, the haughtiest woman she knew, she raised an imperious eyebrow.

Mr Stewart was a hard man to unsettle, and he looked back at her with a raised eyebrow of his own.

'You thought I would be upset to see you with another woman, even though we agreed it was a silly mistake, nothing to ever be repeated.'

'We did agree that.'

'Yet you think I am not capable of moving on, of accepting it meant nothing?'

'I just thought…'

Jane held up a hand, hating how cold her voice sounded but knowing she could not let him see how unsettled she really was. She didn't want to feel this way. She didn't want to have a longing to reach out, wrap her arms around his neck and kiss him until she was ruined, but it wasn't something under voluntary control.

'The kisses we shared,' she said, hoping she could maintain her composure as she spoke, 'Were perfectly pleasant, but they were both at moments of high drama. People do reckless things when they have been in danger, and that was all there was to it.'

'Perfectly pleasant,' he murmured, frowning, as if no one had described his kiss as 'perfectly pleasant' before.

'We had an agreement, Mr Stewart,' Jane said, pressing on. 'I promised you I would tell you if I started to fall for your charm.'

He nodded, his eyes all the while searching hers.

'I do not break promises lightly, and I have no qualms in telling you that I do not have feelings for you, past perhaps the developing of an unlikely friendship.' She looked at him directly now, willing herself to stay strong. 'I like you, Mr Stewart, more than I ever thought I would, but my regard for you stops there. There is no ulterior motive in wanting to spend time with you. I have no desire to ensnare you into marriage.'

The silence stretched out between them before finally Mr Stewart nodded, satisfied. 'I like you too, Jane.' He said it so softly, so gently, that all of her resolve was almost dashed in those five little words. She felt her heart squeeze in her chest at the prospect of what could be before she could harden it. Mr Stewart might have kissed her, but his reaction immediately after, and his presence at the theatre with a stunning young lady, showed her there was no chance of anything more between them.

For her own self-preservation, she needed him to believe she was as uninterested as he was. Shaking her head, she told herself again she *wasn't* interested. Mr Stewart had no place in her life's plans. She wanted neither a husband nor a lover. For so long she had strived for something more, something she could call her own. She wanted to achieve something more than getting married and pushing out babies every year or two for the next twenty years.

'I'm sorry,' he said, waiting for her to look up again. When she didn't, he stepped forward, placed a finger under her chin and tilted it ever so gently. Jane felt as though everything around the faded away and it was just the two of them suspended in the darkness together.

She swallowed, wondering if he could hear the pounding of her heart, and cursing how her body was betraying her after she had given such a convincing speech.

'I'm sorry,' he said again. 'I shouldn't have doubted you.'

He paused and for a moment Jane thought he was going to kiss her again.

'Will you grant me a favour?'

She nodded, her chest feeling as though it were being squeezed from the inside out.

'Call me Tom. I hate the formalities of society.'

'Tom,' she said softly.

'Good. We should get back before anyone finds us here. Then we really would be in trouble.'

They both moved at the same time, her body crashing into his, and as he reached out to steady her his hand brushed against her breast. Jane inhaled sharply and looked up into his eyes, wondering if she imagined the flash of intense longing before he quickly turned away.

Chapter Thirteen

'Captain Weyman and Mrs Weyman have been kind enough to invite us for drinks,' Mrs Burghley said as Tom strolled back into the rapidly emptying foyer of the theatre.

He felt his heart sink a little. This evening had not gone to plan. Mrs Burghley had been introduced by a mutual friend and he couldn't deny she was beautiful and superficially charming. Tom had been cajoled into inviting her to the theatre as a favour to this friend, who had told him she was in need of company after being dropped by the group with whom she used to socialise after her late husband's money had started to run low. From the hints she had been dropping all evening, she was looking for a protector, a man to swoop in and save her from the precarious position she was in.

Normally he would have given the widow more of a chance, but today everything she did seemed to grate on him. Even her laugh had annoyed him, and he had quickly stopped the wandering fingers she had placed on his leg as everyone's attention had been directed towards the stage at the start of the play. He wanted to go home to bed and forget about Mrs Burghley.

Glancing at Jane, he felt that same thrum he had every time he looked at her now. He didn't want to admit this was one of the reasons he had found Mrs Burghley's company so trying this evening, but he knew his mind was distracted by Jane.

At this moment, she was trying her hardest to be inconspicuous, as he had seen her do many times before. Even so, he couldn't rid himself of the memory of their kisses. He found himself thinking about it at inappropriate moments, then having to spend time and energy chastising himself for making such a big deal out of it.

He had kissed dozens of women in his life. There was no reason for him suddenly to obsess over these two kisses with a perfectly ordinary woman.

He grimaced, admitting to himself that Jane was not perfectly ordinary. Perhaps that was the reason he was dwelling so much on the kiss; he had allowed himself to like her, to think of her as a friend, before he had kissed her. Normally he didn't let the women with whom he conducted his liaisons to get too close, showing them only his superficial self. Jane had crept under his defences, becoming his friend.

'Enough,' he murmured to himself. She had assured him that to her it was nothing more than a mistake. He needed to forget their kisses too. 'That is very generous of you. I would not wish to impose.'

'Nonsense,' Mrs Weyman said, her eyes sparkling. 'The evening is young and it would be our pleasure to entertain you.'

'Thank you.'

'I'm sure we can squeeze into our carriage,' Mrs Weyman said, motioning to a carriage as they left the theatre. 'It'll be a little tight, but it is not far.'

'A little tight' was an optimistic way of putting it and for a moment, as he climbed into the carriage, he doubted whether they would all fit. It required a great deal of shuffling until they did, and when they finally lurched forward as the carriage departed Tom was sitting squeezed in the middle of one seat with Mrs Burghley to his left and Jane on his right.

'This is fun,' Jane murmured in that dry way of hers.

He had to suppress a smile but didn't dare move to see her expression lest he upset their precarious balance.

Thankfully the journey was short, as promised by the Weymans, and in five minutes the carriage slowed. It took a little manoeuvring to get everyone out but finally they were all standing in front of a smart house with black metal railings outside.

'Oh, how pretty,' Mrs Burghley said. 'I used to live not too far away, and I've often walked past these houses and thought how well positioned they are, overlooking the park.'

'It isn't big,' Mrs Weyman said with a contented expression on her face. 'But for now it is a very pleasant home. We're renting it for a few more weeks until my husband gets his orders.'

Inside, the Weymans led the way into a comfortable drawing room and a maid bustled around, ensuring the fire was well stoked and drinks poured. Captain and Mrs Weyman excused themselves for a moment, leaving their guests to make small talk in their absence.

'Tell me, how do you know each other?' Mrs Burghley asked, her eyes flicking between Jane and Tom, seated on opposite sides of a low table.

For a moment he thought about saying something shocking and provoking. Perhaps that Jane had punched him in an alley in Southwark and their friendship had blossomed from then.

'Oh, you know,' Jane said with a dismissive flick of the hand. 'The usual mutual friends, attending the same social events.'

'I thought you said you didn't attend many events of the *ton*.' She turned to him with confusion in her eyes.

'I don't. I met Miss Ashworth at one of the few I do attend.'

'I would wager Mr Stewart is a fine dancer. Am I right, Miss Ashworth?'

'Alas, I am not the right person to ask. I stumble at even the easiest of dances,' Jane said. He remembered the waltz they had shared, that wonderful feeling of gliding around the ballroom together. 'He is very much in demand on the dance floor, though, so I think you are right. How do you know each other?'

Mrs Burghley shifted a little closer to Tom.

He was powerless to move away, pressed up against the arm of the sofa.

'We were introduced by a friend,' the widow said, looking up at him with a seductive smile. 'They thought we would enjoy one another's company.'

'Mrs Burghley, I wonder if I could have your opinion in the dining room?' Mrs Weyman said as she bustled back into the room. 'Your dress is exquisite and I have a few samples of fabric I am struggling to choose between. Perhaps you might be able to help me.'

Tom and Jane watched as Mrs Burghley left the room, throwing him a glance filled with both regret and promise as she exited.

'Fabric?'

Jane snorted. 'Lucy normally is more subtle than this.'

'What does she have to be subtle about?'

Jane gestured at the space between the two of them. 'No doubt she is hoping to return to us cinched in a passionate embrace.'

'She knows?' He hadn't meant to exclaim in such horror.

'Of course she doesn't know we kissed,' Jane snapped. 'I'm not an idiot.'

'What *does* she know?'

Jane looked at him without speaking for

thirty seconds then must have decided to put his mind at ease.

'She is aware of our little arrangement.'

'Fine,' he said slowly, nodding his head. 'That's not disastrous.'

'But she is under the impression that our agreement does not preclude us developing feelings for one another.' She sighed and slumped back in her chair. 'I do wish you weren't so damn attractive.'

This made him smile. He loved how she spoke her mind, often the words flowing out before she had a chance to consider the impact of them.

'It is a burden I have to bear,' he murmured.

Her head snapped up. 'I'm not saying *I* find you attractive,' she said quickly. 'Just that objectively you are attractive, and that means everyone thinks I must be falling for you.'

'Objectively I am attractive,' he mused, trying his hardest to look puzzled rather than amused. 'So does that mean you do find me attractive or you don't?'

Jane opened her mouth to speak and then pressed her lips together so hard, they turned white.

'We don't need to have this conversation.'

'I think we do,' he said, unable to stop the grin spreading across his face.

'Stop it.'

'Stop what?'

'Looking so pleased with yourself.' She let out a long-suffering sigh and gave a dismissive wave. 'It is how people describe you. You are Mr Stewart, the charming and handsome bachelor who has no plans to settle down.'

'Is that what people say about me?'

'Yes. As if someone can be summed up in a mere sentence.'

'What do they say about you?'

She pulled a face and shook her head. 'I don't know. Probably something along the lines of Miss Ashworth, the dull and plain debutante who has no interest in society.'

'Don't be ridiculous.'

'I'm not. Society likes to put people in their boxes. I am an unattractive woman destined to be a spinster.'

'You are not.'

'I don't have any plans to marry.'

He waved a dismissive hand. 'You're not unattractive. You're not even plain.'

A hand flitted to her hair, where she had it pulled back into a tight bun.

'You may try to look plain, so you can fade

into the background,' he said quietly. 'But you do not succeed.'

She scoffed and he saw the disbelief in her eyes.

'You believe it, don't you?' he said, realising now that she didn't choose the unflattering dresses and hairstyles solely to remain unnoticed. 'You believe that you're not beautiful.'

'No one, ever, has thought I am beautiful,' she said, her chin jutting out in defiance.

'That's why you do it, why you choose clothes that don't fit that well and have your hair in such a severe style.'

'Enlighten me,' she said softly. 'Seeing as you are suddenly the expert on my innermost feelings.'

'You truly believe you are plain, and you think if you made an effort it would show you care. It is about preservation, at not having to listen to anyone laugh because you tried to be more than you think people expect.'

She shrugged but Tom could see he had got to the core of it.

Knowing he should stay in his seat, he stood, hating how Jane had wrapped her arms across her chest protectively. With a glance at the door, he came and crouched down in front of her, taking both her hands in his own.

'You're beautiful, Jane Ashworth.'

At first she wouldn't meet his eye. Instead she shook her head and kept looking down at her lap.

'Look at me.' He waited, the seconds stretching out until finally she lifted her head a fraction and looked him in the eye. 'You are beautiful.'

'No. I'm the plain one, the clever one, the dull one.'

He frowned, wondering who it was she was comparing herself to.

'You are clever, I am not denying that, but you are so much more than those three words. You are witty and sharp, you are kind and generous, you are beautiful…and you are a hundred more things.'

Knowing he was on dangerous ground, he reached up and trailed a finger down her cheek. It was intimate, far too intimate, for a couple who only an hour earlier had agreed there was nothing in the kiss they'd shared, but he did it all the same.

Jane took a sharp breath and he saw her eyes darken as she looked at him.

'Beauty is not just about the thickness of a woman's hair or the clarity of her skin, it is about so much more,' he said softly. 'But, even if it were based purely on the physical, you are an attractive woman, Jane, even when you try so hard not to be.'

For a long moment she looked into his eyes and he felt as though he might be getting through, then she gave a violent shake of her head and stood abruptly, almost knocking him over, fleeing from the room out, of the glass doors into the garden beyond.

Tom stood, debating whether to follow her. It was a cold night, but he doubted the Weymans' garden was large, and she could return whenever she wanted. She would probably tell him she wanted solitude, but he couldn't bring himself to leave her out there alone, believing the lies her own mind told her.

With a cursory glance at the door to the hall, he satisfied himself no one was returning to the drawing room yet, and dashed out into the garden to follow Jane.

It took him a few seconds to adjust to the moonlight, but after a moment he saw Jane's figure in the corner of the little garden.

'Go back inside,' she said as he came and touched her gently on the arm. Already her skin was cool to touch, and he quickly shrugged off his jacket to drape around her shoulders.

'No.'

'If we're found out here together...' She trailed off, leaving the consequences to his imagination.

'All the more reason for you to tell me what has upset you and how we can fix it.'

She shook her head.

'Who were you comparing yourself to, Jane?' he asked, watching as her eyes flicked up in surprise at the question. 'When you said you were the clever one, the plain one, the dull one?'

'It doesn't matter.'

He reached out and ever so gently took her hand, hearing her sharp intake of breath. A spark passed between them, setting his skin on fire, and Tom desperately tried to ignore it. Nothing good could come out of this attraction he was feeling, and he had resolved to think of Jane as a friend. If one of his other friends were having a crisis of confidence like this, he would calmly but firmly help them through it.

'It's my sister,' Jane blurted out, her eyes darting up to meet his. 'Harriet.'

'Harriet?'

'I didn't mention her before. She was my twin. She died a few years ago. I find it difficult to talk about her.'

'I'm sorry. It must be difficult to lose someone so close.'

'She was beautiful with such a gentle temperament.'

Tom stayed quiet, allowing Jane to talk now she had started to open up.

'Everyone would joke she had stolen all the gifts when we were in the womb. She was beautiful whilst I was plain. She was kind whilst I was spiky…'

Slowly he began to see what this would have done to a little girl, raised to think she was not conventionally attractive or worthy.

'I didn't mind,' Jane said in a voice that hinted she had minded, at least when she'd been young. 'I determined I would play to my talents. Beauty might be the most treasured attribute in a young woman, but I would not dwell on the fact I had not been blessed. Instead I would look for another way to make those around me proud.'

'Was it your parents who made you feel second best?' Tom felt a sudden flare of anger that anyone could do this to a young child.

'Not directly. No one was ever cruel to me, no one came out and told me I was ugly or lacked charm.' She shrugged and Tom squeezed her hand. 'It was more subtle than that. People from the village would stop and make a fuss over Harriet and say how lovely she was, then they would turn to me and purse their lips, and ask me if I was a good girl and helped my parents as I should.' Jane pulled away, shaking herself a little, as if ashamed to have indulged in so much self-pity. 'I should be thankful, really. It made me realise when I was young the conventional path of marrying a man who could provide for me might not be open to me.'

'So you started to explore your other talents.'

'Yes, my writing and my painting.'

'I think I understand,' Tom said, choosing his next words carefully. 'It is all nonsense, of course, but I understand.'

'Nonsense?'

'I did not know your sister, so I cannot comment on her appearance, but I do know you. Shall I tell you what I see when I look at you?' Tom didn't wait for her to answer before pressing on. 'I see a perfectly shaped face with striking high cheekbones and gently arched brows. I see full, rosy lips and eyes that are deep and intelligent. I see thick, shiny hair, even when it is pulled back into the most severe of buns. I see you.'

For a moment he thought she was going to launch herself at him, fling her body into his arms and take advantage of the darkness.

'It is kind of you to say,' she said eventually, her voice even and under control. 'And I dare say it is true that beauty is subjective—although I am sure, if you were to be completely truthful, you would choose a woman who looked like Mrs Burghley over a woman who looked like me every time.'

Tom couldn't deny that normally the women with whom he conducted his affairs did often have certain physical attributes in common, but he was acutely aware of the attraction he felt towards Jane.

He stepped forward and took her into his arms, looking into her eyes before he lowered his lips to hers. He kissed her gently, tasting the sweetness of her lips and enjoying the way she melted into him after a few seconds. Pushing away all the self-recrimination, the voice that told him this was beyond foolish, he kissed her, loving the way she pressed her fingers into his back, not caring in that instant if they were found.

In his rational mind he knew this was reckless, needlessly so. He didn't want to marry Jane, he didn't want to marry anyone, yet here he was kissing a young woman who would be ruined if they were found. All of this he knew. He'd told himself again and again.

Normally he didn't have a problem with keeping his impulses under control. He might dart through life in search of the next pleasure, but he did it mindfully, never dallying with anyone who wasn't as free and enthusiastic as himself. Yet here was Jane, the young woman no one seemed to take any notice of, and he couldn't keep his hands off her.

'What are you doing?' Mrs Burghley's voice rang out clear and loud through the darkness. 'You're kissing *her*?'

They sprang apart, Jane knocking into the wall behind her and bouncing back off again into Tom's arms. Carefully he set her right and then stepped away, trying to form a useful thought instead of the pure panic that was threatening to consume him.

'Mrs Burghley…' Jane started to say, but was interrupted by the widow.

'I am not talking to you. I am talking to Mr Stewart.'

He saw Jane recoil and knew it would take a lot for her to hold her tongue.

'What is happening?' Mrs Weyman said as she stepped out from the drawing room. He watched as her eyes roamed over their positions in the garden before widening in surprise.

'Why did you invite me tonight?' Mrs Burghley asked, taking a few steps towards Tom in the darkness. He didn't answer immediately, knowing his future was now in this woman's hands. He doubted Mrs Weyman or her husband would do anything that might tarnish Jane's reputation, but he barely knew Mrs Burghley, and couldn't rely on her discretion.

'Lord and Lady Otterby thought we might enjoy one another's company,' he said, taking a few slow steps towards the widow. 'And I thought we would both enjoy a night at the theatre.'

'Then what is this?' She gestured at the Jane and him, a look of disbelief still on her face.

'Shall we all go inside?' Mrs Weyman said, clutching her husband's hand as he stepped out of the drawing room. 'It is a very late and I am sure some of our neighbours are asleep.'

'You invite *me* to the theatre, set up hopes there may be something between us, and then kiss *her* in the darkness?'

'He kissed you?' Mrs Weyman sounded shocked, a hand flying to her mouth.

Tom felt as though his head was spinning and about to explode from his shoulders. He had the urge to run, to push through the Weymans and Mrs Burghley and flee into the night. Every muscle in his body was tensed, preparing to flee, and then he caught sight of Jane's panicked face, her eyes darting everywhere. As much as he didn't want to be forced to marry her, she didn't want to marry him either.

'Perhaps we can all go inside and sort this out,' he said, hoping the uncertainty in his voice was audible only to his own ears.

'Forget it,' Mrs Burghley said, spinning on her heel and pushing past the Weymans. 'Goodbye, Mr Stewart.' Her words sounded ominous, like a threat, and he heard Jane gasp from behind him.

The front door slammed and for a long moment no one moved.

'I think we'd better go inside,' Captain Weyman said eventually, ushering his wife in ahead of him. Tom waited for Jane, but as she moved past him she wouldn't meet his eye.

'Sit down,' Mrs Weyman instructed gently. Tom sat on one side of the room, Jane on the other, and he was glad when the Captain placed a generous glass of whisky in his hand. 'Now, tell me everything and we will see if we can work this out.'

'What am I doing here?' he murmured and leaped to his feet, throwing back the glass of whisky. 'I will go after Mrs Burghley,' he said, addressing Jane. 'I will ensure she sees sense.'

Before anyone could voice a word of protest, he was out the door, following in Mrs Burghley's footsteps from just a few minutes earlier. With luck he might catch up with her. She would be on foot for at least the first part of her journey, until she found a carriage for hire to take her home.

It was imperative he caught her and implored her to keep what she had seen to herself. Otherwise the repercussions did not bear thinking about. Either Jane would be ruined or he would have to marry her.

Chapter Fourteen

'Calm down,' Lucy instructed, rubbing Jane's back. 'It's not worth your tears.'

Jane sniffed, trying to regain her composure. Very soon she would have to return to Lady Mountjoy's and face the questions of the older woman, enquiring how her evening had been. Any hint of redness around her eyes and Lady Mountjoy would spot it and soon prise the story out of her.

'It's late,' Jane said, glancing at the clock on the mantelpiece for the hundredth time. 'Why isn't he back yet?'

'There are a hundred reasons,' Lucy said soothingly.

'He's run away.'

'No, I'm sure that's not true.'

'Perhaps he is on board a boat to France as

we speak. Better to flee the country than be saddled with a dull spinster for a wife.'

'Oh, Jane. You care for him, don't you?'

'No. Not one bit.'

It was clear from Lucy's expression she didn't believe her, but thankfully she dropped that line of questioning.

'What happened in the garden?'

Jane buried her head in her hands, trying to work out the chain of events that had led to them kissing again.

'I was unsettled,' she said slowly. 'I made an offhand comment about being a plain spinster and Tom... Mr Stewart...told me I was beautiful.'

'Was he trying to seduce you?'

'No.' She shook her head slowly. 'He's not like that.'

'He does have a certain reputation, Jane.'

'Not with debutantes.'

Lucy considered for a moment and then seemed satisfied. 'Do you love him?'

'No,' she said a little too quickly. 'No, it was a mistake, a collision of bodies in the darkness. In any other circumstance, nothing would have happened.'

Lucy fell silent and Jane considered her own words. She had been trying hard not to think about anything but the possible consequences. Grave as they were, they didn't scare her anywhere near as much as the feeling she got when she allowed herself to relive their kiss. She had felt as though she were finally alive, finally allowing that spark of joy to run free within herself. It was frightening, and she knew she had to push the feelings away.

'We need to get you home,' Lucy said decisively. 'Act like nothing untoward has happened.'

'You don't think he is coming back?'

'It is almost midnight. Maybe he thought it better to discuss things in the morning.'

Lucy was right, he wasn't coming back. Perhaps he would send a note in the morning, perhaps he wouldn't. She didn't think he would abandon her to face the gossip alone, but how well did she really know him?

'Yes,' she said wearily. 'I shall go home.'

Going off to find her husband to accompany them on the short walk back to Lady Mountjoy's house, Lucy pulled the door closed behind her, giving Jane a few minutes of much-needed privacy. She slumped back in her chair, allowing her mind to wander, to remember the heat of their kiss. She hated that her subconscious mind was still yearning for Tom, that the rebellious part of her wasn't scared or nervous, but hopeful that this could be the beginning of something wonderful.

'He doesn't want this,' Jane whispered to herself. 'And you don't want him like this.'

None of this had been planned. She didn't think he had ever set out to seduce her, just as she hadn't expected to feel an attraction to the Season's most notorious rake.

With a burst of resolve, she checked her reflection in the small mirror hanging over the mantelpiece. Carefully she smoothed her hair, glad of its simple style which allowed her to fix the stray strands of hair easily. Her eyes looked a little red but hopefully the cold air on the walk back would make her cheeks flush too and she could blame the chill breeze.

'Come on,' Lucy said, re-entering the room with Jane's coat draped over her arm. 'Let's get you home and you can have a good rest. Things will seem better in the morning.'

Jane buried her head under the covers as the maid bustled across the room, lighting the fire for the new day. She hadn't slept at all, tossing and turning through the night with her mind whirring with all the possible consequences of the night before. This morning she was no closer to having things worked out and her head was pounding. She hated that her fate was in another person's hands—really all she could do was wait to see what Mrs Burghley decided to do.

The maid finished with the fire and quietly left the room, and Jane considered pleading illness and hiding from the world in bed all day. Quickly she dismissed the idea. The last thing she needed was more time to worry about what the future would hold.

Instead she rose, pulling on her dressing gown to ward against the chill in the bedroom, and crossing to the desk to take out some papers. She was working on a story about three little field mice trying to outwit an owl, but couldn't quite get the owl's eyes right in the pictures she was creating to accompany it. For a while she sketched, trying one thing after another, enjoying the simplicity of her task, which forced her to concentrate but did not need her to be well rested or overly alert.

After about half an hour she sat back in her chair, satisfied. She had changed the shape of the owl's eyes and added some tiny tufts of fluffy feathers. Later she might try adding some colour to the picture with her paints, but at this moment it was a big improvement on what she had managed before.

There was a soft knock on her door and then Lady Mountjoy poked her head in.

'You're awake. I wasn't sure if you would be after your late night.'

'I'm awake,' Jane said, tidying up her papers and stashing them in a drawer.

'Have you looked out of your window?'

Jane shook her head then moved to the window, pulling back the curtains.

Outside the street was buried under a thick layer of snow and delicate snowflakes were still falling from the sky.

'That's fallen quickly,' Jane said, surprised. It had been after midnight when she had walked home with Lucy and Captain Weyman and although it had been overcast there hadn't been any hint of snow. Lord Mountjoy had been predicting more snowfall for weeks despite the colder months supposedly being over and she knew he would be pleased his predictions had come true.

'I do love the snow,' Lady Mountjoy said, coming in and perching on the cushions of the window seat. 'Years ago, Lord Mountjoy and I considered spending a prolonged period abroad. One of the things that made us decide to stay in England was the way the country-side looked in the snow.'

'A snowy day in London is a little different, I suppose,' Jane said. They'd had some snow a month or so earlier, a few days where the rivers had frozen over and the streets had been treacherous in the ice. At the time Jane had been focussed on finishing the book she'd been working on and had ventured out only once or twice.

'It does not hold a patch on Somerset in the winter,' Lady Mountjoy said with a smile. 'But London does have charms of its own. Perhaps Mr Stewart might take you to experience some of them.'

Jane looked up sharply, knowing Lady Mountjoy was not aware of anything that had gone on the night before, but feeling her cheeks burn all the same.

'I expect he will be busy with Edward.'

'Of course, it will probably be Edward's first time in the snow.'

Jane nodded, trying to ignore the ache inside that made her yearn to be there with them. This was an unacceptable feeling. Pure desire, physical attraction, she could dismiss as something primal and subconscious, something she was not in control of. Admitting that there was anything more than the physical was far too perilous. She shouldn't even have had a flash of an image of Tom, little Edward and her co-cooned together as a happy family.

'You could offer to accompany them on whatever outing they decide,' Lady Mountjoy said, trying to look nonchalant.

'I wouldn't want to impose.'

'I doubt it would be an imposition. Mr Stewart seems to enjoy your company.' Lady Mountjoy paused, as if considering whether to say any more. 'You mustn't fear his reputation, Miss Ashworth. Mr Stewart is a good man, one of the best, despite the awful example his father set for him.'

Jane knew she shouldn't pry, knew that if it was something Tom wished her to know he would have divulged it himself, but she was intrigued by Tom's past, by his background.

'Was his father that terrible, then?'

'He's always kept the details close to his chest, but the Stewarts are an incredibly wealthy family,' Lady Mountjoy said, gazing out of the window. 'Yet at the first opportunity Rebecca Stewart elopes and is never heard from again and Thomas Stewart joins the army. He's the only son, in a family richer than most of the titled aristocracy, yet he goes and risks his life unnecessarily.'

'I can't imagine wanting to get away so badly.'

'No,' Lady Mountjoy agreed. 'Even when Mr Stewart was injured his father visited only once, I am told.'

'No wonder he isn't keen to tread the traditional path of marriage and family.' Jane's eyes widened as she realised what she had just said. Lady Mountjoy was an astute woman; it would only take one slip for their whole deception to come crashing down.

Trying not to overreact, Jane threw a cautious glance at the countess and gave a silent groan as she saw the quizzical look on the older woman's face.

'Has he told you that?'

Jane shook her head. 'No, but it is what everyone says about him. They tell me he is a rake, a man who does not care for the niceties of polite society, yet he is still accepted into the ballrooms and dinner parties with open arms. He is forgiven his sins because of his charm and his easy smile.'

'And what do you think?'

'He's not a rake,' Jane said thoughtfully. 'Not in the traditional sense. He knows what he enjoys, and allows himself to indulge in that enjoyment, but never if it would hurt someone. The sins that people whisper about, they aren't real, that is why he is so easily forgiven. There is no one he has wronged, no one to hold a grudge.'

'I think that is a very astute observation, Miss Ashworth. You obviously know him well.'

Jane thought of the way their bodies had swayed together in the darkness, the softness of his lips on hers.

'I know him a little, but what I do know I like.'

'And I can tell he likes you,' Lady Mountjoy said.

Looking away, Jane tried to stop the tears forming in her eyes. She knew he did like her. She could tell it by how easy they were in each other's company. They could talk for hours, debate the issues that interested them, speak more gently about personal matters. She also knew that he desired her from the flare of passion in his eyes, the firm way he had grasped her and pure hunger in his kiss. Even though she couldn't quite understand it, she knew it was true.

He might like her, might even desire her,

but Jane knew it wasn't enough. From the very start he had made his priorities clear, and a few fumbled kisses he probably already regretted would not change that.

'I do not know the intricacies of your family's situation,' Lady Mountjoy said slowly. 'But I am aware you are the eldest of six girls and there are likely some hopes you will make a match. You may not be searching for a wealthy husband, Miss Ashworth, but perhaps you are searching for a good man. Do not discount Mr Stewart because he happens to be wealthy. One does not preclude the other.'

Lady Mountjoy stood and crossed the room, pausing by the door. She motioned at the small desk in which Jane had secreted her pictures and writing. 'Some places of business may end up closing early if the snow really becomes a difficulty. Maybe you can take one day to enjoy the company of a man you admire.'

Jane blinked, unable to do anything but look open-mouthed after the countess as she left the room. Although she knew Lady Mountjoy was sharp, with friends everywhere, she had been convinced her search for a publisher had gone unnoticed. She had shared so much of her life with Lucy and the other debutantes over the past few months yet even they had been unaware of her secret mission.

If Lady Mountjoy knew… Jane shook her head, unable to comprehend the enormity of her realisation. These last few months, she had truly believed no one had known her secret, and here was Lady Mountjoy announcing calmly that she was aware of Jane's ambition.

Pulling out the drawer, she looked at the bundle of papers, and then carefully took them out of their dark hiding place and set them carefully on the desk. Maybe it was time to stop sneaking around. She lovingly ran a hand over the topmost of the papers, scrutinising the picture with an artist's eye.

She had received her first box of watercolour paints when she'd been eight years old and at first not paid them much attention. Only after she and Harriett had both been sick in bed with measles had she taken them out, eager for anything to assuage her boredom. Jane had found she was talented, able to study something and quickly create its likeness, and from there her love of painting and drawing had been born.

For once she had been the one receiving praise. Harriet had found the intricacies of creating something beautiful with the paints too laborious and had quickly given up. It meant, for the first time in her life, Jane had emerged from the shadows and in this one thing had outshone her beautiful and graceful sister. She didn't like to admit that had been one of the main reasons she would take out the paints at first, but as the months had gone by the satisfaction she'd got from creating something from nothing had been motivation enough.

The stories she wrote to accompany the pictures had come later, but her first love had been drawing and painting to create the pictures that now made the stories come alive. With a nod of satisfaction, she shut the drawer, leaving the pile of papers on the desk.

Chapter Fifteen

'I want to go sledging and ice-skating and build a snowman and have snowball fights,' Edward said with the enthusiasm of someone experiencing his very first snowfall.

'We can do all of those things,' Tom said as he squeezed his nephew's hand. The little boy was wrapped up against the cold in bulky layers, happily skipping along beside him. Tom had been out late the night before, trying to find Mrs Burghley, and then spending some time attempting to persuade her to keep quiet about what she had seen. When he had returned home, Edward had been curled up in his bed and the maid had apologised, saying it was the only way she had been able to settle him. Tom had carried the little boy back to his own bed and had sat with him a while, glad of the distraction of Edward's rhythmic breathing.

'Miss Jane promised she would come with us,' Edward said. 'She lives in the countryside and she knows how to go sledging.'

For an instant he allowed himself to indulge in the image of Jane hurtling down a hill, hair streaming behind her, wild whoops of joy coming from her mouth.

'In a few minutes you will be able to ask her if she would like to accompany us.'

'Of course she will,' Edward said with a small smile. 'She likes you and she likes me even more.'

Tom wasn't sure how he would be received this afternoon at the Mountjoys' house. So far he hadn't heard of any rumours circulating about an illicit embrace between Jane and him in a darkened garden, but without a doubt Lady Mountjoy would be the first to hear of any whispers. He might already be unwelcome in the smart townhouse he was approaching... unwelcome or expected to prepare a proposal.

As he knocked on the door he felt his stomach flip, a sensation that only settled when they were shown into the drawing room without any fanfare.

'What a lovely surprise,' Lady Mountjoy

said as she glided in to greet them. 'Edward, you must be so excited about the snow.'

Tom watched as the older woman ushered his nephew over to the window and she was soon listening intently to all the things the boy was planning to do in the snow for the first time.

'Mr Stewart.' He hadn't even heard Jane enter the room and spun suddenly at the sound of her voice. She looked tired, her skin pale and her eyes without their normal sparkle. Immediately he felt a cad. He could have sent word somehow to let her know the outcome of his talk with Mrs Burghley. Even though there wasn't a conclusive answer as to what she might do, he could imagine Jane had spent an unsettled night, kept in the dark, left only to speculate as to her fate,.

'Good afternoon, Miss Ashworth,' he said, trying to read her expression. 'Edward reminded me you promised to accompany us to the park in the event of snow.'

'Yes, Miss Jane, please say you will come,' Edward said, dashing over and giving Jane a big hug.

'Of course I will come,' Jane said, dropping a kiss on the little boy's head. For an instant Tom had a vision of what his future could be like. It involved Jane doting on Edward, a life of comfortable routine.

'Is something amiss, Mr Stewart? Are you unwell?' Lady Mountjoy enquired.

He shook his head, unable to speak. Suddenly his cravat was awfully tight around his neck.

'Do you need a glass of water?'

Again he shook his head. Jane moved closer, peering at him in concern. 'You're making strange noises,' she whispered.

He tried to smile but by the reaction of everyone else in the room the result could not have been very reassuring.

'I do not know who will be free to chaperon me,' Jane said, flashing a concerned look in his direction. He was grateful she was trying to move the conversation on.

'I am sure a maid will be a satisfactory chaperon. You will be out in public and accompanied by Edward. It is hardly a scandalous outing,' Lady Mountjoy said after a moment's thought.

'Would you like to join us this afternoon, Miss Ashworth? I do not know how long the snow is due to settle for.'

'Of course. Let me gather my hat and gloves

and change my dress for something more suited to a spell outside.'

Tom marvelled at how quickly Jane was able to change and collect the things she needed. Many women he knew took hours just to select the right outfit, but in a mere fifteen minutes they were standing on the pavement outside Lady Mountjoy's house with a frowning maid a few feet behind them.

'Come, let us walk to the park,' Jane said, taking hold of Edward's hand. She glanced over the young boy's head to Tom, and he could see she was eager to hear his news, but unsure what to ask in front of Edward.

'I am sorry you did not get home until late last night,' Tom said, knowing that at six Edward might not understand everything they talked about, but was very capable of taking it in and repeating it at inopportune moments.

'I understand you also had a late night,' Jane said, looking pensive, then shaking her head. Tom felt a rush of relief. No doubt she only meant to delay their conversation until they reached the park, but it gave him a few minutes' respite.

They walked slowly. The snow had been fresh in the morning, but over the course of the day the pavements had become slippery and in places treacherous. It was a relief to go through the gates of the park and step into the thicker, fresh snow covering the grass where no one else had set foot.

Edward was off immediately, running over the snow and marvelling at his footprints.

'Come and play!' he shouted, whooping with joy.

Jane turned to him and Tom felt as though he were on unsteady ground. He didn't want to jeopardise what they had, didn't want to tear her out of Edward's life by his mistakes.

Slowly she shook her head, her eyes following Edward. 'He's been waiting for this since he arrived in England. Whatever it is we need to say to one another can wait.'

Tom nodded slowly. 'Are you sure?'

'Completely.'

He felt a rush of relief and, even though they were in the middle of the park, he reached out and grasped her hand as she went to move away. For a long moment they both looked down, staring at where his fingers entangled hers, both encased in thick gloves.

'You're a good person, Jane Ashworth,' he said quietly. 'We're both lucky to have you.'

'Come on!' Edward shouted again and after one final moment Jane pulled away, running in the direction of the little boy and leaning down to talk to him. Tom hurried over, but before he could get close two perfectly round snowballs came whizzing towards him. One fell short but the other hit him squarely in the chest before crumbling and falling to the ground.

'I'm going to get you,' he called, gathering up a handful of snow.

It was not a fair fight, two against one, although his aim was true on a few occasions. Jane had a surprisingly strong arm and was merciless in her attack, and before long she and Edward were giggling with laughter as they hit him over and over again.

Changing tactics, Tom made a run for them, gathering a squealing Edward up in his arms and running off to a safe distance.

'Help me, Miss Jane!' Edward giggled.

Now he was under attack from two sides. Retreating from the relentless snowballs from his nephew, he ran back towards Jane as she tried to dart away, laughing.

'Don't even think about picking me up like you did him!'

'Now, that is an idea,' Tom murmured, lunging towards her.

'No!' she shrieked, dodging away. 'Think about the consequences, Mr Stewart.'

'I can only see benefits. One, I would lift you away from your endless supply of ammunition. Two, I could pin your arms to your sides and you wouldn't be able to launch any snowballs. And three…'

He trailed off, knowing he couldn't say three out loud.

'Three?'

Luckily they were both distracted by Edward barging in, screaming and throwing snowballs as if he were in the final charge of a battle.

'I surrender,' Tom called from under the barrage of snowballs.

'Do we let him surrender?' Jane crouched down to confer with the little boy. Finally, she nodded. 'We accept your surrender on two conditions.'

'What are they?'

'You donate your gloves to Edward—his are completely soaked through.'

'Gladly, and the second?'

'You take us to see the sledgers.'

'I know the perfect spot.'

He took a moment to adjust Edward's outer layers, ensuring his nephew was still warm despite the freezing temperatures, and then took off his gloves and handed them over.

'Your prize,' he said, helping Edward slip them on.

With his nephew skipping on ahead, Tom offered Jane his arm. The maid who was chaperoning them trailed behind, looking more and more unimpressed with her job out here in the snow, when the other maids were working in the warmth of the Mountjoy household.

'What did she say?' Jane asked when she was sure Edward was far enough ahead not to hear. 'You never came back. I didn't know if that meant good news or bad news.'

'I'm sorry, it just got so late. It took me ages to find Mrs Burghley. She was almost home by the time I caught up with her.' He passed a hand over his brow, trying to rub away the headache that was threatening to return. 'She was angry.'

'She thought there was going to be something between you?'

'I think she may have got the wrong impression. The friend who introduced us thought we might be a good match for one another. She is looking for a…protector.'

'And are you looking for a mistress?'

'Good lord, no.' He shook his head. 'I think Mrs Burghley is short on funds after her husband's death and hoped I might be the one to save her from having to rethink her current lifestyle.'

'So what did you say to her?'

'I apologised for behaving poorly towards her and explained what she had seen was a mistake. I begged her to think of your reputation.'

Jane looked up at him and he felt awful that he couldn't guarantee Mrs Burghley would stay quiet.

'She said she was tired, and needed time to think, and asked me not to contact her again.'

Jane bit her lip, her expression troubled.

'It doesn't seem terribly promising.'

'At least she didn't say outright she was going to tell everyone what she saw.'

For a moment their eyes met as they remembered the kiss and then Tom quickly looked away. He knew he needed to put an end to the inappropriate thoughts he kept having about Jane. It might have already ruined both of their futures. He couldn't allow himself to slip up again. If by chance they managed to get away with Jane's reputation intact, he could never do anything again to jeopardise it.

'So what do we do?'

'I suppose we wait.' He shook his head, knowing how unsatisfying that was as an answer. 'I lay awake last night and tried to think through all the possible solutions.'

'Did you come up with anything else?'

'I could try to bribe her,' he said, frowning into the distance. 'She is struggling financially and may be open to a payment or two to keep our secret.' He shrugged. 'It isn't as though it would need to be for ever. In a couple of months you return to Somerset, and I might take Edward to the country for the summer, so I don't think I would need to pay her more than once or twice.'

'It sounds like you don't think it is the best idea.'

'No, I worry it might be a misstep. Although she does need the money, I wonder if a bribe will seem too dirty, too offensive, and then she will feel it is her moral obligation to tell society about what she saw.'

'It's a nightmare.'

'I know.'

'Miss Jane, look. There are children sledging over here.' Edward ran back and grabbed hold of Jane's hand, pulling her with him across the snow.

Tom watched as they hurried in front of him and wondered if things would be terrible if the rumours started and he had to make things right with Jane. Edward would have someone to look after him, someone else to love him, and he would get Jane. Shaking his head, he knew that couldn't happen, but perhaps there was a way he could continue with his normal life and preserve Jane's reputation. A marriage in name, a marriage to provide Edward with a mother figure. For an instant, he wondered if he could ever keep to an arrangement of convenience like that—whether he would be able to keep his hands off Jane if she was his wife, looking up at him with yearning in her eyes.

Quickly, he shook himself. Anything else wasn't an option. It wasn't what he wanted from his life, the quiet domesticity of a married man. After his accident he had promised himself he would live every day for pleasure, for seeking out the different, the unknown. He wasn't made for a life spent with one person day in, day out. He didn't want the responsibility of someone's love, someone's trust. He wasn't a good enough man for Jane, a selfless enough man. If things went wrong between them… He shook his head, hating the idea he could ruin her life the way he'd ruined his sister's.

'Come on, Zio Tom,' Edward called over his shoulder and Tom tried to push the thoughts out of his head. At this moment the only decision he had to make was whether to try offering Mrs Burghley a bribe or not. Everything else was a mess of *what if*s and uncertainty. It was no use debating what his marriage to Jane would be like when hopefully nothing would force them into making that decision.

'He is so keen to join in,' Jane said as they watched Edward inch forward, eager to be whizzing down the hill with the older boys they were observing.

'He hasn't mixed with other children since he arrived.'

'That will come in time,' Jane said, placing a hand on his arm. 'Perhaps in the summer, when you take him to your country residence, he will get to know the local children in the village.'

'Perhaps,' Tom said.

They stood watching for a moment and then Jane stepped forward and grasped Edward's hand. 'Come with me,' she said, gently guiding the young boy behind her.

As he watched them, Tom saw Jane approach one of the older boys in the group and speak to him for a minute before Edward stepped forward. To Tom's surprise, a minute later Edward was speeding down the gentle hill on the back of the sledge, whooping in delight.

After a couple of runs down the hill, Jane slowly retreated until she was back standing next to Tom.

'I know how lucky we are to have you,' Tom said quietly. 'When you suggested this little arrangement, I had my doubts. I thought it would benefit you more than me, but it has been the opposite. I don't think Edward would be nearly as settled as he is now if you weren't in our lives.'

Jane smiled at him, but it didn't quite reach her eyes.

'I wouldn't let a scandal ruin your life, Jane,' he said softly.

'It may not be in your hands.'

'I agree I may not be able to control whether Mrs Burghley starts any rumours, but I would not leave you to face them alone.' He shook his head to try and emphasise his point. 'I am not that sort of man, and I respect you far too much for that.'

She looked at him, her eyes wide and her cheeks flushed, although he couldn't tell whether it was with emotion or the cold.

'What are you saying?'

'I would marry you, if needed.'

'If needed?'

He heard the slight change in pitch of her voice and tried to work out why she was getting upset over this.

'If there is a scandal, I will marry you.'

She turned to him fully. 'You would ask me to marry you?'

'Yes.'

'I might not accept.'

'You would be a fool not to.'

'I could just return to Somerset.'

'You could, but gossip has a long reach.' He shrugged. 'Hopefully it won't come to that.'

'Hopefully not.'

They stood in silence for a while, watching Edward speeding down the hill, laughing with his newly made friends.

'I should go,' Jane said after a few minutes.

'I've said something wrong.' He searched her face, trying to work out exactly how he had offended her. Neither of them wanted to get married, that much he knew, but he thought it might alleviate some of her worries to know he wouldn't leave her to face the potential scandal alone.

Jane took a shuddering breath and then turned fully to face him. 'No, you haven't.

It's just been a long day and I worry about the future.'

He had the sudden urge to reach out and cup her face. The feeling was so strong, he had to take a step back to make sure she was out of reach, otherwise he couldn't trust himself not to do it.

'Go home,' he said, suddenly. 'Rest. I am sure everything will look a bit better after we have both had some sleep.'

Giving a short, sharp nod, she called over to her maid, who had been loitering twenty feet away, and then hurried over to say goodbye to Edward. Tom watched her leave, wondering why he felt as though he had handled the situation badly, not knowing what to say to make it right.

Chapter Sixteen

'It's quiet in here tonight,' Tom said as he took a seat at the bar.

'The locals all know Rose has her night off on a Thursday. It makes me wonder how many come in here just to see her.'

'You do have a beautiful wife, Western,' Tom said, taking another gulp of his drink.

'I know. I'm a lucky man. Rose doesn't let me forget it.'

Tom trailed a finger around the top of the glass. His head had been pounding most of the afternoon, and he had even tried to go to bed soon after Edward had collapsed into an exhausted slumber, but he had felt the pressure building as he'd lain there between the sheets. Instead he'd opted for fresh air and had taken the route across the river to see Western.

'You look like you've been dragged to hell

and whipped by the devil himself,' Western said as he looked Tom up and down.

'Thanks,' Tom murmured.

'Is it a headache?'

'Yes. They've been coming more frequently these last few weeks.'

'The doctor told you to avoid any unnecessary conflict, didn't he?'

'It is hardly anything I can avoid. Anyway, the doctor also told me I would never walk again. I don't place much faith in him.'

'By rights you shouldn't be walking. I saw that head of yours get trampled. Any other man would be dead.'

'I've always had a thick skull.'

'And the luck of the devil.'

Tom grimaced. 'A lucky man would never have been trampled in the first place.'

'True.'

Western moved away for a moment to serve two men at the other end of the bar, chatting with them easily whilst he poured their drinks.

'Why are you looking so morose?' Western asked as he returned.

'I upset someone today. I said something I perhaps shouldn't have, but I don't understand why they were quite so upset.'

'Does this person matter to you?'

'Yes.'

'A woman?' Western shook his head. 'Damn it, Rose is always right. She will be gloating about this for weeks.'

'What is she right about?'

'She was convinced you have a woman, someone special you weren't telling us about.'

Tom let his head sink into his hands.

'Smith,' Western called to the young man clearing tables at the other end of the room. 'You're in charge of the bar for ten minutes.' Leaning under the counter, Western brought out a bottle of whisky and two glasses and motioned for Tom to come into the private room at the back of the tavern.

As Tom sat down, Western poured out two glasses of whisky and pushed one towards Tom. 'Drink that down and then tell me everything. Maybe we can work out a solution before your head explodes.'

'Cheery thought.'

Western shrugged. 'You'd better start your story, then.'

'You remember when I came here a few weeks ago, early in the morning, the day Edward arrived?'

'Of course.'

'When I left, I bumped into a young woman

I recognised from a society event. I was worried that she was out alone in Southwark so offered to escort her home.' Even though it was only a few weeks ago, it felt much longer. So much had happened between then and now. 'She accepted but we were spotted by the woman looking after her whilst in London. She has the idea we will be well suited.'

'Surely it is a simple matter to disabuse her of this notion?'

'Since that day, Jane has been helping me with Edward. She's good with children, and I have been helping her dodge too many engagements with other potential suitors.'

'It sounds a dangerous game. The young women do see a certain charm in you, and if she is spending that much time with you surely there is great potential for something to go wrong?'

'We kissed,' Tom said, dropping his voice until it was barely more than a whisper.

'And is she insisting you marry?'

'Good lord, no. Jane isn't like that. She does not wish to marry anyone, but there is a certain attraction between us.'

Western stayed quiet, waiting or Tom to get to the crux of the matter. Tom sighed, not sure how to put the complicated mess of emotions into words.

'We were seen when we kissed. A widow I was meant to be escorting for the evening caught us in a darkened corner. I don't know yet if she is going to expose our secret to the world or keep quiet.'

'And if she does expose you to the world?'

'Then I'll marry Jane.'

Western puffed out his cheeks and leaned back in his chair.

'I can see why you're so worried.'

Tom shook his head. 'It might not happen.'

'Is there not another way? You've always been so against settling down. You've never wanted that life of humdrum routine.'

'But maybe it wouldn't have to be,' Tom said slowly. 'Maybe we could agree on a different arrangement.'

Western scoffed. 'What? You continuing on your life as a happy bachelor in all but name whilst this woman looks after your home and your nephew?'

'It doesn't sound good when you put it like that.'

'It's not the way I'm phrasing it that's the problem.'

Tom threw back his whisky and poured himself another.

'She might not even accept my proposal.'

'I doubt she's that much of a fool.'

Tom fell silent, remembering the hurt look in Jane's eyes that afternoon when he had mentioned marriage. He knew he hadn't handled it well, but it was hardly a normal situation. He'd never had to deal with anything like this before. How did you say to a woman, a friend, that you would marry them if necessary without making it sound as if you were reluctant to do so?

'Ah, I made a mess of it,' he said, frustrated.

'It *does* all sound a mess,' Western murmured.

'When I told her I would marry her if necessary, I don't think I looked too thrilled.'

'So now she thinks you would only marry her out of charity.'

'That's not good, is it?'

Western shook his head and Tom pressed his palms into his eye sockets. The pressure felt good.

'I can't see anyone taking it as a compliment, but perhaps it is for the best.'

'What do you mean?'

'This woman... Jane, is it?' He waited for

Tom to nod before he continued. 'She clearly has something about her to make you break your rules. You've always said no married women and no debutantes. It is important to you, and in all the years I've known you I don't think you've ever broken them. Until now.'

Tom thought back over the years and the liaisons. Western was right—never before had he even kissed a debutante or a married woman. It wasn't worth the hassle, but more than that it wasn't worth the guilt that accompanied it.

'I need to make things right with her, don't I?'

'Don't do anything stupid,' Western said, pouring him out another glass of whisky. 'I would love to see you settled down and happy, but I wouldn't want you to be forced into it.'

For a few minutes they drank in silence, Tom considering his options but not able to come to any conclusion.

'I think I'd better go,' he said eventually, standing and stumbling. He grabbed hold of the wall, steadied himself and blinked half a dozen times until the world looked straight again.

'How much have we drunk?'

On occasion, he and Western would share

part of a bottle of whisky as they laughed and talked and reminisced through the night into the small hours, and normally he could handle his liquor well. It must have been the speed at which he'd gulped back the four large glasses combined with not eating for most of the day that affected him tonight.

'Are you safe to get home or do you need an escort?'

'I can manage. Give that beautiful wife of yours a kiss from me.'

Western scowled at him and Tom grinned as he weaved his way back through the main room of the tavern and out into the street.

Chapter Seventeen

Jane awoke with a start, finding it hard to shake off the last remnants of a dream and for a moment feeling disorientated in the darkness. Only as her eyes adjusted did she remember where she was and allow herself to sink back down into the pillows. She closed her eyes but a few seconds later there was a light tap on the window. For an instant, her body stiffened as she listened, but there was nothing further for at least a minute. Forcing herself to relax again, she looked at the ceiling for a while and then sat bolt upright as there was another tap.

She debated whether to hide under the covers or stride boldly over to the window and pull open the curtains.

'You're on the second floor,' she muttered to herself. 'Don't be ridiculous. No one is going to be outside.'

All the same, she crept over to the window and braced herself before wrenching open the curtains.

Of course there was no one there, no flying monster ready to chase her, not even a confused bat knocking into the window. Jane was about to pull the curtains closed and return to bed when she glanced down.

At first she wondered if she were still asleep, still dreaming a bizarre dream. It would be more plausible than what she saw happening for real.

Standing on the lawn was the outline of a man, a man she knew was Tom, even in the darkness. He was throwing little pebbles at her window, but either he was a very poor sportsman or he was inebriated, as his aim was truly terrible. A pebble skittered across a window further along the house and Jane sent up a silent prayer of thanks that Lord and Lady Mountjoy's rooms were on the first floor.

Quickly she pushed up the window and leaned her head out, sucking in a quick breath as the icy air whipped at her face.

'What are you doing?' she whispered as loudly as she dared.

'Jane!' Tom shouted.

He waved and swayed. Definitely inebriated, Jane thought, unable to fathom why he was in the Mountjoys' back garden in the middle of the night.

'Be quiet,' she said, leaning out a little further to check there was no movement at any of the other windows.

'Jane, I'm down here,' Tom called.

'I can see you. Wait there. Don't move.' She knew she should send him away but she didn't want to have a conversation out of the window. Every shout from Tom seemed to cut through the air and she was worried soon the whole neighbourhood would be awake.

She had the forethought to pull on her dressing gown and slip on some shoes before descending the stairs, listening every few steps to see if anyone was stirring in the rest of the house.

It was with a flood of relief she reached the back door that led out into the garden. The keys were on a hook next to the door and carefully she inserted the key into the lock and turned, slipping out through the open door into the night.

'I had to see you,' Tom said as she stepped out onto the patio. His words were a little slurred, and Jane could see he was trying really hard to be quiet, but his mouth wasn't quite cooperating.

'It's the middle of the night.'

'You look lovely,' he said, taking a step back to take all of her in. Jane pulled her dressing gown across her chest a little tighter.

'Go home. We can talk tomorrow. Or any other time.'

'I think I said the wrong thing earlier.'

'It doesn't matter,' Jane said, reaching out and turning him so he faced the garden gate. 'Go home and we will talk tomorrow.'

'I'll go,' he said, even taking a step in the right direction. 'Tomorrow we'll talk.'

'Yes, tomorrow. I promise.' She felt relieved he was leaving so easily. In two minutes Tom would be on his way home and she would be safely ensconced back in her bed.

'Goodnight, Jane,' he said, half-turning back to her and giving her that smile of his.

'Goodnight, Tom.'

Before he could take another step, there was a scraping noise from above. Jane stiffened, unable to move. She knew it was a window opening and knew that at any moment she would be caught in the garden with a notorious rake. There would be no saving her reputation after this.

Even though he was inebriated, Tom moved quickly, lunging forward and grabbing hold of her, deftly spinning her round and through the open back door. Their bodies were pressed together, with his back against the wall, and hers pinning him in place. With one hand he reached out and pressed a finger to her lips, silencing the exclamation of surprise and lingering for a moment as his eyes sought out hers.

Jane felt the beat of his heart even through the layers that separated them and was sure hers was beating exactly in time.

They heard the creak of the window a few floors up and Jane hoped the open back door wasn't visible from above. Slowly she extricated herself from Tom's arms and inch by inch eased the door shut. For half a minute they stood completely still, listening to the faint noises of the house at night, and then with a sense of impending doom they heard the opening of a door and the patter of faint footsteps.

'We need to move,' Tom whispered, his breath tickling her ear.

Jane nodded, wondering if this situation could get any worse. From the position of the window opening, she knew it must be one of the servants, but if they had heard anything they would be sure to come to investigate.

Quickly she locked the back door and replaced the key on the hook and then, grabbing hold of Tom's hand, pulled him along the narrow corridor that led to the main hallway. She paused by the servants' stairs, listening again, only to feel the solid thud of Tom's body careening into hers. It took a moment to steady herself, but in that time she was convinced she could hear the soft creak of wood signalling someone coming down the stairs.

It was a gamble to head to the main staircase with Tom in tow. If she had misjudged the situation, if it was in fact Lord or Lady Mountjoy who had woken and were coming, then it would be an utter disaster. She and Tom would be caught and there would be no explaining away this scandal. Jane just had to hope it was a servant and they had subconsciously chosen their habitual route downstairs, using the narrower servants' staircase.

Silently they climbed the stairs. Jane's heart pounded even harder every time there was a creak, and a couple of times she thought her chest might explode from the awful anticipation of being caught. They made it up past the first floor, circling round and continuing up the second staircase to the second floor.

Jane didn't pause at the top of the steps, entwining her fingers through Tom's and pulling him into her bedroom. Quickly she closed the door behind them and turned the key in the lock.

She rested her head on the cool wood for a few seconds, unable to believe what she had just done. Eventually she turned to find Tom right behind her.

'What were you thinking?' she whispered, wishing she could see him better in the darkness.

'You were upset earlier,' he said, reaching out and placing a hand on her arm. 'I didn't want to leave things badly between us.'

'So you thought you would pay me a visit in the middle of the night and force me to sneak you into my bedroom.'

He shrugged, looking around, as if only now realising that he was in her bedroom.

'I didn't think that far,' he said simply. 'I knew I wanted to see you, but I didn't think about the practicalities of it.'

'You didn't think about the practicalities?' Jane repeated, still unable to take in the enormity of the mess they were in. 'What are we going to do, Tom? If you are found here, it won't matter if Mrs Burghley says anything or not. We'll be marched down the aisle as soon as Lady Mountjoy can persuade the archbishop to give us a special licence.'

She was glad to see a flicker of a reaction in his eyes, then he shrugged again and moved away, flopping down in the chair by the writing desk.

'You're going to sit down? At a time like this?'

'Someone in this house is awake,' he said, sounding a lot more sober than he had outside. 'But it is after midnight and I doubt they will be awake for long. I suggest we sit quietly for half an hour, maybe an hour, and then I will slip out and no one will be any the wiser.'

Jane opened her mouth to protest and then closed it again as she considered his words. This was far from the ideal situation but, now they were in it, perhaps he was right. Perhaps they needed to sit it out and then hope they could slip Tom out of the house when everyone was back asleep.

She looked around for the best place to sit, but with the chair occupied there weren't many options. The window seat was far too cold at this time of night, so it only left the bed. At first she perched on the edge, feeling fidgety and jumping at even the slightest sound.

'You can sit back,' Tom said, observing her through heavy-lidded eyes.

'I don't want to get too comfortable.'

'We're hardly likely to fall asleep, are we?'

He had a point. Jane felt so on edge, so nervous, she doubted she would sleep for three days.

'I am sorry,' he said, as she plumped up the pillows and then positioned herself so she was sitting up against the headboard, her legs stretched out before her on the bed. 'It was stupid to come here.'

'Why did you come here?'

'I couldn't stop thinking of the look on your face yesterday, whilst we were watching Edward sledging.'

'I didn't have a look on my face.'

'You did after I said I would marry you.'

She felt herself bristle and stiffen again. It was something about the phrasing, the way he'd made it sound as if he'd be doing her a favour by saving her reputation if needed. Not that it wasn't true, but she hated being made to feel that way.

'It came out wrong, and I'm sorry. Any man would be lucky to have you as his wife.'

Jane snorted, allowing herself to slip down

a little further on the cushions to get comfortable.

'They would.'

'Apart from you,' she said quietly. 'For you it would be an obligation.'

There was a long silence and Jane had to peer through the darkness to see if he had fallen asleep. When she was satisfied his eyes were still open, she returned to staring up at the canopy of the four-poster bed stretched above her.

'I don't think I've ever told you exactly why I have never wanted to get married,' he said eventually.

'I know about your desire to enjoy every moment of your life, after the accident.'

'Yes, that is much of it,' Tom said quietly. He sounded pensive, as if working out how to phrase the next statement. 'I had a very unhappy childhood, Jane. My father was cruel. He took pleasure in finding little ways to make our lives miserable, my sister's and mine.'

Jane turned a little to face him, wondering why such people became parents.

'Outwardly he did all the things he was supposed to as a parent. We were clothed and fed, I was sent to a good school, Rebecca had an expensive governess.' He fell quiet.

'Being a parent isn't just about fulfilling the most basic of needs, though,' Jane said softly.

'He was a clever man, and he used that intelligence to torment us. Mainly in small ways—pitting us against each other for snippets of affection, warping our perception of what was normal.' He shuddered, and Jane wanted to reach over to him and pull him into an embrace, but she kept still, knowing it would make tonight even more difficult. 'Then I left. I bought a commission in the army and I went away without ever looking back.'

'Your sister was still at home?'

'She was. Every day I hated myself for it, but I couldn't spend another month in that house—it was suffocating.' He paused, and in the moonlight Jane could see the angst on his face. 'I left her behind to save myself.'

'You can't have been very old.'

'I was eighteen. Old enough.'

'What happened to her?'

'We wrote, a lot. She begged me not to blame myself, begged me to go out and live my life without the shadow of our father hanging over me. And then she disappeared.'

'She disappeared?'

'I was away at the time, but when I returned home the servants said one day she was acting normally, going about her daily routine, and the next she was gone. She didn't take a single thing with her except the clothes she was wearing.'

'You must have been so worried.'

'My father paid for investigators—not out of concern for Rebecca, you understand, but because he hated not being in control. They uncovered nothing.'

'What did you do?'

'When I returned to London I met with some of her friends and one told me she had fallen in love. This friend informed me she had no clue who the man was, just that he was foreign. Rebecca had gone, vanished, and left no trace behind her.'

'Did you feel guilty?'

For a long moment Tom remained silent, his lips pressed together and a frown on his face.

'I should never have left her. It was selfish. I put my own future, my own chance of happiness, above hers.'

'You were eighteen, barely more than a child yourself. A child who had lived through a whole lifetime of cruelty. Subject a hundred people to that, and show me anyone who wouldn't have taken the opportunity to escape as you did.'

'I loved my sister more than anyone in the world,' he said, shaking his head. 'But I still put myself first.'

Realisation slowly dawned on Jane. 'That is why you don't want to get married. You don't feel you would be good enough, selfless enough.'

'I can't trust myself to put someone else's needs ahead of my own. I didn't do it before, and no one deserves that in a husband.'

It was as if the final piece of the puzzle had fallen into place. She had always wondered if there was something more to his adamance that he would not marry. The pursuit of pleasure was one thing, but she had wondered what would happen if he ever fell in love. Now she understood he wouldn't let himself fall in love for exactly this reason.

'I searched for her. I spent a lot of money trying to find her, but I never did. She had hidden herself too well.' He shrugged. 'At least I know now she had a good life, a kind husband, a beautiful son. All the things she always dreamed of.'

'All the things you deserve too.'

He shook his head and ploughed on, as if needing to get everything off his chest now he had started. 'Then I had my accident and when I woke up I realised how lucky I was to be alive. It took a long time to learn to walk again, to be able to concentrate for more than a few minutes without getting a blinding headache, but I made progress month by month. When I was fully recovered, I decided I would dedicate my life to finding pleasure. That way I wouldn't hurt anyone. I wouldn't betray anyone like I had my sister.'

He fell silent and Jane wished there wasn't such a distance between them. She wanted to pull him into her arms, to smother him with love, to make him see that he was more than worthy.

'Now you see,' he said after a long silence. 'I can't marry, not unless the alternative is much worse.'

The pain in his expression made her heart break and all Jane could do was nod silently. Nothing she could say tonight was going to change his mind. He'd held on to this belief for over a decade. It was firmly entrenched in his mind.

They sat for a long time, completely quiet, the only sound their rhythmic breathing. Jane couldn't stop thinking of the heartache Tom must have carried round, the burden of guilt pressing down on him over the years. Nothing could change how he had acted when he had fled at the tender age of eighteen, but she wondered if there was some way to make him see he'd not been the same man then as he was now.

Chapter Eighteen

Tom shifted, wondering why he was quite so uncomfortable. He reached back to pull a pillow into place but his hand grasped only air.

It took a moment for him to remember where he was, his eyes shooting open and taking in the darkness in the room. He breathed a sigh of relief. It was still dark. Hopefully he had merely dozed off, not slept half the night in Jane's bedroom, chaste though the experience had been.

He stretched and reached for his pocket watch, patting himself down for it, cursing when he realised he must not have brought it out with him the night before. Slowly, working out the stiffness in his muscles as he went, he levered himself up from the chair, pausing as he caught sight of Jane on the bed. Her hair was loose, fanned out on the pillows, one arm thrown up over her head in a casual manner. She still wore her dressing gown, tightly secured, but it had risen up a little, exposing the creamy white skin of her legs.

He shook his head in disbelief. Over the years he'd had liaisons with the most desired courtesans, dallied with women said to be the most beautiful in Europe, but here he was, unable to draw his eyes away from Miss Jane Ashworth's ankles.

'Jane,' he whispered, aware that he needed her to accompany him downstairs to lock up after he had sneaked out through the back door.

'No,' she murmured, not opening her eyes and turning away from him.

Smiling into the darkness, he tried again. 'Jane, you need to wake up.'

This time she flopped an arm over her ear so she wouldn't have to listen.

Gently he laid a hand on her shoulder and gave her a shake. 'Jane, you need to let me out before anyone wakes up again.'

He didn't think she was going to rouse, but after a few seconds his words seemed to sink in and she remembered their predicament. She sat up so fast, they almost banged heads, leaned over her as he was. Luckily he moved quickly, taking a step back and avoiding a sore head for them both.

'What time is it? Did we fall asleep? This is a nightmare.'

She had leapt out of bed and was already pacing the floor, her words delivered in a low whisper. Tom spotted the clock on the mantelpiece and went over to look, an icy flood of horror spreading through him when he realised it was much later than he had thought. Far from dozing for a few minutes in the chair, he must have been asleep for hours.

'It is a quarter to seven.'

Jane let out a panicked squeak, a hand flying to her mouth.

'Cook will be up. The maids will be up. Any moment one of them will be coming in to light my fire.'

'Can we sneak past them?'

Jane paused for a moment and then shook her head. 'To get to the back door, you have to go straight past the kitchen.'

'How about the front door?'

'I don't have a key and there isn't one kept anywhere accessible.'

Tom ran a hand through his hair, aware of the minutes ticking away. Every second they wasted standing here, debating the best way out instead of moving, increased the chance they would be found and if they were found there was no way he was getting out of marrying Jane.

He glanced over at her, taking in the way her hair was ruffled and loose, flowing over her shoulders. There was a beautiful pink glow to her cheeks and a brightness to her eyes. Perhaps it wouldn't be so bad waking up to Jane every morning. Or tumbling into bed with her each night.

Silently he reprimanded himself. *If* they got caught he would, of course, do the right thing and marry Jane, but that didn't mean it would be a conventional marriage. Already, sometimes when he looked at her he saw a flash of true affection in her eyes. He couldn't risk that growing any more. Their lives would have to be separate, a marriage in name only, for he knew if he spent even just one night in her bed he would never be able to leave her behind. There was a primal pull between them, something he couldn't quite describe...something that was very hard to fight.

'I can't just stay here,' he said. 'We'll have to risk the kitchen door.'

'There's too many people. There is a door leading onto the patio in Lord Mountjoy's study. The key is in his desk. We might be able to sneak in there if the maids are upstairs lighting the fires.'

'Good. Let's go.' He paused for a second and then turned back to Jane. 'I'm sorry I came here last night and put your reputation in danger. It was beyond foolish to get that inebriated and allow my head to follow my heart.'

She looked up at him with her big green eyes and Tom got the overwhelming urge to kiss her. He wanted to fold her in his arms and kiss her until the whole household was hammering on the door, demanding to know what was happening inside the room.

'I forgive you,' she said with a little half-smile. 'Now, wait here whilst I go and fetch a glass of water from the kitchen and see where everyone is positioned. If a maid comes in...' She trailed off, glancing at the wardrobe behind him.

'You want me to hide in the wardrobe.'

'It's better than under the bed.'

'Be quick,' he instructed her, watching as she adjusted her dressing gown and smoothed down her hair. It was nice to see her this early in the morning, to see the version of her only her husband would see in the future.

Jane slipped out of the door, clicking it

closed behind her, and he slumped back in the chair by the window. He felt drained, probably hung over, but also emotionally drained from being so honest the night before.

Not completely honest. The thought popped into his mind. He had told her everything about his past, all the reasons he could not marry, but he had not told her how much he was tempted to throw all of that to the wind. *She* tempted him. Every night he fell asleep with her face in his mind, he dreamed of her body pressed against his. Never before had he felt an infatuation like this, the need to be close to her.

Looking down, he noticed a sheaf of paper half-sticking out of a closed drawer in the desk. There was a flash of colour on it, a beautiful golden yellow, and immediately it piqued his interest. Aware the drawer was closed and private, he reasoned he would open it, ensure the piece of paper was undamaged and place it more carefully back inside.

As he opened the drawer he felt a flicker of surprise. On the piece of paper was the most beautiful painting of three little field mice hanging on to sheaves of golden corn. The detail was exquisite, down to the miniscule whiskers on their faces, and it felt as though you were just about to step into a real farmer's field.

He picked up the piece of paper, unable to quite believe the quality of the painting.

Underneath was a page of writing, and then sticking out from under that he could see another painting. Knowing he shouldn't, he picked up the paper with the writing on and looked at the picture under it. This one was of an owl, tawny brown and looking fierce as it stretched its wings to fly.

He longed to read the writing that accompanied it, but knew he had already pried too much. When she was ready, maybe Jane would let him see it, let him read the entirety of her work.

Carefully he placed the papers in the drawer and pushed it closed. As it thudded shut, the door opened, and for a second he felt as though his heart had stopped beating.

Jane slipped inside, closing the door softly behind her.

'Cook is busy in the kitchen,' she said. 'I can hear the maids on the first floor, probably seeing to Lord and Lady Mountjoy's fire. I think if we are going to move it needs to be now.'

He stood, moving swiftly to join her, and then taking her hand in his own. She looked up at him and he saw the worry on her face, hating that he was the cause of it.

'If anyone spots us, the scandal will be of gigantic proportions. Whether we are holding hands or not won't even feature.'

'That is very true.' She took a shuddering breath and then smiled up at him. 'Let's go.'

With her heart pounding in her chest, Jane opened the door and stepped out into the hallway. There was no one in sight. She knew their best chance was to move quickly, but she had an overwhelming urge to creep quietly rather than rush. Thankfully, Tom gripped her hand a little tighter and together they hurried forward.

Never before had she realised quite how big the Mountjoys' townhouse actually was. There was the second-floor hallway to navigate, then a sweeping staircase down to the first floor, where anyone might be coming out of a room and spot them on the stairs. After they had navigated that gauntlet, there was the final grand staircase to the ground floor. This would deposit them in the wide hallway where there was nowhere to hide until they dived into one of the downstairs rooms.

Without looking round, Jane hurried to keep up with Tom, feeling as though her feet were barely touching the stairs as they raced down them. In no time at all her toes were on the cool marble of the downstairs hall. They both froze for a second as voices approached and Jane was certain they were about to be caught. Tom lunged through one of the doors, pulling her with him and closing it with a quiet click. Her back was pressed up against the wall and Tom's body was firm against hers. For a long moment, neither of them moved, and then Tom dipped his head just a little. Jane longed to reach up and kiss him, to abandon herself to the red-hot desire that was burning inside her. She wanted to loop her legs around him, to pull him to her and forget where they were.

She almost gave in, pushing herself up on her tiptoes a fraction, but then she thought of Tom's words the night before. His anguish had been so raw, even all these years later. It was not merely a story, an excuse for not getting married. She could see he truly believed every word he had said. He didn't think he could trust himself to put another's needs above his own.

Jane knew this was nonsense. Time and time again over the last few weeks Tom had made sacrifices for both his nephew and her without being asked, without really thinking about it, because it was the right thing to do. He had a strong moral compass, a sense of right and wrong, and even if it did not match up with the strict rules of society it didn't mean it wasn't a good way to live his life. She might know it was nonsense, but Tom believed it.

Slowly she sank down from her tiptoes, a flood of disappointment flowing through her as her heels touched the floor.

'I'll get the key,' she said, her voice sticking in her throat. She wriggled out from her spot against the wall and walked over to the desk, telling herself that soon she would be back home in Somerset. Soon she would be far away from Tom Stewart and his alluring smiles.

Lord Mountjoy's desk was meticulous. Everything was neat and ordered and had its place. It made finding the key easy, kept as it always was in the bottom drawer in a little container at the back left. Her fingers gripped it and she pulled it out triumphantly, wondering for the first time whether they might actually get away without being caught.

Tom crossed the room in four strides, joining her by the desk, relief blossoming on his face too. Quickly Jane moved to the glass doors that led out to the patio area beyond and inserted the key into the lock. She had opened the door a few times before, and knew it was stiff, so set about jiggling the key to try and get the mechanism to work.

With a start she felt Tom's fingers on her hand, gripping her wrist. Voices were approaching and she watched in horror as the door handle began to move. There was nowhere to go, nowhere they could hide in the time it would take to open the door.

Jane let out a little whimper, hating the feeling of helplessness, the feeling her entire future was about to be decided for her.

Tom looked at her, and in the moment before the door opened he smiled. There was no dread in his eyes, no recriminations, just pure reassurance. Jane felt her heart constrict and knew in that moment that she was in love with him.

'I'll clean out the fire in Lord Mountjoy's study,' one of the maids said as she pushed the door half-open. 'Then I will be down to help with heating the water for bathing.'

The door was open wide enough for someone to see in, but the maid was looking back over her shoulder at her companion and hadn't yet spotted Jane and Tom. The companion must have said something for the maid paused and then sighed.

'No, of course that is fine. I'll get to the fire

later this morning.' Without even looking into the room, the maid shut the door again with a click.

'What just happened?' Jane whispered, unable to believed they were still undiscovered.

'I think we have tested our luck enough,' Tom murmured, reaching for the key in the lock and giving it one final jiggle. The door opened and quickly he stepped out, pausing for a moment on the threshold. 'Get back to bed,' he said with a grin. 'I'll call on you later. I am sorry for all of this.'

Before Jane knew what was happening, he leaned forward and kissed her quickly but firmly on the lips, then turned and hurried down the side of the house.

Too stunned to move for a moment, Tom was already around the side of the house before Jane had recovered. Her fingers were stiff and fumbling as she locked the door and returned the key to the drawer. It only took a few seconds then to sneak out of the study and hurry upstairs, her heart still racing even though she knew the worst of the danger had passed.

Once inside her room, she collapsed into bed, unable to believe Tom had spent the best part of the night in her bedroom and they had got away with not being caught.

She had barely pulled the bed covers up to her chin when one of the maids bustled in, ready to set her fire for the morning. Jane wasn't quick enough to close her eyes and pretend to be asleep, but the maid seemed happy enough to chatter as she worked, holding both sides of the conversation, except for the occasional murmur of agreement from Jane.

'Will you stay in bed a little longer, Miss Ashworth?' Dorothy asked as she finished with the fire. 'Shall I bring up your morning tea?'

'That would be lovely.'

Dorothy darted round the room for another minute, tidying anything out of place. As she reached the chair by the window, the one on which Tom had spent an uncomfortable night, she paused. Jane's eyes darted to where she was standing, taking in the silky fabric of Tom's cravat hanging over the back of the chair.

'Do you like it?' she said, forcing her voice to remain calm and nonchalant.

Dorothy's eyes darted to hers. 'It's a cravat, miss.'

'I know. One of Captain Weyman's. He hates the colour, so Lucy has given it to me to cut up and make ribbons.'

She couldn't tell if the maid believed her, but

at least it was a passably plausible story, something hopefully the maid would file away and not think about further. Jane did her best not to stare at the young woman, knowing acting out of the ordinary would make the implausible story even less believable.

'It is a lovely colour, miss. It will make beautiful ribbons.'

It was all Jane could do not to let out a huge sigh of relief. Instead, she leaned back on her pillows and closed her eyes. Perhaps today would be a little less stressful.

Chapter Nineteen

The snow was beginning to melt, turning into a dirty grey sludge underneath her feet, and Jane was glad of the thick-soled boots she'd brought from the country for occasions such as this. They were not the most elegant boots ever but it hardly mattered with them hidden under her dress with only the toes visible if she took a particularly big step.

'Where are we going?' She pulled her cloak a little tighter around her ears, shivering at the cold whip of the wind. It made her clench her jaw and sent an ache all the way from her ears to her chin.

'I don't know,' Lucy said, giving her friend's arm a squeeze as they walked along side by side. 'I had my instructions to bring you here for two o'clock, so that is what I am doing.'

It was all very mysterious. Jane had spent

the morning restless and unable to settle, flitting from trying to read a book to taking out her watercolours, but not able to paint anything, to aimlessly staring out of the window. She'd felt as if she was waiting for something to happen although she wasn't quite sure what.

'I haven't heard any whispers,' Lucy said, lowering her voice. 'Although I will admit I haven't been out much in the last few days. I didn't want to be anywhere someone could stop me and question me if Mrs Burghley had spilled her secret.'

'You are too good, Lucy,' Jane said, leaning in to her friend. 'Perhaps she won't tell anyone. The waiting, the not knowing, is so hard. I wish I could hunt her down and just ask her. It is awful, waking up each day and not knowing whether your whole world will come crashing down.'

'It must be. I do not envy you that, Jane.' She shook her head as they waited for a carriage to trundle past before crossing the road. 'Have you seen Mr Stewart since that evening?'

Closing her eyes for a moment, Jane thought of waking up this morning with Mr Stewart gently shaking her arm. For an instant she had allowed herself to believe that that was their life, and she had awoken with a contented feeling before the panic of reality had crashed back down on her.

'Yes. We took Edward sledging yesterday.'

'Did he…?' Lucy trailed off, looking as if she didn't know how to phrase the question without causing upset.

'He proposed.' Jane scoffed and corrected herself. 'No, that's a lie. He didn't propose. He said if things went badly, of course he would marry me.'

'Did you want him to propose? Properly, I mean?'

Jane couldn't bring herself to look at Lucy, knowing her friend's expression would be one of complete concern and affection. She felt the prick of tears in her eyes and tried to suppress the wave of emotion that threatened to overwhelm her.

Taking in a deep, shuddering breath, she nodded, feeling relief as she finally admitted it.

'Yes,' she said quietly. 'More than anything else, and that scares me so much.'

'Why does it scare you?'

'I hate how easily I have given up my promises to myself.'

'To focus on your work?'

'Yes.'

'Marrying Mr Stewart wouldn't mean you

would have to give up your ambitions. I know many men would not want you to continue with passions that might take your focus away from looking after the home and any children you might have, but I don't think Mr Stewart would be one of them. He seems to be very relaxed. I think he would make a wonderful husband for you.'

'He doesn't want to get married. He has his reasons, reasons he thinks are very valid. He isn't going to move away from his beliefs unless we are forced into it.'

'Do you think his reasons are valid?'

'No, at least I do not believe the worst in him, as he does himself.'

'Oh, Jane, what a mess.'

It was so frustrating, knowing the future was out of her hands. She knew if she looked at things rationally the best thing would be for Mrs Burghley to keep quiet and for Tom and her to move on with their lives. She didn't want him to be forced to marry her, even if she did want to be with him, and she knew the option she dreamed of, the option where Tom suddenly realised he was deeply in love with her and *wanted* to spend the rest of their lives married, wasn't going to happen.

They splashed through some deep puddles,

both having to lift their skirts to avoid getting completely soaked. Already the hem of Jane's dress was wet and grey in colour, soaking up the moisture from the melting snow.

'There he is,' Lucy said, pausing as they rounded a corner. 'Perhaps you should tell him, Jane.'

'What?'

'Tell him how you feel about him. Tell him you love him. I wager you haven't been truthful with him yet.'

Jane thought of the kisses, the surge of emotion that had passed between them. He knew she desired him, that she enjoyed his company, but she had never really let him see the depth of her feeling.

'It wouldn't change anything,' she said quietly. 'It would only serve to make things more difficult between us.'

They fell silent as Tom spotted them and raised a hand in greeting.

'Thank you for coming today, Mrs Weyman,' Tom said, taking her hand and bowing over it. 'I know it was short notice.'

'I do not mind at all. In fact, I am intrigued as to the secrecy of where we are going.'

'Are you well, Miss Ashworth?' he enquired, sounding as if he didn't have a care in the world, but Jane knew he was really asking if everything had been calm after his departure from the house that morning.

'Very well, thank you, Mr Stewart.'

'I have done something I think you are going to be annoyed about, Miss Ashworth, but I hope with time you will be able to forgive me.'

He was smiling at her, but she could see the earnest expression on his face. She felt a roiling of nerves in her stomach. Tom had sent a note this morning, inviting her for a walk and telling her that there was a new book publisher opening up close to Bond Street. He suggested she bring her manuscript and illustrations so she could see if the publisher would grant her an audience. The heavy packet of papers was tucked under her arm.

'You're making me nervous.'

'There is a shop I am going to take Miss Ashworth into, Mrs Weyman. I know the weather is cold, but I don't expect us to be more than a few minutes. There is a little shop that serves tea across the road you could wait in. Is that acceptable?'

'Of course,' Lucy said, pulling Jane in as Tom stepped away a few paces. 'Maybe he's going to buy you a wedding ring.'

'Don't be ridiculous,' Jane whispered, hating the trickle of hope that ran through her.

'Are you ready, Miss Ashworth?'

Jane stepped over and took his proffered arm, looking up at the signs that hung above the shops. It wasn't a part of London she knew well, but she never had been one to enjoy shopping, tolerating the trips to the modiste with gritted teeth and a book stowed in her bag for the quieter moments.

'Where are we going?' Jane murmured as they walked a little way down the street. Out of the corner of her eye, she saw Lucy crossing the road and escaping from the cold into the little shop.

'Did anyone notice anything was amiss this morning?'

'You left your cravat.'

'Did someone see?'

'The maid found it, I invented some story about it being Captain Weyman's and said Lucy had given it to me to make into ribbons.'

'Quick thinking,' he said, nodding in approval. 'I must have removed it as I was dropping off last night.' He gave her a rueful smile. 'In the panic this morning, I didn't even notice. I am sorry I put you in that position. I don't know what came over me last night.'

'You were inebriated.'

'It's no excuse. I shouldn't have let myself get like that to begin with. I'm far from a man obsessed with sobriety, but I do normally know my limits.'

Tom slowed his pace and then exerted a small amount of pressure on her arm, indicating they should stop. Jane glanced around, wondering where he was taking her with such secrecy, but before she could work it out Tom pulled her attention back to him.

'You might not forgive me so easily for this.'

She frowned, not understanding him.

'This morning, whilst you were checking the coast was clear downstairs, I saw a piece of paper sticking out of one of the drawers in your desk. It had the most wonderful painting on it.' He held up his hands as if to defend himself. 'I didn't look further than the top two sheets, and even that I know is a gross invasion of privacy.'

Jane felt the blood flood to her cheeks. Even though she dreamed of being published, she hated showing people her work. It was unusual for a woman to have such ambition, to want to strike out on her own and pursue her talents beyond using them to amuse herself and her close friends and family. Hardly anyone except her younger sister had ever laid eyes on the pictures she painted, and the stories were guarded with even fiercer need for privacy.

'You shouldn't have…'

'I know. Believe me, I know, but once I had seen them I couldn't stop thinking about them.'

Jane spun round, finally realising where they must be.

'There is a man I know from my school days. I have requested an appointment with him.' Tom reached out as if to take her hand and then seemed to remember they were on a public street. 'I have told him there is someone I would like him to meet, someone who's work I think merits his attention, but I have not told him anything else.'

Jane looked over her shoulder. It was not a publisher she had been to before, although the name was familiar. When she had first arrived in London, she had begun by writing to a few of the more prestigious book publishers rather than traipsing round to their shops. It had not been very successful, but she did recognise the name above the shop here as one who had at least replied and told her gently they were not accepting new manuscripts at present.

'The man who owns the business is Richard Hambly. As I said, I know him from school, but we were not close. He was older than me. He owes me nothing and the courtesy he does me is just for a meeting. If anything comes of this, it will be because of you, not because of me.' He paused, looking at her earnestly. 'I think your work has merit, Jane, and sometimes we have to take the small advantages granted to us in life.'

For a long moment Jane's eyes flicked between Tom and the bookshop and then finally she nodded. Doing things her way hadn't achieved anything so far. Perhaps having someone who was open at least to viewing her work was what she needed.

'Good, come on. I will introduce you.'

They entered the shop and Jane paused for a moment, overwhelmed by the volume of books on display. They were beautifully bound and lined on the shelves with precision and care. Some had little stands that allowed the books to be displayed open, with their innermost secrets on show to the world. The shop seemed to stock a mixture of adults' and children's books and for the first time in a long time Jane felt a frisson of excitement. There was a reason this had originally been near the top of her list of publishers she wanted to approach.

'Mr Stewart, good morning,' a young man said as he stepped out of the room behind the counter. There was another man there, a clerk, who moved aside and busied himself with arranging a new stack of books on the shelves.

'Good to see you again, Mr Hambly,' Tom said, taking the other man's proffered hand and shaking it. 'May I introduce a good friend of mine, Miss Jane Ashworth?'

'Delighted to meet you, Miss Ashworth. Why don't you come through to my office and we can talk?'

He led the way through the door at the back of the shop to a neat office beyond, motioning for them to have a seat. There were some crates piled high in one corner and it looked as though he was still unpacking.

'Sorry for the mess. I moved in here six months ago and I still haven't got the room how I like it.'

'It is a lovely shop, Mr Hambly,' Jane said, trying to suppress the nervousness she was feeling.

'Yes, I'm rather pleased with it. I moved from a few streets away as this is more prominent and gets more passing trade. I kept the old shop for all the printing equipment, but I do miss the whir and bang of the printing press as I work.' He leaned back in his chair. 'Mr Stewart said you have some work you would like me to consider.'

Jane picked up the packet of papers from her lap and slid out the manuscript she had spent so much time on. The paper felt heavy in her hands and she hesitated before handing it over.

'I write children's stories, Mr Hambly, and draw and paint the illustrations for them.'

The publisher leaned forward in his chair and took the proffered bundle.

Her heart was fluttering in her chest, feeling like a butterfly that was fighting to break free. Although she had been visiting publishers for the last few months, this was the first time that anyone had actually invited her to sit down and show her work. It felt like a momentous moment, although Jane was acutely aware any rejection now would be a direct response to her work.

'What age group is this for, Miss Ashworth?'

'For slightly older children, although I think younger children would enjoy the stories if read to them by someone else. I often read my stories to my younger sisters before bed and they enjoy them.'

He nodded, turning over the first page. Jane

watched him carefully, seeing his eyes widen at the beautiful illustration she had chosen to be included on the title page. It showed the three field mice dashing through the cornfield with the owl swooping down behind them, wings spread wide.

'Did you paint this?'

'Yes.'

'It is beautiful. With just one picture I feel I am already inside your story.'

A warm glow swept through Jane and she felt the first flickering of hope.

'Are there more pictures like this?'

'Yes, a lot more.'

'Good.'

He settled back to read, turning the pages slowly and spending a long time scrutinising the pictures. It was the most agonising half hour of Jane's life, watching him read and form a judgement on her manuscript. She struggled to sit still, having to lace her fingers together to stop them from tapping on the table or playing with the fabric of her dress.

Finally, Mr Hambly looked up, placing down the last of the sheets of paper in the pile. For a long moment he did not speak, as if formulating a response in his mind. Jane felt her hopes crashing down. Surely if he loved it he would come out and say so straight away?

'Do you have more?' he asked eventually.

'Yes. Five completed manuscripts.'

'All illustrated?'

'Yes.'

'All in a similar theme?'

'Yes.'

'You have talent, Miss Ashworth. When I first looked at the illustrations, I thought of inviting you to work as an illustrator for some of the other children's books I am publishing, but your stories are charming and unlike anything I have come across before. Uniqueness is a good thing in our business.'

Jane couldn't quite believe what she was hearing. She glanced across at Tom, and saw his encouraging smile, before turning back to Mr Hambly.

'I would really like to see the rest of your work, but I think you have real promise, Miss Ashworth, and I would like to work with you.'

For a moment Jane couldn't react. She felt stunned and realised she had never truly believed she might ever get to this point.

'You want to publish my book?'

'Send me the rest of your work, and if you would grant me a few days to think things over

I will come back to you with an offer within the week.'

He stood and Jane scrambled to her feet as well.

'I will send the manuscripts over later today.'

'I will treat them with the utmost care. I am looking forward to working with you, Miss Ashworth.'

Unable to believe what was happening, Jane let Tom escort her out of the shop and a hundred feet down the road before stopping and turning to him.

'Did that really just happen?'

'That really just happened.'

'He liked my work.'

'He loved it, Jane, and who can blame him? I only managed to read some of it, upside down as it was, but you have real talent.'

She beamed, looking up at him. All her worries seemed insignificant now. The only thing she could think of was what the future might hold.

'Jane,' Lucy's voice called out, and they both spun to face her as she hurried across the street. There was a look of alarm on her face and she was moving quickly, far quicker than was deemed appropriate for a young lady when out in public.

'Is something amiss, Lucy?'

'I was enjoying a cup of tea, watching the world go by, when I was approached by an acquaintance, a woman I do not know well. She is the wife of another captain in the army who my husband knows a little.' Lucy paused, taking in a deep breath before continuing. 'She asked me about the rumours surrounding you and Mr Stewart, dropping in she knew we were friends.'

'Rumours?' Jane felt all the elation of a moment ago being sucked out of her.

'I was a bit sharp. I was taken by surprise, and said I knew of no rumours,' Lucy said, a look of deep concern on her face. 'I should have questioned her more, found out what it was she had heard and who she had heard it from, but then I saw you two out here on the street alone together and thought it more important you did not appear to be without a chaperon.'

Next to them, Tom let out a sharp exhalation and began to shake his head. 'I thought we were safe.'

Jane had allowed herself to hope so too when they hadn't been assailed by gossip on the first morning after Mrs Burghley had witnessed the illicit kiss. Glancing around, wondering if everyone was looking at them, Jane suddenly felt self-conscious.

'We need to get away from here and find out what has been said.'

Lucy looked at her and must have had the same thought at the same moment, for together they said, 'Lady Mountjoy.'

'She will know,' Tom agreed. He leapt into action, guiding them round to his waiting carriage and helping them inside.

They travelled in complete silence. Jane was too shocked to be able to say anything. Even though she had known there was a very real possibility of Mrs Burghley telling everyone what she had seen, Jane had always considered this outcome in an abstract way, like a puzzle needing to be solved. She had never allowed the emotion to overwhelm her, had never really allowed herself to think about all the consequences. Risking a glance at Tom, she took in the pallor of his complexion. He didn't look like a man happy to be considering his impending nuptials.

Of course, she had a choice. Tom would offer her marriage. He was a gentleman, but more than that, he was a man who had his own set of morals, and abandoning a friend in need would not be acceptable to him. Already he had told her he would offer marriage, but that didn't mean she would have to accept.

Jane knew most people would view her as a fool for even considering turning down Tom's proposal. He was an extremely eligible bachelor and a good man. He was kind, easy to get along with and devastatingly handsome. In theory, there was nothing but positives.

Jane turned and looked out of the window, trying to distract herself with the view of the streets of London flashing past, but it was impossible. She was always aware of Tom when he was in close proximity and now the closeness felt overwhelming.

Digging the nails of one hand into the other, she relished the bite of discomfort for a second, finding the pain the only way to take herself away from the decision. Then the carriage slowed, the Mountjoys' townhouse came into view and she knew she had no more time for distractions. She needed to make a decision.

Chapter Twenty

'I need a moment,' Jane said as she leaped from the carriage when it had barely stopped moving. She rushed towards the house, brushing past the footman as he opened the door, and disappearing before Tom could even step down to the pavement.

Slowly he stepped out, turning round to help Mrs Weyman down as well. Together they walked up to the house. Lady Mountjoy came to greet them by the door, her expression serious.

'Come in,' she said, ushering them inside. 'Lucy, why don't you go and check on Jane—see if she needs anything. I need to talk to Mr Stewart.'

Mrs Weyman looked glad to be able to escape, although Tom had hoped he would be able to go after Jane himself. Perhaps it was better they both had a few more minutes before they committed to each other for the rest of their lives.

Lady Mountjoy led him through to the drawing room and closed the door firmly behind them. Tom waited for her to sit, and then almost collapsed into one of the comfortable arm chairs.

'How bad is it?' He knew Lady Mountjoy would have heard every piece of gossip there was to hear and would be fully apprised of the situation. She knew everyone, was a friend to many and was even respected by the few who were not part of her inner circle.

'It is bad, Mr Stewart, very bad indeed…' She paused, and then seemed to take pity on him, for her expression softened. 'But not unsalvageable.'

'What are they saying?'

'The rumours were started by Mrs Burghley—a friend of yours, I believe.'

'A short-lived acquaintance.'

'A woman scorned?'

Tom shook his head. 'We went to the theatre together once. I did not feel there was anything between us, but perhaps Mrs Burghley thought differently.'

'I do not know the woman well. I came

across her a few times whilst her husband was still alive. She's beautiful and I assume she is used to getting the things she wants.'

'Undoubtedly.'

'And she couldn't have you.'

They both remained silent for a minute. Tom had regretted the decision to take Mrs Burghley to the theatre ever since that fateful night.

'What has she said?'

'She has told everyone that after your trip to the theatre she accompanied you and Miss Ashworth to a friend's house. Whilst there, you and Miss Ashworth sneaked off into the garden and she found you entwined and kissing in the darkness.'

Tom let his head fall into his hands. It was a very accurate retelling of what had happened. She hadn't embellished it at all, which made it all the more plausible.

'She hasn't said who the friends were, although I assume it was Lucy and her husband.'

Tom nodded. At least they hadn't been pulled into it, branded as a couple with loose morals.

'It *could* be a disaster,' Lady Mountjoy said. 'If you refused to marry Jane—but I think you will do the right thing.'

'Of course,' he said stiffly.

'A quick wedding, and a show of being to-gether in wedded bliss, and the *ton* will soon find something else to gossip about. In a couple of months, no one will even remember the circumstances of your marriage.' She scrutinised him for a moment. 'You do not look convinced.'

'Of course I will marry Miss Ashworth,' Tom said slowly. 'I respect her too much to do anything else. I got us into this mess, and I will do the right thing and get us out of it.'

'That sounds an awful lot of duty and not much romance,' Lady Mountjoy said with a sigh. 'I know you care for her.'

Tom remembered all the times Jane had swooped in and helped him with Edward. He remembered the quiet, unassuming way she listened to him and made him laugh when he didn't think there was anything to laugh about. The way she'd looked at him before they had kissed and the way he had felt that irresistible pull towards her, that need to be with her.

'I care for her, but I cannot offer her the sort of marriage she wants. She will have my name as protection, she will have a comfortable life-style. She will want for nothing material.'

'What about affection?'

He sucked in a raspy breath. Of course he cared for her, but he couldn't offer her love. If their arrangement was more practical, it would be easier to keep the boundaries that kept her safe. He couldn't trust himself always to put her needs first—he had shown he couldn't be trusted when he had abandoned his sister. He would be better able to protect Jane if she knew the limits of their marriage.

'I cannot offer her love,' he said, supressing the part of him that was shouting protestations inside his head.

Lady Mountjoy smoothed her skirts. 'I do not pretend to be able to read minds, but I think I can see when one person cares for another, and you care for Jane.'

'That is why I cannot risk her heart,' Tom said softly. 'This way will be better. She will be my wife in name, and free to pursue whatever path she wants without me tying her down.' He shrugged, trying to brush off the weight that was pressing down on him, trying to suffocate him. 'We will both benefit. I will gain a mother figure for Edward, and she will avoid the scandal of the gossip that is circulating.'

'I do not believe your true feelings are so practical, Tom.'

He shook his head, refusing to let out the storm of emotion building inside him. It was better this way, better for both of them. There was no way of avoiding the marriage, but he could still protect Jane.

Jane was pacing up and down when Lucy knocked on the door and entered immediately.

'You look frantic, Jane,' Lucy said, catching her by the arms and forcing her to stop moving for a second. 'Take some deep breaths.'

Slowly Jane obeyed, feeling some of the nervous tension flow from her.

'This is a nightmare,' she said, clutching hold of Lucy and looking at her imploringly, as if there was something her friend could do to stop it.

'I agree it is hardly ideal,' Lucy said slowly. 'But is it really a nightmare?'

Jane looked at her as if she had grown a second head. 'Yes.'

'A scandal is not what any of us want, but all it really does is speed things along.'

'What do you mean?'

'It is obvious that you love Mr Stewart,' Lucy said, as if she hadn't just exposed Jane's biggest secret. 'And he loves you. All this gossip has done is speed up your engagement and wedding.'

Jane spluttered. 'I do not love Mr Stewart.'

'Of course you do. It is obvious in the way you look at him, the way you talk about him, the way you two share little jokes and intimate looks. You forget, I have been in love with William for a long time, Jane, much of it illicitly. I know how a woman acts when she is in love.'

'He does not love me.'

Lucy took her hands and squeezed them in her own. 'He loves you, Jane. He may not have admitted it to himself yet, but that man loves you.'

Jane bit her lip, wondering if there could be any truth in what Lucy was saying. Her friend was romantic, always sure that things were going to turn out for the best. She thought of their kisses, of the easy companionship they had together, the way they laughed and talked. For her, that all translated into the deep emotional connection she felt for this man—maybe it did for him too.

'I don't have to marry him,' she said quietly.

'Don't do anything rash.'

'I'm considering my options. I have a publisher interested in my books. I could go home to Somerset and write and draw and paint and support myself.'

'Is that what you want?'

For the first time, she let go of any of the little lies she'd told herself, of the doubts and boundaries holding her back.

'No,' she said eventually. 'I want to write and draw, but I want to do it with Tom.'

'You have your answer, then.'

It felt like a long walk downstairs, and Jane paused on the first floor landing before starting on the final steps that would take her to her future husband. The door to the drawing room had come open a crack, and she could hear Lady Mountjoy's voice, followed by Tom's. She wondered what they had discussed, and whether the older woman was angry at the idea of a scandal or elated at the thought of a wedding. Knowing Lady Mountjoy, probably the latter. The countess had never shied away from a brewing scandal in the time Jane had known her, and always seemed able to twist the situation so the young couple she was championing came out on top.

'This way will be better,' Tom was saying, his voice clear but with a dejected note. 'She will be my wife in name, and free to pursue whatever path she wants without me tying her down. We will both benefit. I will gain a mother figure for Edward, and she will avoid the scandal of the gossip that is circulating.'

It was as though someone had reached into her chest and ripped her heart in two. Here she was, convincing herself that Tom loved her, and all he could do was think about the practical reasons it would not be so bad to have her as his wife. Suddenly, she felt foolish and naïve. A vision of a marriage of convenience to Tom burst into her mind, with her stuck at home, pining after the husband she secretly loved whilst he continued to seek his life of pleasure.

She let out a little sob, angry with herself for almost falling for the fantasy, and devastated that she would not get the happy ending she had conjured in her mind. Clamping her hand over her mouth, she realised they must have heard her inside the drawing room. She ran, not even taking the time to grab her coat, and burst out into the street as if she were being chased by hungry wolves.

Somewhere behind her she heard Tom calling her name, but nothing would have enticed her to return in that moment. Not caring where she ended up, Jane ran, darting down streets and dodging people out for a stroll now the snow had melted. She ran until the tears had stopped falling and the sobs had left her body empty and aching. Finally, she sank down onto a bench, gasping for breath, wondering when she had let herself get so vulnerable.

Chapter Twenty-One

'You are in a foul mood,' Western said as he eyed Tom up and down. 'And you look a state.'

'Don't be afraid to speak your mind there, Western.'

'I'm only saying what I am seeing.'

Tom grunted and went to set up the line of plates thirty paces away. They were out in the country, an hour's ride from central London, and so far they hadn't seen another soul since having arrived at the spot. It was a favourite retreat of theirs, somewhere they came every few months to shoot pistols without being disturbed. Sometimes they would even talk, although Tom hoped this time they could just shoot and ruminate on their problems in silence.

He walked the thirty paces back and picked up the pistol Western had left in the case. It was a beautiful weapon, shiny and well maintained. Tom had inherited it from his father and, as much as he'd hated the old man, he had to admit he had good taste in pistols. This pair not only looked good but shot straight and were reliable, everything you wanted from a weapon.

When he was satisfied the pistol was in good working order, he loaded it and then took up his position. Western stood next to him, the other pistol in his hand, his stance identical to Tom's.

Tom fired first, pleased to see one of the plates shatter, the pottery exploding outwards and tinkling to the ground. Western fired a moment later, also hitting a plate at the other end of the row.

'Nice shot,' Western commented. 'It looked to be right in the centre of the plate. Did you know you always have the best aim when you're angry?'

'I'm not angry.'

Western scoffed. 'I've known you a long time, Stewart. I know when you're angry.'

Tom bent over his pistol, concentrating on reloading it. He *was* angry. Angry at himself for how he had handled the situation with Jane, angry with Jane for not granting him a few minutes to explain himself, angry with Mrs Burghley for forcing his hand and starting the gossip that was going to destroy Jane's reputation.

He turned and aimed again, taking his time and shooting as he exhaled, feeling a surge of triumph as another plate shattered.

'I can guess, if you would prefer it,' Western said.

'You can be annoying as hell, Western, did you know that?'

'My wife tells me on a daily basis.'

Tom sighed and put down the pistol, knowing Western wasn't going to stop until he had the whole story from him.

'I've messed up,' Tom said quietly.

'With the woman you were telling me about?'

'Jane, yes.'

Western took another shot, smashing one of the plates, and then motioned for Tom to go on.

'Mrs Burghley told a few people about having seen us kiss,' he said, still unable to comprehend how he was in this situation when a couple of days ago he had been sure he would marry Jane. 'The rumours spread quickly.'

'Were you forced to propose?'

'I had told Jane I would—I promised her I

wouldn't abandon her. Even so, when we heard the rumours it was a bit of a shock. I think part of me thought Mrs Burghley might do the kind thing and keep quiet.'

'Did you react poorly?'

Tom thought back, wondering if Jane had seen it as so. He hadn't jumped for joy when he'd realised her reputation had been destroyed in one swoop, but he didn't think he had reacted particularly poorly.

'I wasn't ecstatic,' he said slowly. 'But I accepted what had to happen. We were out when we heard the rumours and hurried to get back to Lady Mountjoy's house.'

Western nodded, starting to reload his pistol, handing it to Tom before picking up the one Tom had abandoned. Tom aimed and fired, finding it easier to think when part of his brain was distracted by shooting the pistol.

'Jane went upstairs to take a minute and I spoke to Lady Mountjoy.' He paused, trying to remember the exact words he had said. 'I told Lady Mountjoy it couldn't be a marriage fuelled by love, but that it would suit both of us perfectly well. Jane would keep her reputation and I would gain a mother figure for Edward.'

Western looked at him with an expression of surprise.

'I thought you were meant to be good with the ladies. I take it she heard this?'

'Yes, unfortunately she did.'

'Is she in love with you?'

Tom was about to say no, but then he stopped himself and considered. Jane was always practical, always sensible, but he knew there was a layer of deeper feeling there. When they had kissed, he'd seen it burning in her eyes, and even when they were together innocently, strolling through the park or dancing in the ballroom, he felt a warmth from her.

'I think maybe she is.'

'Then your words would be devastating to her. She probably harboured hopes that you loved her as she loved you.'

Tom tamped down the little voice that declared he did love her, trying to brush it away.

'I didn't even get the chance to talk to her about it,' he said quietly, shaking his head. 'She ran away, and I searched and searched, but couldn't find her. Later that day, she went home, but has refused to see me since.'

'I'm not surprised.'

'This will ruin her life, Western. *I* have ruined her life.'

Tom began to reload the pistol, taking his time to combat the shaking of his hands.

'Her reputation,' Western corrected softly. 'Not necessarily her life.'

'She will become a pariah in social circles.'

'But from what you've told me she doesn't sound the sort to really care.'

'Even some of her friends will turn her away.'

'Not true friends.'

Taking a few deep breaths to steady his hand, Tom aimed again, cursing when the shot went wide. Lowering the pistol, he considered Western's words and realised his friend was right. All this time Tom had been treating her like an ordinary young woman, a normal debutante, but Jane was nothing of the sort. She was fiercely independent and knew what she wanted from her future.

She might not be welcome in polite circles in London with a ruined reputation, but he didn't doubt her family would welcome her back. Jane had always spoken fondly of them, even if she was lost a little in amongst so many children. She had somewhere to go and, with the likelihood that Mr Hambly was going to publish her books, she had something that would occupy her time and hopefully bring her an income.

'She doesn't have to marry me,' he murmured. All this time he had assumed she needed him, that the only way for her to survive this was to marry him. It had meant he hadn't really thought about what was best for her.

Tom felt a coldness spread through him as he realised he had probably lost her for good.

'I don't want to lose her,' he said quietly.

'Why?' Western asked, the question sounding harsh. 'You only want to marry her to give Edward a mother figure.'

Tom knew his friend was deliberately provoking him, but he couldn't help but react all the same.

'That's not true.'

'Do you want to marry her?'

Tom didn't speak for a long moment, allowing the memories of the last few weeks to flood into his mind.

'Yes.'

'Why do you want to marry her?'

'I love her.' He blinked, surprising himself at the answer. Western clapped him on the back, throwing his head back and giving out a whoop of joy.

'In all the years that I've known you, nothing has been so hard as getting you to confess that.'

'I love her,' Tom repeated, realising it was true. He loved the way she smiled and the way she was always so direct. He loved the sparkle she got in her eyes when she wanted to be kissed and the enthusiastic way she tried anything new. He loved that she didn't care what people thought of her, forging her own path, even if people stared and whispered.

Shaking his head, he knew this realisation didn't solve all his problems.

'That only makes things worse,' he said quietly.

Western regarded him for a long time and then turned away to take his shot.

'You've never put into words what it is that stops you from allowing yourself to be happy,' he said quietly. 'But you do not fool me with this carefree act of yours. You have too big a heart to keep it locked away, pretending that you would rather have purely superficial relationships.'

Tom opened his mouth to make a flippant remark but nothing would come out. He thought of all the years keeping people at arm's length. Western was the only one who truly knew him and that was because they'd been through hell on the battlefield together. No one else had come close in his adult life, and Tom knew that was because he was an expert at knowing the exact moment to step away.

Until Jane. Somehow she had slipped under his defences, she had clung on when he had attempted to keep his distance and their friendship had bloomed alongside the desire that burned between them.

'You don't have to tell me,' Western said, lining up another shot and smiling in satisfaction as the penultimate plate broke a second after the pistol shot rang out. 'But ask yourself if it is truly worth your happiness. Sometimes the ideas we create in our youth, we hang on to for far too long.'

He handed Tom the pistol with the final shot and took a step back. With his thoughts racing, Tom took his position, knowing if he didn't concentrate the shot would go wide again. He cleared his mind, pushing all the irrelevant noise to one side, and aimed, pulling the trigger with one lone thought left in his head: *I love her*.

The plate shattered and Tom felt a momentary thrill of triumph. Western took the pistol from him and went to start clearing up the shards of pottery from their makeshift targets.

Tom sat down, half-collapsing to the ground.

He looked up at the clear sky above, trying to find answers that weren't there.

I need to see her, he realised. Perhaps everything would become clearer if he could see Jane, if he could tell her how he felt. It might not change anything for her, but it would mean they were both making decisions without hiding anything from one another.

'I've been going about this all wrong,' he murmured to himself. Not that he hadn't tried to see Jane since she had fled into the street and disappeared, but each time he'd been denied. Lady Mountjoy had been sympathetic, inviting him to wait in the drawing room on each occasion he had called, but each time she had returned downstairs, shaking her head and telling him Jane would not come out to see him today.

He'd given up too easily, sometimes secretly relieved, as he had not known what he wanted to say to her. There was an urgency inside him, pushing him to make things right, but he had been unable to work out how.

'You get back to the city,' Western said as he returned with all the pieces of broken pottery. 'I'll tidy up here. I'll clean the pistols and drop them off in a day or two.'

Without a word of argument, Tom nodded,

already striding over to where his horse was loosely tied to a fence post. It was an hour's ride back to central London. If he went straight to Lady Mountjoy's, he could confess how he felt to Jane by three o'clock. They would still have much to work out, and she still might refuse his offer of marriage, but it was better than standing around here, feeling wretched and not acting on anything.

'I'm going to miss you so much,' Jane said, squeezing Lucy hard as they embraced.

'I will be coming to visit before you know it.' Lucy had tears in her eyes and suddenly they spilled over onto her cheeks.

'Promise you'll write to me every week. I want to know every little snippet of news.'

'I promise.'

They hugged again, neither wanting to be the first one to let go.

'If we are to make the coach to Bath, we really should leave now,' Lady Mountjoy said, her tone gentle.

Jane nodded, looking around at the plush drawing room, sad that her time in London had come to an end like this.

'Thank you for your hospitality,' Jane said to Lord Mountjoy.

'You are welcome to stay with us any time,' he said magnanimously. 'I do hope you get all the happiness you deserve, Miss Ashworth.'

Jane took one last look around and then allowed Lady Mountjoy to lead her out to the waiting carriage. There was a coach leaving London at noon to start the first leg of the journey to Bath. Lady Mountjoy had offered to accompany Jane, to give her the use of the family carriage, but Jane felt that she needed some time alone before she was swept back into family life. Perhaps a few days on the road would be enough time for her to learn to hide her heartbreak.

They stepped up into Lady Mountjoy's carriage that would take them to the coach and Jane caught a glimpse of all the luggage strapped to the back. It was much more than she had brought to London, and it reminded her of her hostess' generosity during her stay.

'I want to thank you too,' Jane said as they settled on their seats.

'Don't thank me,' the countess said. 'I've made such a mess of all this for you. I deserve to be condemned.'

'No. You are the kindest person I know. You saw what it would mean to take five girls like us and show us the world of the debutante.

Even I, who was determined not to enjoy myself at first, have had the most incredible experience these last six months.'

'That's kind of you to say, my dear,' Lady Mountjoy said, leaning forward and placing her hand over Jane's. 'I worry that my motivation was selfish, that I missed escorting my daughters to the balls of the Season so much, I tried to recreate those times I loved without acknowledging enough that you are all your own people with your own aims and goals.'

'You have nothing to reproach yourself for. Everything you have done for us has been wonderful.'

'Are you sure you wish to leave, my dear?'

Jane nodded. Over the last few days, she had thought about little else. After she had heard Tom declaring their marriage would be nothing but a practical arrangement, she had felt her heart crack and crumble. In that moment, she'd realised quite how much she had been hoping for the fantasy. Even though she had tried to hide it from herself, she loved Tom and had desperately wanted his love in return.

'It is your decision,' Lady Mountjoy said, leaning back in her seat. 'And it may be the right one, as long as you are sure.'

'I can't stay here, not knowing I will have to face Tom at some point.'

'No, I can see that would be difficult.'

'I know the mature thing would be to talk to him, but I just can't do it. I can't listen to him tell me all the reasons we should get married when I know he wishes it weren't so.'

Lady Mountjoy bit her lip and looked as though she wanted to say something.

'I want to run away and get swallowed up by the noise and chaos at home so I do not have to think about Tom or the scandal or my ruined reputation.'

'The gossip may follow you.'

'I know,' Jane said with a sigh. 'But what harm can it really do me in my tiny Somerset village where people have known me all my life? They won't believe it. I'm steadfast Jane, sensible Jane.' She scoffed. At least her reputation as being dull and undesirable was good for something. 'There may be rumours, but I doubt anything will stick, and it is not as if I am trying to land myself a husband.'

'And what of Tom?'

Jane felt a piercing pain slice through her heart every time she thought of the man she loved. 'I suppose I won't see him again.' At least the scandal wouldn't hurt him. If anything, it would enhance his reputation as a rake, and mean he escaped the machinations of society debutantes and their mothers.

'This is all wrong!' Lady Mountjoy burst out suddenly. 'He loves you. I know he loves you.'

Jane shook her head sadly. She had hoped he did, even convinced herself he did. She remembered the heat in his kisses, the affection in his eyes when he'd looked at her. They had talked to one another like old friends and she knew marriage with him, the right sort of marriage, would have been easy.

'I know he has reasons why he thinks he should not marry,' Jane said, unsure how much Lady Mountjoy knew about Tom's sister and how he blamed himself for leaving her behind. 'But if he loved me, truly loved me, then none of that would matter—not enough to keep us apart.'

'Sometimes he can be so stubborn,' the countess murmured, then fell silent, staring out of the window.

Jane tried not to think about it, tried not to think about what their lives could have been like if she had said yes to him, tried not to wonder if she was making a mistake in refusing to marry him even if he was only offering her a match of convenience.

'If you change your mind, do remember you are always welcome to stay with us, here or in Somerset. No matter what you decide, you are family now, and if you need anything at all I want you to ask.'

Jane nodded, realising she was going to miss Lady Mountjoy as much as she would miss Lucy. The rest of the debutantes had fallen one by one, finding their husbands and their happiness. Jane longed to catch up with Charlotte, who had stayed in Somerset with her husband, and with Eliza, who was on her honeymoon. Perhaps soon they could all reunite. She tried to dampen down the tears that threatened to come when she realised she was the only one of the five debutantes who had not ended the trip to London with the man she loved. Love and marriage had never been her aim. She should be proud she had achieved what she had set out to do and had garnered the interest of a publisher for her stories.

The carriage rolled to a stop and the driver set about arranging the transfer of her trunk and bags across to the coach to Bath. Jane felt a wrench of emotion and sprung forward in her seat, embracing the older woman who had given her so much.

'I will miss you,' she said, her voice muffled by Lady Mountjoy's dress.

'And I you, Jane. Do write and let me know you have reached home safely, and I will pay you a visit when we return to Somerset in a couple of months.'

It felt as though the walk to the coach were a mile rather than a mere twenty feet and Jane couldn't bear to look back, getting on and taking her seat whilst desperately trying to stop herself from breaking down.

Slowly the coach filled up, the space quickly becoming hot despite the freezing temperatures outside. Everyone had on multiple layers, thick dresses or jackets layered over with coats and gloves, and it took a while for people to shed some of those layers to get comfortable. As a result, Jane felt crushed in the corner of the coach, pressed up against the side by a large middle-aged woman, and barely able to move her legs, as they were precariously placed so as not to touch those of the tall man opposite her. It was going to be a long few days.

Chapter Twenty-Two

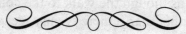

Having ridden as fast as was possible on the busyroads back into the centre of London, Tom now paused for a minute outside the Mountjoys' townhouse. Whilst riding, he had mulled over the right way to phrase things a hundred times, but now he was standing here he did not have a clue what he actually wanted to say.

'Stop delaying,' he muttered to himself and forced his feet to move.

The door opened immediately, and Tom was surprised to find Lady Mountjoy standing there, her eyes red-rimmed.

'Is something amiss?'

'Come in, come in,' the countess said, ushering him inside. 'Foolish boy, asking me if something is amiss.'

'What has happened? Is it Jane? Is she unwell?' He had an awful sinking sensation in his

stomach and almost pushed past Lady Mountjoy, determined to climb the stairs and check
for himself that Jane was unharmed.

Lady Mountjoy turned and walked away,
motioning for him to follow her through to the
drawing room.

'Jane's health is as robust as always. On that
front you do not have to fear.'

'I really need to speak to her.'

'That won't be possible…'

'I know she has refused the last few days,
but I am adamant I will succeed today.'

'It isn't possible, Tom, because she has left.'

Tom felt the world shift under his feet.

'She can't have left.'

'I assure you, she has. Three hours ago I
waved her off on the coach to Bath.'

'No.' He staggered backwards and sat down.
This wasn't how this afternoon was meant to
go. As he had been riding over, he had thought
and thought about what he was going to say
to Jane. He knew he had to tell her he loved
her, that the scandal and his desire for a happy
family for Edward were not the only reasons
he knew marriage to her was the right thing.
He had hoped when they were together, when
he could hold her hands and look into her eyes,

the words would come naturally and she would be able to see what lay in his heart.

'She decided to return to Somerset.' Lady Mountjoy looked at him with a dejected expression. 'She is convinced you do not love her.'

Tom closed his eyes and shook his head. 'Of course I love her. How could I not?'

'Then whatever has been stopping you from telling that poor girl you feel the same way she does?'

'I need to find her. The coach left three hours ago, you say?'

'Yes. It will be on the road out of London now.'

He took his pocket watch out of his jacket and checked the time. Nightfall was only a few hours away and it would be treacherous to ride in the dark on the poorly maintained roads. Conditions were worse the further you got out of London and, as much as he wanted to reach Jane as quickly as possible, he knew he couldn't risk his horse's safety to do so.

'I will bring her back,' he said, standing abruptly.

'Be careful.'

He bowed and then strode from the house. Even though he wanted to set off immediately, he knew charging out into the darkness unprepared was beyond foolish. Tonight he would ready his horse and ensure his affairs were in order and tomorrow he would leave at dawn. Even with the head start, the coach would make slow progress, and he would likely catch up with it tomorrow evening before it stopped for the night.

Rationally, he knew twenty-four hours was hardly any time to wait, but it felt like an eternity. He had a sense of urgency, a need to tell Jane how he felt now he had worked it out for himself.

Twenty-four hours later, Tom was wet and cold, cursing the English weather and wondering whether the warmer days of spring would ever arrive. A steady drizzle had plagued him all day, slowly soaking through his coat and penetrating his clothes layer by layer. He was now so stiff he doubted he would be able to straighten up if he dismounted and he had ceased being able to feel the ends of his fingers about an hour ago.

The light was fading fast and, although a local had assured him it was only another few minutes to the coaching inn, he was beginning to doubt whether this stage of his journey would ever end.

Time and time again throughout the day he had been splattered by thick mud as coaches rolled past, and for one of the only times in his life he wished he had been sensible enough to travel in the comfort of his own carriage rather than on horseback.

Sending up a silent prayer of thanks, he murmured a few words of encouragement to Rupert as he spotted the faint glow of an oil lamp ahead. Slowly the coaching inn came into view, a long, squat building that looked as if it had stood in the same position for hundreds of years. The yard was large and well maintained and Tom was thankful when a stable boy ran out to greet him as he entered through the gate.

'Give him a good brush down for me,' Tom said, passing a couple of coins to the young boy.

'Yes, sir. I'll make sure he is fed and watered too.'

'Thank you.'

Tom peered around him, noting the two carriages stationary on one side of the yard. It was highly likely that one of the coaches was the one headed to Bath, the one Jane was travelling on. Unless they had made extraordinarily good progress, they couldn't have reached much further before the light had begun to fail, and Tom knew there wasn't another coaching inn for ten miles.

Looking down at himself, he grimaced. He was hardly the suave and charming man the gossips liked to paint him, splattered top-to toe in mud and grunting at the stiffness in his muscles. All the same, he moved as quickly as he could towards the entrance, wondering if Jane would be sitting in the dining area or if she would have already retired to her room.

'Filthy weather still, I see, sir.' An older man with a friendly smile greeted him as he entered.

'Indeed.'

'Will you be wanting a room?'

'Yes.' He hoped they had something available as, now he had dismounted, he doubted he would be able to get back on his horse.

'I will show you up in a moment, sir. Would you like a drink or something to eat first?'

There was an enticing smell coming from the dining room and Tom knew his body would appreciate a good meal and a spot by a roaring fire.

'Later, perhaps, but first I need to know—has the coach to Bath stopped here?'

'Yes, sir. Filled most of our rooms.'

'Good. I've been riding all day to catch up with it. I am looking for a Miss Jane Ashworth.'

The innkeeper's eyes narrowed and Tom glanced down, realising in his current state he didn't look particularly trustworthy.

'My sister,' he said in explanation. 'She is returning to our home in Bath but I have some sad news of a relative.'

'I see, sir. I can deliver a message to the young lady and see if she wishes to meet with you. Excuse the caution, but you can't be too careful these days. There are so many ne'er do wells about.'

'Thank you. Perhaps you could arrange for some hot water so I can clean up before dinner.'

'Of course, sir.'

The innkeeper disappeared for a moment, shouting instructions to a weary-looking maid before reappearing with a bunch of keys. He led Tom upstairs and down a narrow corridor to the room at the end.

'I only have our most expensive room left,' he said as he opened the door.

'That is fine.'

It was a good-sized room with a four-poster

bed and an arm chair in front of the fire. There
was no blaze burning in the grate but the wood
was piled high, ready to be lit.

'I will send Sally up to light the fire and
bring you some hot water.'

'Thank you.'

Tom waited for the innkeeper to leave before sinking into the chair and kicking off his
boots. He felt restless, as if he wanted to pound
on every door, shouting for Jane, but knew
he needed to be patient. In a few minutes the
innkeeper would deliver his message and Jane
would agree to meet him. After chasing her for
a day, he could wait another half hour.

Glad of the warmth when the maid arrived
and started the fire, he unpacked the small bag
he had travelled with. It contained only a single change of clothes. He hadn't expected the
weather to be quite so foul, and in his haste he
hadn't thought ahead to what would happen if
he didn't catch up with Jane in one day.

Soon the maid reappeared with a steaming bowl of water and he set to work, peel-
ing off his wet clothes and hanging them up
to dry. When he had stripped down to just his
breeches, he took a moment to stand in front
of the fire, feeling the heat seep through his
skin and start to warm his core.

The hot water was bliss and he was grateful to be able to wash away the grime and mud from the day. As he stood in front of the mirror combing his hair, there was a soft knock on the door. Thinking it would be the maid or the innkeeper, he called for them to come in, not bothering to reach for a shirt.

'Oh, you're naked.' Jane's voice was shocked, but he barely even registered the tone, so glad was he to see her.

'Hardly,' he said, indicating the breeches.

She coughed and then slowly raised her eyes to meet his.

'Perhaps I should come back later.'

'You are not going anywhere,' he said, adamant now he had found her he was not going to let her out of his sight until he had said all he had come to say.

Striding over to the door, he ushered her inside and closed it firmly behind her, turning the key in the lock so no one could burst in on them.

'What are you doing here, Tom?'

'You ran away.'

'I didn't run away. I decided to go home.'

'Without telling me.'

'It is no longer any of your concern what I do.'

There was a flare of defiance in her voice but he could see she was sad too.

'Of course it is,' he said, and then forced himself to breath slowly. There were so many things he needed to say to her and it was vital he did it in the right way. 'Will you sit down? I would like to talk to you, properly, without rushing.'

She hesitated and then went and perched on the edge of the arm chair by the fire. Tom took a moment to look her over. Her eyes were red-rimmed, and he wondered if she had been crying, but apart from that she looked well. He didn't know what he had expected—perhaps that she wouldn't cope without him, as he felt he hadn't coped without her, but at first glance she seemed to be fine.

He took a step towards the bed and then sat down, wishing he was closer but knowing Jane needed to hear his words before he reached for her hand.

'I am sorry for what you heard me say to Lady Mountjoy,' he said quietly. 'I was panicked and worried about the future.'

'That is understandable,' Jane said, her face impassive. 'Thank you for the apology, but it really wasn't necessary for you to race all this way to say you were sorry how things ended.'

She stood and turned to leave and for a moment Tom was stunned. Recovering as quickly as he could, he leaped from the bed and grasped hold of her by the arms.

'That was not all I came to say.'

Jane looked down, swallowing as her eyes skimmed across his naked chest and arms.

'Please put on a shirt,' she said, her voice low, and he could see there was a flicker of desire in her eyes when she looked back up at him.

Tom complied, taking a moment to pull on the clean shirt he had hung up a few minutes earlier. When he turned back to Jane, she looked as though she wanted to flee.

'I've been beyond foolish,' he said, realising if she left now he might never get a chance to say what he needed to. 'It took losing you to make me realise what we had, what we could have in the future.'

'I don't understand.'

Reaching down, he took both her hands in his own.

'I love you, Jane.'

She looked up at him as if he had just declared he was off to live on the moon.

'No, you don't.'

He laughed, loving how certain she was about everything, even now.

'I do. I didn't realise it at first. I think I tried not to admit it to myself because it would mean confronting things I have tried to hide from for a long time.'

'You love me?'

'Yes. I love you. I love *everything* about you. When I pictured my life without you, it made me so miserable. It was a life without laughter and happiness and love.'

Shaking her head, she pulled away. 'How have you gone from thinking our marriage would be a convenient arrangement, something done to preserve my reputation with the added benefit of providing a stable family for Edward, to this?'

'I think I knew I loved you even then. I just couldn't admit it.'

'Because loving me is so shameful.'

'No,' he said firmly. 'You are worth the love of a hundred men. It was my problems, my stubbornness, that stopped me from being able to accept what my heart was trying to tell me.'

Jane fell quiet, her head bowed and her eyes darting back and forth across the floor.

'I need some time,' she said abruptly, turning to leave.

'Jane,' he said, softly now. 'All I am asking for is some time to explain.' He was asking for a lot more than that—they both knew it—but first they needed to sit down and talk.

She nodded. 'I'm not going to run again,' she said with a half-smile. 'But I just need a few minutes.'

'Have you eaten?'

'No.'

'Shall I ask the maid to bring something up and we can talk over dinner?'

'That sounds like a nice idea. Perhaps in half an hour.'

Without waiting for his answer, she left, walking away quickly so he couldn't try to stop her. Normally he was good at reading people, at knowing what they were thinking or what they were going to do, but at this moment he had no idea what was going through Jane's head.

Jane burst out of the double doors into the courtyard, gasping for breath. She felt as though she were suffocating and tried to suck in great lungfuls of air. The cool raindrops that landed on her face were a shock to her body and this seemed to help her, to ground her a little, and slowly she felt some semblance of normality returning.

Glancing up, she was grateful to see there were hardly any windows looking out over the courtyard. The last thing she needed was for Tom to witness her panic and come rushing down.

Leaning back against the wall, she tried to empty her mind of everything but the air going in and out of her chest. It took a few minutes but after some time she felt much calmer.

He loves me. Jane knew if he had told her this a week ago she would have been dancing with joy, planning out their lives together. Now everything was different. She did believe him. Tom wasn't cruel. He wouldn't tell her he loved her if he didn't. Despite everything that had happened between them, she still knew he was a good man, a man who would never intentionally go out of his way to hurt her.

He loves me. Part of her wished she could ignore everything else—ignore the fact he didn't want the responsibility for someone else, that if he had the choice they wouldn't be getting married—but this was her life, her future, and she refused to go into it blindly.

Jane knew she had to listen, to hear what he

had to say, and then she could consider whether they would be better together or apart.

'I love you, Tom Stewart,' she murmured, wondering if love was going to be enough.

Half an hour later, there was a delicious aroma wafting out of Tom's room as Jane approached. Quietly she knocked on the door, not wanting to announce to all the other guests at the inn that she was going in to have dinner alone with a man, unchaperoned.

'Come in,' Tom said as he opened the door. He was dressed properly now, in a shirt and jacket. They were a little crumpled but fresh. As usual, he looked devastatingly handsome.

Someone had set up a small table and brought in another chair, placing it so it faced the arm chair that was already in the room. On the table were two steaming bowls of stew—the delicious smell she had detected on walking along the corridor. There was also a plate of bread and a selection of meats and cheese. Jane had taken some bread and an apple for her lunch from the inn she had stayed at the night before, but apart from that she hadn't eaten since breakfast, and suddenly she realised quite how hungry she was.

'That smells wonderful.'

'I know. I had a hard time not eating both portions before you arrived and pretending they only brought bread and cheese.'

'I applaud your restraint. Shall we eat?'

The stew was delicious, warm, flavoursome and filling, just what Jane needed after a long day being rocked in the uncomfortable and crowded coach. She felt herself relaxing and didn't object when Tom started to talk about everyday things. He told her of his time in Italy and the skirmishes he and his friend Western had got into in the army. It felt good to listen, to not worry about the future for a little while.

Once the meal was finished, they placed the plates outside the door and Tom took her hand, leading her to the bed.

'Sit with me,' he said, his eyes holding hers. 'Sit with me while we talk.' Hesitantly, she nodded. There was a knot of nerves in her stomach, swirling and squirming. In the next few minutes, they would decide what their entire futures looked like.

'I meant what I said earlier,' Tom said quietly. 'I love you. I didn't allow myself to admit it, because it would mean confronting all the demons from my past, but it is the truth.'

'I believe you.' She hesitated, wondering how she could make him see it wasn't his love she was questioning. 'I know the heartache you went through with your sister. I know you still blame yourself for leaving her behind. I understand that is why you have never wanted a relationship where the other person becomes reliant on you, but if we marry that will happen.' She paused and looked him directly in the eye. 'If we marry, I will be your wife.'

'I know.'

'And the last thing I want to do is make you feel trapped or as if you have been forced into this.'

Tom reached out and took her hand. 'I have been doing a lot of thinking over the last few days and I realised something you said to me a few days ago was true. I was a young man when I left for the army, a young man who had experienced nothing but cruelty and disdain from my father. If could turn back the clock and have my time again, I wouldn't leave my sister there, but that is said with hindsight and growth.'

Jane felt a surge of hope begin to build inside her. This was exactly what Tom needed to see, needed to realise, but she hadn't thought it possible, given how long he had been holding on to his guilt.

'If placed in that situation again, I know I would act differently,' he said, looking at her with affection in his eyes. 'So I have to believe the same is true for my life with you and with Edward.'

'I know you would always put that boy first and do your best by him.'

'I would. I still feel guilty about leaving my sister behind, but I need to move forward in my life as the man I am now, not the boy I was then.' He paused and then took her hand. 'I am sorry it took me nearly losing you to realise this. For so long, I've felt so guilty. Any time the subject has come up, I've hurried to suppress it. I didn't want to examine what had happened and that meant I was stuck in a perpetual loop of guilt and regret.'

'I think everything you've said is true,' she said, knowing it meant they might be able to share a future.

'I want it all, Jane. I want you and I want love and I want us to be a family with Edward. I stand by part of what you overheard me say to Lady Mountjoy—Edward's life will be much better with you in it. So will mine. We would be lucky to have you. *I* would be lucky to have you.'

'I would be lucky to have you too,' Jane said quietly.

Tom raised his head a little so his eyes held hers.

'You mean that?'

'Yes. I love you, Tom. I've loved you for longer than I could admit to myself. I want nothing more than to make a life with you.'

'I would never take away your independence.'

'I know. It is one of the many things I love about you.'

With a gentle hand, Tom reached up and cupped her cheek, and Jane felt the inevitable pull between them. His fingers caressed her skin, sending little shocks through her body and making her want to collapse into him.

'I have something very important to ask you, Jane,' he said, his voice low. 'Will you marry me?'

'Yes.'

He kissed her, his lips brushing over hers, teasing her exquisitely until she couldn't help but tangle her fingers in his hair and pull him closer. She moaned as he pulled away and then started trailing kisses down from her earlobe and onto her neck. Somehow they had collapsed backwards on the bed and Jane felt the wonderful anticipation of what was to come.

'I propose we don't have a long engagement,' he murmured as he ran a hand over her body, catching the bottom of her skirts and lifting them to expose the bare skin of her legs beneath.

'Six months?' she offered.

'You are ridiculous,' he said, a hand climbing up higher on her leg, passing her knee and making her gasp in anticipation.

'Four months?'

'If you think you can keep our nightly visits secret for four months, then you are deluded,' he whispered in her ear.

'Two months?'

'Still far too long.' His hand was midway up her thigh now and he paused, making her almost cry out with frustration. 'How about I make you an offer?'

'Go on, then.'

'Tomorrow morning I ride back to London and petition the archbishop for a special licence. He will not refuse. Then you become my wife within the week.'

'People will think we have something to hide.'

'We do,' he said, his hand tracing circles upwards. 'We have so much to hide.'

He kissed her again, long and deep, and in that moment Jane would have agreed to anything.

'One week,' she murmured as he pulled away.

'One week. Then we can do this every single night.'

Jane was surprised when he pulled her to her feet and spun her so she faced the door. For a second, she felt a crushing disappointment, thinking he was going to send her on her way, then she felt his fingers on the back of her dress, unfastening the ties that kept it in place.

He worked quickly, loosening it off until it was ready to fall past her hips and pool on the floor. Underneath she had on a chemise, stays and a long petticoat, so she was not yet naked, but she could feel his eyes raking over her body all the same.

'You're beautiful, Jane,' he said as he unlaced her stays and threw the piece of clothing to the floor.

She shook her head. It was inconceivable to her that he should find her this attractive, that he could desire her the way she desired him.

The petticoat was next, falling around her

ankles, leaving her with only her chemise to cover her body.

Jane let out a little gasp as he gripped the hem of her chemise, even though she knew this was coming. With one swift movement he lifted it off over her head and Jane felt the chill of the air prickle her skin.

'Look at me,' he instructed her. 'You are beautiful. I cannot resist you. I don't know what you have done to me, but I am enchanted, bewitched.'

Again she shook her head.

'You're beautiful, Jane, and I will tell you so every day of our lives until you see it for yourself.'

He moved in closer and kissed her, this time his hands running across the bare skin of her shoulders. It felt exquisite, like nothing Jane had ever felt before, and she leaned into him, wanting to hold him closer. Although Tom had dressed for dinner, he had already shrugged off his jacket and loosened his cravat, so it was quick work to pull free his shirt from his trousers and manoeuvre it over his head. Jane felt clumsy and inexperienced, fumbling a little, but as she ran her hands down his naked chest all her doubts and uncertainties went away.

As they kissed Tom tumbled her back onto

the bed, his body over hers. His fingers danced over her skin, caressing and building up a wonderful tension inside her. Instinctively she felt her hips rise to meet his, her body arch to enjoy his touch.

Tom trailed kisses down her neck and along the length of her collar bone. There was a wonderful moment of anticipation as he paused, before dipping lower and kissing her breasts, circling her nipples until she couldn't bear it any longer, and pressed his head into her. He grinned up at her and then ever so slowly took one of her nipples into his mouth. Jane almost screamed at the jolts of pleasure that shot through her body, hoping he would never stop, whilst also wondering how long she could bear the exquisite sensation.

At the same time his hand moved lower until his fingers touched her most private place. Jane gasped, throwing her head back on the pillow and wondering why anyone ever left the bedroom if this was what it could feel like. Slowly, ever so slowly, he began to move his fingers, caressing and stroking, as Jane felt a ball of tension start to build in her belly. Even as she writhed underneath him, he didn't stop, coming up to kiss her lips as she felt every muscle in her body tense and then glorious waves of pleasure spread out from her very core.

She felt as though she were floating and it took a while for the sensation to subside. Her breath was coming in short gasps and for a minute she could do nothing but enjoy the feeling of pure ecstasy.

As she opened her eyes, she saw Tom pushing down the waistband of his trousers, a question in his eyes.

'We can stop if you want?'

'No,' she said, pulling him to her. 'Don't stop.'

She reached out and touched him, loving the way he threw his head back as she grasped hold of him, feeling the silky softness over his hardness. She felt a moment of panic as he positioned himself but that was soon replaced by a wonderful anticipation.

'I'll go slow,' he said, seeing the expression in her eyes.

He pushed into her and Jane felt a fullness like nothing she had ever experienced before. He moved slowly, as he had promised, even though Jane could see it was taking great effort on his part. Little by little she started to raise her hips to meet his, marvelling at how wonderful it felt. She let her head fall back on the pillow and abandoned herself to the moment, moaning as Tom started to move faster and faster until she felt the waves of pleasure crash through her again as they climaxed together.

After a moment, Tom collapsed down on the bed next to her, pulling her into his arms, and they lay like that for a long time, neither able to speak.

Once she felt a little recovered, Jane turned over so she was facing him, and Tom pulled at the sheets, covering her body so she didn't get cold. His hand was resting on her waist, the position so intimate Jane felt a swell of happiness.

'Is it always like that?' she asked.

'I have heard,' Tom said slowly, choosing his words, 'That making love is best when you are actually in love. I expect that was why it was so good.'

'You truly love me?'

'With all my heart.'

Jane snuggled down under the bed clothes, feeling a wonderful contentment wash over her. This was not how she had expected this day to end, but she would take the happiness over the heartbreak she'd felt this morning any day.

Chapter Twenty-Three

Tom jolted awake, his reflexes quick enough to stop himself from hitting the floor as he toppled off the chair. He checked his pocket watch as he stood, eyes widening as he realised the time. Ever since Edward had come to live with him, the little boy had struggled to get to sleep, then would awake about midnight, crying for his mother. Tom often stayed up working or reading in his study until he heard the young boy stir and then headed upstairs to comfort him.

Quickly he took the stairs two at a time until he reached Edward's bedroom on the first floor. It was looking more like a child's room than when he had first arrived, with Edward's pride and joy, a wooden rocking horse, in one corner.

Edward was sleeping peacefully in his bed, cheeks rosy and hair tousled on the pillow.

Leaning over the slumbering boy, Tom kissed him gently on the cheek. He felt an overwhelming love for him. Although he knew one night without the nightmares and tears Edward shed for his mother was only a start, it felt like a new chapter was dawning where some of the pain could be soothed.

'Is it morning?' Edward muttered as Tom retreated to the door.

'Not yet. You keep sleeping. Today is a big day.'

Tom debated whether to bother going to bed. It was five o'clock and already he felt the rush of anticipation for the day. He wished Jane were here, waiting for him in his room. He wanted to tell her about Edward sleeping through, about his hopes that they had seen the last of the night terrors and sobbing from the little boy. There was still a long way to go, but he felt optimistic that this was the first step of many.

'I'm so excited!' Edward shouted as he bounded up the stairs and into Jane's room, throwing his arms around her to cuddle her. Jane pulled the boy into a tight embrace, not caring that he was wrinkling the silk of her new dress. She would take a cuddle from Edward over a pristine appearance any day.

'I'm sorry, miss,' the harried-looking nanny said as she rushed into the room. 'I couldn't keep up.'

The agency had sent the nanny a week earlier and she had been worth the wait. Young and energetic, she was a welcome addition to the household. Edward seemed to like her, although would often sneak off to find the company of Jane or his uncle.

'You are just the person I wanted to see,' Jane said, crouching down to face the boy. 'Your uncle and I have been talking about a honeymoon. Not yet—perhaps in a few months.'

She saw the little boy's face drop. 'I don't want you to go.'

'We wouldn't ever go anywhere without you, Edward.'

'You mean I could come?'

'Yes. We were thinking of taking a trip to Italy, and I wondered if perhaps you would like to go back to where you lived with your mother and see all your friends?'

He nodded, his eyes wide.

'Good. That is settled, then. After the wedding, you can help us plan the trip.'

'Come now, Edward, Miss Ashworth has much to do this morning, I'm sure.'

There was a clatter of feet outside, and as Edward left the room Lucy entered, arm-in-arm with Lady Mountjoy.

'This may be the second happiest day of my life,' Lucy said as she started fussing around Jane, straightening her skirt and smoothing out the creases in the fabric.

'It certainly is one of the happiest of mine,' said Lady Mountjoy. The older woman waited for Lucy to finish and then stepped forward, holding out a small package. 'This is for you, Jane, my final debutante. I always knew you were destined for a great match.' She swiped at her eyes, trying to get rid of the tears that were forming. 'And there is no greater match than one made out of true love.'

The countess embraced her and then handed over the package. Jane opened it, gasping at the beautiful earrings inside. They were elegant and simple, the sparkling diamonds at the centre of the earring resplendent enough that they didn't need any extra adornments.

'Thank you, they're beautiful. It is too generous, Lady Mountjoy.'

'Nonsense. You have given me a wonderful gift this year, all of you debutantes who came to join me. It has been one of the most eventful but fantastic years I have ever known. I feel privileged to have been even a small part of your journey.'

'None of this would have been possible without you,' Jane said, trying not to cry herself.

Lady Mountjoy took her leave, making her way downstairs for the ceremony, leaving Jane and Lucy alone.

'Charlotte has just arrived,' Lucy said as she helped put the finishing touches to Jane's hair. 'She is so happy to be here.' Charlotte was another of the debutantes selected by Lady Mountjoy for her long trip to London. She had never made it to the capital, though, having fallen in love during the few weeks they had spent on the Mountjoy estate prior to leaving for London, and marrying Lady Mountjoy's nephew.

'I'm glad she's made it.'

Eliza was the only one missing from their little friendship group. Jane had written, but Eliza had set off on her honeymoon a few weeks earlier, and she doubted the letter would reach her friend before the wedding happened.

'I think it is almost time,' Lucy said, giving Jane's arm an excited squeeze. 'Do you need a moment?'

'No.' Jane shook her head. She didn't feel nervous, not really. Ever since the night in the coaching inn, she was convinced she and Tom were perfect for each other. It had been an agonising few weeks whilst he had arranged the special licence and all she wanted now was to become Mrs Stewart.

Together they walked downstairs, Lucy handing her a bunch of flowers before she walked into the richly decorated drawing room. They had both wanted a quiet, small wedding and had agreed Tom's drawing room was the perfect place for their nuptials. Jane had never been to a wedding outside of a church before, but as she surveyed the guests in the familiar room she knew this had been the right decision. On one side of the room sat Lord and Lady Mountjoy, Lucy and Captain Weyman and Charlotte and her husband, Lord Overby.

On the other side was Edward, his nanny and Mr and Mrs Western, who Jane had met a few times now, soon realising what an important part of her husband's life they were.

Jane's whole family hadn't been able to

make the journey, but her father sat at the front of the room, beaming proudly, and Jane had assured her mother she and Tom would come and visit very soon.

Jane's eyes took everyone in as they swept over the room and then settled on the man standing at the front. Mr Thomas Stewart, former rake, current charmer and soon to be her husband.

He turned at that moment and smiled at her and Jane felt overwhelmed by love. This wasn't what she had expected from her time in London, and certainly not how she'd thought they would end up when she had first suggested to Tom they feign interest in one another to save her from having to socialise with other eligible bachelors.

'You look beautiful, my love,' Tom murmured as she reached him.

As the ceremony was about to start, she felt a light tug on her free hand and glanced down. Edward had joined them in front of everyone else and was now holding her hand. She beamed down at him and then up at her very-soon-to-be husband as she repeated her marriage vows.

Epilogue

Two years later

Jane sat back in her chair, sipping a glass of orange juice and enjoying the heat of the sun on her face. Somewhere in the distance she could hear an excited whoop and laughter coming from Edward as he ran rings round his uncle and the three other men who had happily agreed to teach the young boy cricket.

'Tell us about your books, Jane,' Lucy said, leaning forward as far as she could in her seat, but floundering as her bump got in the way. It was a surprise to no one that Lucy was pregnant with her third child so soon after having had twins a year earlier. She was a natural mother and bloomed into the role, happily declaring she wanted a dozen children. The twins were sleeping peacefully in a bassinet in the shade and Jane felt a maternal tug as she glanced over at them.

'The first three have been published and Mr Hambly tells me they've been a terrific success. The first editions sold out within a few weeks and he had to get busy printing more.'

'That is amazing,' Eliza said, shaking her head in disbelief. 'I can't believe you were working towards this all the time we were together and none of us knew.'

'You were a little preoccupied with the delightful Lord Thannock,' Lucy teased.

'As were you, with the dashing Captain Weyman.'

'And Charlotte was busy smuggling pigs into country estates and bewitching the man she protested she could not stand,' Jane added.

They all laughed as they remembered that first summer together. It had been two years since Lady Mountjoy had brought them together at her big country estate with the proposal she select a debutante to take to London for the winter months and the spring Season. It had been an eventful two years, with four marriages, four honeymoons and three babies, and Jane felt grateful they were all here together to sit down and enjoy one another's company for a few days.

Lady Mountjoy had invited them all back for a house party, and they had been so eager to come together they had rearranged any other engagements to make sure it happened.

'How are my favourite debutantes?' Lady Mountjoy said as she stepped out onto the terrace to join them.

'Hardly debutantes any more,' Charlotte said, cradling her one-year-old in her arms. 'I am relegated to sit with the matrons at any events we attend now.'

'It's worth it, though, isn't it?' Lady Mountjoy said in a loud whisper, indicating the little girl in Charlotte's arms. 'It's worth it to be a mother.'

Jane found her hand travelling to her belly. She wasn't as far gone as Lucy, but she would soon be adding to their family. Already she felt so lucky to have Edward, who she loved as though he were her own. Another child would be an extra blessing.

'Are you still writing and illustrating more books?' Eliza asked her, fascinated by the process. Eliza had returned from her honeymoon to find Lucy and Jane both married and happily settled, and Jane a published author. She had grumbled about things moving too quickly whilst she'd been away, but Jane had seen by her expression she was delighted by all the news.

'Yes, Mr Hambly has told me he will publish whatever I can write. It is a different feeling. For so long I wrote and illustrated the stories, not knowing whether anyone but me would ever see them. Now I get a rush of nervousness thinking everything will be studied and judged.'

'You have nothing to worry about,' Eliza declared with her characteristic confidence. 'I've bought all three already published and they are nothing short of perfect.'

Jane beamed at her friend, her smile growing even wider as Edward ran back to the table for a drink, followed by Tom and the other husbands.

'I think a toast is needed,' Lady Mountjoy said, waiting until everyone had assembled and found a glass. 'Two years ago we embarked on a fantastic journey. I was lucky enough to meet you fabulous ladies and grow to know and love you like you are family.' She paused, smiling as Lord Mountjoy stepped out of the drawing room and looped an arm around her waist.

'For years, I've been telling every young debutante I meet, every eligible bachelor—anyone who will listen, really—the importance of marrying for love. You spend more time with your spouse than anyone else, and that time can be the happiest if you choose your partner correctly.'

She paused for a moment, looking round at the group of young women and their husbands. 'I am delighted you have all chosen so well. To spend a life with the person you love is a life well spent,' Lady Mountjoy concluded. Lord Mountjoy beamed behind her and leaned round to give his wife a kiss on the cheek.

She raised her glass in a toast. 'To love and friendship.'

That was a toast Jane could agree with, and it seemed apt, given she was surrounded by people she loved and wonderful friends.

'Love and friendship,' she said, feeling her heart soar as Tom leaned in and kissed her.

* * * * *

COMING SOON!

We really hope you enjoyed reading this book.
If you're looking for more romance, be sure to
head to the shops when new books are
available on

Thursday 19th
January

MILLS & BOON®

Coming next month

A SEASON OF FLIRTATION
Julia Justiss

Maggie gave her a shrewd look. 'What do you think of him? You've met, I trust?'

'He's an impressive young man,' Laura said carefully, trying to keep her tone neutral.

"Is he handsome?" Eliza prodded with a grin.

"Quite." Laura laughed. "Also quite dismissive of Society ladies. He thinks we are all empty-headed and frivolous."

"You'd be the lady to convince him otherwise," Maggie said. "Laura the mathematician. Not that you need to win his favor, of course. A banker's rich daughter may find an aristocratic husband, but a banker's son would be entirely ineligible as a match for you."

"How fortunate I am not angling for a husband," Laura retorted. No matter how appealing she might find the admittedly unsuitable Mr. Rochdale.

Continue reading
A SEASON OF FLIRTATION
Julia Justiss

Available next month
www.millsandboon.co.uk

MILLS & BOON

THE HEART OF ROMANCE

A ROMANCE FOR EVERY READER

ODERN

Prepare to be swept off your feet by sophisticated, sexy and seductive heroes, in some of the world's most glamourous and romantic locations, where power and passion collide.

STORICAL

Escape with historical heroes from time gone by. Whether your passion is for wicked Regency Rakes, muscled Vikings or rugged Highlanders, awaken the romance of the past.

EDICAL

Set your pulse racing with dedicated, delectable doctors in the high-pressure world of medicine, where emotions run high and passion, comfort and love are the best medicine.

ue Love

Celebrate true love with tender stories of heartfelt romance, from the rush of falling in love to the joy a new baby can bring, and a focus on the emotional heart of a relationship.

Desire

Indulge in secrets and scandal, intense drama and plenty of sizzling hot action with powerful and passionate heroes who have it all: wealth, status, good looks…everything but the right woman.

EROES

Experience all the excitement of a gripping thriller, with an intense romance at its heart. Resourceful, true-to-life women and strong, fearless men face danger and desire - a killer combination!

To see which titles are coming soon, please visit

millsandboon.co.uk/nextmonth

JOIN US ON SOCIAL MEDIA!

Stay up to date with our latest releases, author news and gossip, special offers and discounts, and all the behind-the-scenes action from Mills & Boon...

 @millsandboon

 @millsandboonuk

 facebook.com/millsandboon

 @millsandboonuk

t might just be true love...

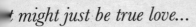

MILLS & BOON
True Love
Romance from the Heart

Celebrate true love with tender stories of heartfelt romance, from the rush of falling in love to the joy a new baby can bring, and a focus on the emotional heart of a relationship.